CONTI

Love Crafted

RavensDagger

PROLOGUE

THERE WAS a brilliance to Fivepeaks at dawn, an interplay of light and fading shadow that was—as far as Abigail was aware—unique to the city.

The royal palace had its great clock, the dials lit from behind by a thousand glass tubes filled with Aether. It was the first thing to catch the sun's light as it slipped over the horizon, like a beacon announcing that morning had arrived and it was time to start moving or else start plotting excuses for why one was tardy to work.

Then, as the sun rose, the lamp men would move across the city, the vanguard of the working class, each one shutting off the street lights with a touch to their circles. They always started near the Parliament building on the second peak and worked their way down, lights flicking off like twinkling stars just ahead of the wash of morning sunlight.

On the opposite end of Fivepeaks, atop the tallest hill, the Academy would open its gates and the twin braziers on either side of the school would burst to life. They were bright beams of eldritch light that turned the mundane stone building into something ethereal, something that was beyond the normal sort of magic everyone and their mother used daily. Statues would come to life, paintings would begin to move, and the school prepared to receive a thousand inquisitive minds.

As the sun finally crested the horizon for good and lit up the fields around the city, the other mounts would awaken. The Conclave of the Inquisition remained dark, the entire complex hidden from the light by a towering mound of stone, but Merchant's Hill, where Abigail worked from sunrise to sunset, didn't shy from the light. Red lamps sputtered out with sparks of wasted Aether and neon tubes fizzed to life with a press of a thumb and a bit of focus.

There was a strange sort of quiet in the early morning hours. The streets outside were busy with the hubbub of morning crowds and the grinding of rune carts across the cobbles, but those noises were distant and easily forgotten, save for the occasional rattle of glass jars when a cart rushed by.

The city was awake, and it was alive. Magic circles flashed to life and left the air smelling of ozone and lightning, the Familiars of a thousand mages rushed ahead of their masters to the Academy on the hill, and gossiping shopkeepers walked in tight knit groups to their stores.

All that energy and life was locked behind a thick wooden door.

Two girls stood around a circle painted onto the floor, lit only by lamp light. "It stinks," Abigail said, her nose scrunching up as she inspected her handiwork.

Her friend shrugged one shoulder, an unladylike gesture that would have been inappropriate in any other circumstance. "It'll work," she said. "I don't think you made any mistakes."

"Yeah," Abigail said as she traced the circle with a discerning eye one more time. Each reagent was in its place. The sulphur in a non-reactive glass dish, the alum flower in a neat pile, the lime and lunar caustic in their positions. There were other ingredients of course, more than she had ever seen in a single circle before.

Then, in the middle of it all, on a slightly raised pedestal, was a smaller circle, connected to the first by lines of salt and magnesia. That's where the more esoteric ingredients rested. Five points, each with a smaller circle. One had a drop of her blood, another the hair of a virgin maiden (easy to obtain, that), then a dollop of aged ent sap. There was a bit of gold in the form of a medallion she had found and which she hoped wouldn't be lost in the casting, and finally a single unicorn cock, freshly butchered.

"Are you sure?" she asked again, eyes looking up from the intricate spell and to her friend. "Daphne, I've never cast anything this strong before," she whined.

Her friend smiled, just a twitch of the lips and a folding in the corner of her eyes. "Don't worry Abi, I'm here for you. I'm sure it'll be fine. The spell's a bit old, but it's usable, if non-standard."

"That's not helping," Abigail said. She shifted on the spot a little, weight going from side to side as she hesitated even more. It was, of course, too late to back out. The ingredients were laid out already, some would be lost if she tried to store them now.

Daphne stepped closer and wrapped Abigail in a tight hug, only having to bend down a little to do it. "It'll be fine. There's always a bit of leeway with these things. My summoning went super well. You love Archie. Do this right and you'll have an Archie of your own, then it'll be super easy to get into the Academy."

"Archie was summoned with a proper circle," Abigail said. "And you had supervision."

Daphne snorted, an indelicate gesture that had her nose scrunching up. "I'm supervising you."

"By a professional," Abigail shot back.

"Ouch. Abi, you're being mean," Daphne said. She let go of the hug to poke Abigail in the ribs. "Now push some Aether into that thing and let's watch the sparks fly."

Abigail nodded, took a deep breath, and hesitated just a little more.

Then, when she heard Daphne sighing from her place near the wall, she fell onto her knees next to the circle, reached in, and pushed her bare hand onto the cold ground. Eyes closing, she pushed with all of her will. Her hopes, her dreams, all depended on that one moment.

And then she summons you.

You float in the Void. In the Darkness where Light doesn't dwell. Only the things that are In Between lie dormant here.

Meaning is a concept that is as transient here as spring gales. Causality is optional. Willpower dictates the flow of the space between spaces.

There is a tug, a pull, a calling from across what Mortals and Lesser Beings would only understand as a great, unfathomable distance.

It awakens you.

You are vast, larger than any mere mortal could hope to conceive of, and yet the one calling you, your summoner, wants you to squeeze into a form so small as to be insignificant. The little mortal asks for the impossible with a sort of blind faith that, at its base, amuses you.

A twist, a turn, and mass, insofar as you have mass, is compressed. Space is transitory, it does as you wish. With a scream, physics reels from your irreverence to its laws. It batters at what you are doing but that is as easy to ignore as a faint stench.

Between one blink and the next you are an entity of the void no longer.

CHAPTER ONE

THE CEILING has wooden beams, some of them marred by smoke stains and soot. You know this because you are on your back on the floor, which affords you an excellent view.

You wrinkle your nose at the smell of burning sulfur and something sickly sweet, then you wrinkle your nose again just because you can. You have a nose now. This is rather novel.

Of course, that's all perfectly normal. You are a being made flesh now. You have bits that are squishy over hard parts, and some hard parts with squishy bits inside them. It's all quite disgusting and probably unsanitary. It's no wonder that mortals are so mortal. One small impact is all it would take to rend this sack of meat apart.

There's a noise. You know this because you have ears.

You wiggle your limbs and, after a moment of not really moving, decide that your patience for mortal flesh limbs has already reached its end. You reach into the space between spaces for more of yourself and pull a fraction of a fraction of your essence into the mortal coil. There's a tearing sound, and a splash.

Warmth runs across your back and you see inky black blood pooling out around you.

That's probably bad. But at least now you are no longer limited to a mere four limbs. Your new limbs sprout out of your back like the wings of an Angel. Though unlike those weaklings your wings are black, and wiggly, and a little bit slimy with your blood. They are also boneless and featherless.

They're tentacles.

Tentacle wings.

Angels don't have anything on you.

Now equipped properly, you let yourself go limp as your tentacles spear into the floor and raise you up to your feet.

There are two meaty fleshbags in the room. They are small, with delicate little bones covered in mostly beige flesh. One has long brown fur atop her head and the other black. Perhaps the fur means something. You will have to look into it and make sure any fur you have tells the mortals that you are not to be trifled with.

One of the girls steps forwards, the shorter of the two and the one you suspect is your summoner. She opens the hole in her face and noises come out.

You blink at the strange, guttural sounds. This is a problem. But of course, you have a simple solution. You just need to tear the knowledge out of your summoner's head. Everything these mortals know is stored in the meaty organ in their head. A terribly inefficient way of going about things but they're primitive mortals, so what can one expect?

Bringing one of your tentacles back, you prepare yourself to spear through your summoner's skull to get to the juicy brain matter within when you pause.

Would going through the skull break the summoner?

Best to merely apply pressure atop the summoner's head and extract the knowledge of their meat flapping language that way. It is not nearly as efficient, but it will work.

You step forward, then the world shifts and you brand new nose twinges as it meets the floor with a meaty smack.

Curse physics! It is attempting to foil your amusement by dragging your squishy meat body to the ground.

Walking cannot be difficult if the mortals are doing it, but the only two you see are standing still and not assisting you by presenting the art of waking in an easy to digest fashion. Very well, you don't need their assistance anyway. Your tentacles bring you back to your feet.

Raising one arm up, you reach for your summoner's head.

You feel the muscles on your face drawing your brows together as you reach harder. Perhaps you cannot touch your summoner's head because you are not standing at your full height? That must be it, you decide.

You stand to your full height.

...

You stand to your full height.
You blink your fleshy meat eyes, then look down.

The ground is very near.

You look back up. Your summoner is taller than you are. A whole two heads taller.

This is a problem.

But all problems have solutions. And the best solutions always involve tentacles. You wrap your fleshy tentacles around the beams of the ceiling, then push off the ground with others until you are suspended in the middle of the room. Your summoner cowers away from your form which is unacceptable. You wrap a tentacle around her waist in a fleshy cuddle of muscle and drag her close.

You are now taller than your summoner, the perfect height to reach out and...

Hand meets head. Tendrils that are only partially in this realm scour through your summoner's mind, skipping past boring things until the parts that dictate speech and the knowledge of how to move the flaps on your face to communicate are found.

Ah, you were supposed to use your tongue. That is what the small, inefficient tentacle in your face is for.

Disappointing.

You clear your throat as you remove your hand from your summoner's head then gently and reluctantly lower her back to the ground. The moment she's out of your grasp, you feel a lack, as if you had accidentally bumped into a black hole and lost a bit of yourself.

You will have to see if wrapping your summoner in even more tentacles will fix the issue, but that is a problem (which can, again, be fixed with a liberal application of tentacles) for another time. You are nothing if not a paragon of self-control.

"Hello," you say.

"Ah," the girl says in return. Truly, your summoner is lacking in many things. It would be best if you kept her safe, cocooned in a whole pile of your flesh—you shake your meat head and refocus. She is about to continue. "Hi there," she says. "My name's Abigail."

A name.

Yes. You will need one of those. Then you'll need to discover why this mortal called upon you.

Abigail. You taste the name, your new knowledge of the mortal tongue telling you nothing of great importance about it. Perhaps the mortals just name themselves after whatever sound they like most.

Your summoner is a small thing, a human tadpole or whatever they call their young, with brown fur… hair tied in a bun behind her head. She has spectacles, big round bits of glass perched on the very end of a tiny nose. They make her eyes look wider than they are as she gazes right back at you.

"Daphne," she says, and for a moment you are confused, but then the other mortal, the one you had nearly forgotten about, moves away from the wall with cautious steps. "Daph, I think it worked?"

"Yeah," the Daphne girl agrees. "But what did you summon?"

That is a foolish question. You are you, that much is obvious. But perhaps these mortals don't know as much. They are terribly short-lived after all.

Abigail turns back to you and her mouth twitches up, the corners of her eyes creasing up in a strange way. "Ah, my name's Abigail, like I said. Do you have a name? W-what are you?"

Giving her a name is the least you could do, of course. You take a deep breath, filling the sacks in your chest until they're about to burst, then you let it all out in one long wail. Your vocal chords aren't made for the kinds of twists and turns and variations that would be proper in speaking your Name, but you try your best with the faulty equipment you have.

Abigail and Daphne slap their hands over their ears and wince back until you run out of air. You take another deep breath, ready to continue where you left off. That wasn't even the start of your True Name, merely the precursor titles.

"I'm sorry!" Abigail wails. "I didn't mean to hurt you, you don't need to cry," she says before walking right up to you where you still hang off the floor. She reaches out to you with her arms like grasping, bony tentacles and pulls you against her chest.

You are insulted. Infuriated! How dare this, this mortal tentacle-grab you as if... actually it's rather pleasant. Nice and warm. You can feel your summoner's breathing, her little heart thumping away in her chest.

Of course, it wouldn't do not to return the favour before you start in on the questions. It's just proper etiquette when a creature wraps you in its tentacles to wrap them back.

You aren't doing it because it makes you feel nice to cuddle your summoner. Of course not. You have more self control than that.

Abigail squeaks as you wrap her up in layers and layers of tentacular glory. It is probably a squeak of happiness, her teeth are certainly bared as you lift her off the ground. "Your cuddle was appreciated," you say. "I shall return the favour tenfold."

"Um," Daphne says. "I don't think that's a good idea." You disagree, but you do leave Abigail's head uncovered. It's not a proper cuddle this way, but at least she can still breathe, which is important for living and talking, two things you wish for her to continue doing.

"Foolish mortal," you reprimand. "Cuddles are always appropriate recompense for services rendered. Now, if you do not appreciate my true name, then I shall translate it into your meat flapping language." You feel the muscles in your brow contracting as you concentrate. "I am That Which Dreams Eternal Between Space and Time."

Daphne closes her eyes slowly. "I think we'll call you Dream, it's a pretty enough name," she says.

You don't particularly care what they call you. "Summoner Abigail, why did you call upon me? Why did you dare awaken me from my Mostly-Eternal Slumber?"

You realize after a moment's silence that maybe your summoner's face shouldn't be that red and that maybe you're cuddling her too hard. You let go, and she lands with a gasp on the hard packed ground a moment before Daphne moves over to her to help her up. It is obvious that she too, has difficulty with the whole walking thing.

"Some sort of mimic, maybe?" Daphne mutters. "It's obviously magical, so you lucked out there."

Abigail makes a snorting noise that you can't translate and hugs her friend closer. "But we did it!" she says, the red fading to be replaced by an expression that shows off all of her teeth. She turns shining eyes onto you. "I summoned you because I need a Familiar, someone to help me, and who I can cherish and love and care for until we're both really old."

You see Daphne rolling her eyes behind Abigail. "She needs a Familiar to enter the Academy. It's part of the entrance requirements."

"That too," Abigail says. "But I want a friend first. So, can we be friends, Dreamer?"

You are quite speechless. This tadpole has summoned you to be friends? Cuddle buddies? Tentacle pals? How foolish!

CHAPTER TWO

ABIGAIL AND Daphne decide that their time in the dank basement is over, and that even if you are less than presentable—whatever that means—it is time for you to leave the room and be shown around.

Learning that Abigail is in no way a powerful monarch or a sort of god queen of her people is disappointing, but that is the kind of thing that could be fixed in due time. For now, you follow the girl up a rickety staircase and out of a storm door that leads into an alleyway of sorts.

The moment you exit the little room you start to feel the bite of cold nipping at your many, many extremities. This is easily ignored, but perhaps not before Abigail notices you shivering.

"Oh, you poor thing," she says. "I'm so sorry. Wait, wait, you can have my jacket." That said, she removes the simple brown coat she is wearing to reveal an equally simple beige blouse underneath. Bending forwards, she tries to wrap you in the jacket, but your tentacles are in the way. At least, until you retract them a little.

The jacket is nice. It is warm. It smells like your summoner, and even if the material is a little coarse on your back it isn't a bad kind of rough. It is like a small, feeble hug. You wrap the jacket closer around your frame and stare around the alley.

"Seriously Abi, we didn't think of bringing a blanket or something?"

"I didn't expect to summon someone so… you know," Abigail says. "It's okay, we live right across the street." So saying, Abigail points out of the alleyway and across a cobbled street.

The roads here are wide, with tall sidewalks on either side where mortals in strange garb are aggressively minding their own business. The buildings here are tall, all of them at least three storeys high and with gabled roofs covered in brightly coloured shingles.

A cart rumbles by, pulled not by animals but by a strange wheeled contraption like a bicycle crossed with a water heater.

"That one over there," Abigail says, her face twisting back into that expression with her teeth showing as she notices you looking around. She is pointing to one shop in particular.

It's a squat building, wider by some margin than its neighbours and with large windows at its front. *Madam Morrigan's Artifices, Tinctures and Ingredients*, read the scrolling letters across the top.

"I work there, and Madam Morrigan lets me stay in the apartment above for cheap. She has her own house a little ways into the city," Abigail explains. Before you know to react, she reaches down and grabs you by the hand, your soft, new flesh held firm in a calloused grip. "Be careful when crossing the street," she says. "Look both ways and let the carts go by first. The drivers can be very rude."

"Very well," you concede as she pulls you along.

"We're going to need to buy Dreamer here some clothes," Daphne says. "And some shoes. Her feet are going to get torn up walking on the cobbles like that."

"Oh no," Abigail says as she stops, and therefore makes you stop as well. "Did you want me to carry you so that your feet don't hurt?"

You think upon this. On the one tentacle, being carried is similar to a cuddle, and is therefore the greatest method of transportation. On the other tentacle, it would be demeaning in front of all these mortals. You must prove that you are superior and need no shoes to protect the tiny tentacles stuck to the ends of your feet. How will they grow long and wiggly if you confine them within leather and cloth?

"I will attempt walking," you say to her, and her face splits into another one of those strange expressions of joy.

"All right then," she says. "Come, I'll show you to our home. You're going to love it, I'm sure."

The girls wait by the roadside until the traffic clears up, then you scurry across the road, hand still in Abigail's own in order to keep your balance. Walking is still tricky, but there are plenty of mortals walking around to copy from.

The door to Madam Morrigan's is locked until Abigail fishes a key out from the pocket of the jacket you are wearing, it opens with the tinkle of a bell and you all move into the dimly lit room.

Shelves tower above you, filled with jars and dishes and strange dried husks of once-living things. There's not one scent in the air, but millions of them, all mixed together in a way that makes it hard to pinpoint which is which. Abigail lets go of your hand to press her palm over a circle carved into one wall.

There's a... shift in reality, a tiny nudge. Not a scream as physics is rent, but a sigh as it allows something to happen that shouldn't be.

The room lights up as curved elements in glass cases, all stuck to the ceiling, start to glow. "Going to need to change the oil," Abigail mutters as she looks at a jar next to the circle she pressed. "Anyway, welcome to where I work! The staircase is just in the back, in the storeroom. Our house isn't big, but it's ours."

Now that there is enough light to see, you allow yourself to explore with hungry eyes. There are jars with brains and delicate flowers marinating in amber liquids. Bins of dusts and powders are neatly lined up near a far wall next to little measuring bags made of coarse cloth and colourful advertisements are posted on every free space.

At the back rests a tall counter on which a set of complex brass scales wait to be used.

"Hey, Abi, can we talk?" Daphne says. She gestures towards a door leading even deeper into the store, then looks at you. "Alone?"

Abigail hesitates a little, but she gives in to the taller girl's request with a nod. "We'll be right back," she says before they both move towards the far end of the room, and then into a small back area.

You are now alone. Alone in a shop that sells magical reagents to passing mortals for a fee. At least, that's what you assume based on the little cards with numbers next to each ingredient.

You are uncertain of what to do. You want to follow your Summoner, but you also want to investigate this quaint mortal magic she used.

Perhaps you can do both?

As you slowly make your way across the room, ears perked to try and listen in on what's being said in the next room over, you scan across all the jars, powders and neat little things stacked around you.

'Goblin Feet,' reads one little sign above a basket full of tiny feet. You pause before it on your way over to the magic circle on the wall, take a sniff with your new nose and recoil. This does not smell good.

You grab one and pop it into your mouth before retching.

It does not taste good either. Too mushy.

Tiny face tentacle wiggling to get rid of the taste, you search for something to drink and find a bunch of sturdy glass jars with 'Spirit of Salt' written on them. You pop the lid of one of them and take a swallow. It's spritzy and makes your throat tingle. Yummy.

Then you see a display filled with 'Black Widow's Legs' and one with 'Porcupine Quills.' The legs are very good, but a bit dry, and the quills have a nice crunch to them. You find a bowl filled with 'Fennel Leaves' according to the sign next to it, and dump it into a bowl of 'Bay Leaves.' Then you fill the bowl with a handful of Widow Legs and Quills.

The next row over, you find a jar filled with 'Oil of Vitriol' and, after taking a sip, pour it over your bowl. Then you find some yummy, yummy 'Lye' and add that too.

It's a salad!

Truly, you are a chef worthy of much praise.

Grinning to yourself, you bring your snack over to the far wall where the magic circle for the lights is awaiting your inspection. The circle is a bit too high up for you to reach, but that's what tentacles are for. You slide your tentacles out from under Abigail's jacket and use them to lift you up until you're face to face with the circle.

You stare at the intricate carving while slurping up a particularly juicy spider leg. It's filled with tiny little markings, runes, you think, which are laid in a circle within the circle. Everything is connected to the rest by thin metallic lines, like a bent coat-hanger.

That metallic line, in turn, dips into a tank suspended next to the circle. It looks like it's made to be easily removed.

"Abi, it's not a child!" you hear Daphne hiss.

Oh, yes, you're supposed to be listening.

It would be hard to listen from all the way across the room like this with your poor excuse for ears, so instead of trying too hard, you focus a little and the room squishes itself. Physics sobs as the ceiling narrows down into a square that's only a few feet apart while the rest of the room stays the same. You are now only a step away from the room where the girls are talking and you didn't need to move an inch.

"Daph, I summoned her, Dreamer's my Familiar. I… I should be happy. I *am* happy! We did it, and she's obviously magical! Do you know how rare that is?"

"One in six, Abi. One in six Familiars are magical in nature, and that's not a reason to take such a big risk. You don't know what it is yet."

"Familiars don't hurt their masters," Abigail points out.

There is a snort. "I showed you the cuts Archie left on my shoulder with his claws. You know that Familiars can be silly sometimes. They're not magical constructs that need to follow rules."

"I… Well, I won't unsummon Dreamer."

Your chest feels nice and fuzzy as you hear that. So you take a celebratory bite out of a quill and munch on it as you return to inspecting the magical circle.

The whole thing is carved into a plaque, one with tiny writing at the bottom. 'Hubert and Hebert Magical Accomodators Inc. Copyright 24384932. Year of the seventh circle, 345.'

You don't know what any of that means.

"I'm not telling you to get rid of her, Abi, just be careful. It's… it's not normal."

"She, she isn't normal. And not being normal isn't a bad thing, Daph."

Maybe you should poke the circle?

You place your bowl on a handy tentacle that lets it hover near you, then use another, smaller tentacle to grab a bunch of quills and legs and stuff them into your mouth. Abigail had pressed her hand against the circle just… like… this.

Your palm rests against the cold plaque.

Nothing happens.

Hrm.

You poke it harder. Still nothing.

"Look, it hasn't even been an hour yet," Abigail says. "Let's get to know Dreamer before casting stones, okay?"

"Fine, fine. But when it turns out she's on some forbidden creature list I'm not going to be making excuses to the Inquisition for you."

"Daph," you hear Abigail sigh. "Okay. I… I just hope she's enough to get me into the Academy."

"Oh, Abi, you silly girl, of course you'll get in. You're brilliant, and now you have a Familiar, and you've been saving enough for the tuition, right?"

"Yeah, yeah I have everything. Almost. I still need some of the course books, but they're pricey. I'll find used copies somewhere. And robes. I need to get robes soon."

This magic circle thing is very annoying. You could do the light thing without it, but Abigail didn't need to bend nature to her will to make them turn on, she just pressed this plaque. So you're missing something, something vital.

You lick the plaque.

"Dreamer?" you hear a call and notice footsteps approaching.

Quick as lightning, you retract your tentacles, let physics take control of the ceiling again and then stuff the bowl in the cracks between this reality and the next. That way you'll have a snack for later. "Yes?" you ask.

"Ah, there you are," Abigail says as she finds you rubbing a hand across your mouth to remove some of that lye stuff. "What were you up to?"

You point to the plaque with a tentacle. "Magic."

"Ah, right," she said with a suppressed giggle. "I can explain that later. Come on, I'll show you our rooms."

CHAPTER THREE

"AND THIS," Abigail says with a wide, sweeping gesture, "Is my home. Our home."

You stare. Her home—your home, you suppose—is a tiny little place. There's a small room off to one side with a toilet and bathtub and sink. The floor is all cracked and poorly repaired tiles and the walls are made of painted-over plaster that's peeling apart.

The kitchen is the biggest space in the house, with a table that doesn't quite sit straight covered in heavy tomes and a stove off to one side that is covered in a patina of rust.

Deeper in, not even in its own room, is the sleeping area. A bed frame with a thin mattress, quilted blankets all neatly folded atop it. There's a dresser to one side, with clothes stacked on top in careful piles and a bookshelf tucked in another corner, books left all around it in haphazard mounds of knowledge-y goodness. There's no room on the shelves themselves for even a single pamphlet.

"Your place isn't big enough for one person, let alone three," Daphne said. "I should head back home."

"Hey," Abigail protested. "Not all of us can live in mansions."

"I don't live in a mansion Abi, I live in a nice part of the city. You just can't tell the difference because you're such a backwater bumpkin."

"Snooty rich jerk," Abigail shot back.

You blink up at the two of them. They are clearly insulting each other, but the way they're displaying their teeth and the tone of their voices suggest friendly conversation. The mortals are trying to confuse you. This is okay, you can banter right back.

"Both of you are insufficient and worthless," you say.

"Ah," Abigail says.

The two girls look at each other, then back down at your very serious face. The seriousness breaks a moment later as their eyes meet again. They have the temerity to start giggling at each other!

While you stew in resentment, Abigail and Daphne give each other hugs and quick goodbyes, then Daphne pauses before you and leans forwards a little. "Bye Dreamer. You take care of Abi for me, okay?"

"Hrmpf," you say.

She smiles and brings a hand down on your head. As you see it coming, you contemplate taking a bite out of her. It would teach her an important lesson about looking down upon her betters and also you're a bit hungry.

Before you can come to a decision, the hand lands on your head and… you feel your eyes going heavy, your knees going weak, even your tentacles loosening a little as your hair is ruffled.

She stands back up, ending the spell. "I'm off!" she says.

You stand there in a daze for a few long moments until Abigail shutting the door wakes you up. "Are you okay?" she asks.

"I am well," you say. No mere pat upon your head will keep you down! How dare she pat your head. You are the one who pats.

"Alright-y then. You look a bit tired. Did you want something to eat before heading off to bed?"

Why is she talking about travelling to the bed as if it's a big thing? It's just across the room, why would reaching it be worthy of notice? Mortals are strange, but this one is offering food. Maybe she has more lye. "Yes."

She hums a little as she bustles over to the stove and sets a pot onto it. Reaching into a cupboard, she pulls out the only two bowls within and places them on her table. "Going to need to make room," she says as she looks at all of her books. "I don't want to damage my school books."

"School books," you repeat. "For the Academy?"

"That's right," Abigail says, immediately perking up. She opens another cupboard that reveals plenty of tin cans and pulls a pair off the shelf. "That's where we'll be going, the both of us."

"Why?"

She shows her teeth again in a huge grin. "Because the Academy is the best school in all of Fivepeaks. The best magical school in the whole region, really. And if I—we—go there, we can learn all sorts of things about magic. I've been studying a whole lot already just to prepare. I'm going to be a magical researcher, pushing the bounds of what humanity can do with circles and runes!"

Your summoner is very excited. Her talking gets faster and soon she's gesturing with a ladle over a boiling pot of canned food.

"Daphne's going too, but she's not really as interested in the mechanics of magic as I am. Really, she says she's there to find a beau, but we both know that she's actually really passionate about material conversion magics. She's got a real gift for it."

Abigail keeps talking about the school, about how pretty it is, and about how all the professors are great until the food is ready. She grabs the bowls from the table and scoops some meaty sauce into them. There are little pieces of vegetables floating in it. It smells yummy.

She places the bowl before you, then a spoon next to it. As if you would need such an implement.

"Let's eat," she says as she sits next to you and picks up her own spoon.

You pick up the bowl from its edges and tip it into your mouth. It is yummy! Your summoner is the best cook, you decide as you guzzle down the stew. Way better than your salad, and you're basically a god compared to her, which makes her cooking better than godlike according to yourself.

A moment later you place the bowl back down and belch out a bubble of air caught in your throat. It escapes with a bit of steam from the boiling stew.

Abigail is staring. "Okay," she says finally before picking up her spoon and carefully blowing on it.

You watch her eat, tentacles poised to pick any falling food up. Abigail notices, because halfway through her bowl she sighs and asks you if you want the rest.

You do!

Tentacles wrap around her bowl and its contents join the first in your tummy.

"Right," Abigail says. "I think it's time for bed for you."

"I am not tired," you declare before your jaw almost dislocates with a yawn. "I am the night, and the night does not sleep when it doesn't want to."

"Uh-huh," Abigail says. "Not even a little nap? My bed is pretty comfortable." She gestures to the bed in the corner.

Well, you do like naps.

"Okay."

Hopping off the chair, you move over to the bed while your tentacles reach out and wrap around Abigail's thin form. "Dreamer!" she squeaks as you lift her off the ground and bring her to the bed.

Your other tentacles are moving the blankets around to form a proper cocoon. Once you have a nice fluffy pile of them moved aside, you place Abigail down and climb up next to her.

"H-hey, I have things to do," she protests.

"You said it was nap time."

Just to make sure she doesn't misbehave, you wrap her in even more tentacles, then your arms. It's nice and warm and smells like stew and Abigail.

This is good.

"Sleep," you tell Abigail.

She sighs again and wiggles a bit to get more comfortable. "Fine. Good night, Dreamer. It was nice meeting you."

"Yes," you decide. It has been nice so far.

It'll be nicer tomorrow.

CHAPTER FOUR

YOU WAKE up with a jaw cracking yawn, and that, all on its own, is enough to remind you that you have a fragile mortal body hanging onto your non-spatial, non-chronological, non-causality-caring mass.

Waking up from a nap is always a tricky thing. Once, you went to sleep in the great dark only to wake up and realize that there were new things around you. Planets and stars and teeny tiny mortals living on floating rocks.

Physics had pulled a quick one on you while you took a trillion year nap, the sneaky bugger.

But not today. You look down towards your pillow only to find that it is very squishy and soft and breathing a little. It's an Abigail. An Abigail pillow.

This is good. It's warm, and soft, and the little sounds she makes in her sleep are quite adorable.

Unfortunately, you have decided that the nap is over and that it is now time for waking up and action before the next nap. Carefully, you pull all of your tentacuddlers away from Abigail and show your teeth when she mumbles in her sleep and tries to grab onto some of them. Your summoner is beginning to come around to all the fun one can have with tentacles. Most excellent!

A peak out of a dirty window reveals that the sun is just starting to rise, the sky still the dark blue of early morning. That means you napped through the night. Or maybe you've been napping for days and Abigail entered some sort of mortal hibernation state.

Nah, Daphne would have come around to bother you if that was the case.

Hopping off the bed, you do your post-nap stretching. Each tentacle reaches out as far as it can until it's shivering with tension, then pulls back. You're not sure how to work with mortal limbs yet so you wrap a tentacle around your wrist and pull, and pull and pull. There's a pop from your shoulder, and then it feels warm.

With a squelch, your arm is torn out of your shoulder and, freed from its mooring, your tentacle swings it around and into the nearest wall with a splat.

You blink at the gushing wound at your side.

Darn, that's inconvenient.

You pick up your arm, trying to be quiet so as to not wake Abigail from her nap, and push it back into place.

It flops to the ground as soon as you let go.

Sighing at the puddle around your feet, you give up on your old arm, a pair of tentacles bringing it to the bin in the kitchen where fruit peels and empty cans of food are stacked. You shove it in the trash for now.

You glare at your missing arm until it grows back, then test your new fingers a few times. All's well that ends well.

Now, you're up, you're fully armed, you can't make too much noise or it'll wake Abigail and… and you're kinda bored.

There's hardly any room in Abigail's tiny home, everything is all cramped together and it's impossible to move without bumping into things.

You decide to fix that.

It's simple really, there's a limited amount of room here but the Great Infinity has a lot of space. An infinite amount, actually. So, with tentacles that are both here and not here at the same time, you grab some space and start stuffing it around Abigail's apartment.

It's a little messy. The entrance to her bathroom is now bigger than the rest of the apartment, her kitchen counter goes on for quite a ways and one of the legs on the kitchen table plunges into its own shadows, but at least things are bigger.

It's nice, until you notice that the shadows under the bed are bottomless. That won't do.

Getting onto your knees, you tuck your head under the bed and gaze into the Abyss.

The Abyss gazes back.

"Don't you have better things to do?" you ask the Abyss.

The Abyss shrugs a little. "Not really."

You glare at it. "Well go do nothing elsewhere."

With a huff, you take some space away from there. It wouldn't do for Abigail to lose something down there. The Abyss is very rude about giving things back.

You stand up, proud of your hard-ish work and clap your hands onto your bare thighs. Abigail stirs a little, her hair wobbling around in a rat's nest as she shifts her head. She's still wearing her glasses, the silly summoner.

Oh well, she'll wake up in due time.

You head over to the washroom to see if it can be improved too. It takes a few minutes to get there, on account of the distance, but that's alright.

The bathroom is a little dingy, and could use some scrubbing, but that's someone else's job. You put some space in the bottom of the toilet, and more space in the bath until it becomes like a deep ocean, then you use your tentacles to climb up to the vanity.

That's when you catch sight of yourself in the mirror. The girl that stares back is very cute, if you say so yourself, with frizzy brown hair just like Abigail's and pretty black eyes that spin with the slow cadence of a leaf caught in the winds of madness. You also have a button nose. It scrunches left, then right as you try to wiggle it around, eyes crossing as you try to see it yourself. Neat!

"D-Dreamer!" Abigail cries. "What's going on?"

Did Abigail get lost in her apartment? How silly.

You'll have to put off staring at yourself for a while, you need to go save Abigail so that she can make your breakfast.

"Is that blood?! Why is there blood all over? Dreamer!"

Oops?

CHAPTER FIVE

"I NEED TO get to work," Abigail says as she slips on an apron over her dress. The piece of clothing looks constrictive and annoying to wear.

You know this because Abigail, in her infinite cruelty, forced you into a dress and it is constrictive and annoying to wear. Unlike the jacket, it does not even have the benefit of smelling like your summoner. It's too big for you, reaching all the way down to your ankles while the waist is pinched around you by a thick belt, the only thing stopping the dress from slipping off you.

It is uncomfortable and demeaning. You never had to wear clothes in the places between places. There weren't any clothes there to begin with. These stupid mortal rules are stupid.

"I'm going with you," you tell her. You will earn many mortal currencies for your hard work and you will buy the prettiest dresses with them.

"I, I don't know if that's a good idea," Abigail says. She looks at you, then past you to the rest of the apartment. The rooms are all still warped, bigger in some places and smaller in others, the few lights she has insufficient to brighten the whole room up.

You think that maybe changing the room's size made her uncomfortable somehow. The silly summoner.

"It is a good idea," you say. "I will earn many coins with which to buy things." That is what work is for, or so you've come to understand.

"I… fine, but only if you promise not to do any… any sort of magic in the main room."

"Okay." That's an easy promise to make. You've never used magic before to begin with.

Abigail fidgets with her cuffs, then smooths out her apron. "Okay. Okay, we'll just have a quiet morning, and then in the afternoon we'll go see Daphne. Daphne can help."

You don't know what she's supposed to help with, but that's hardly your concern. You follow Abigail down the flight of stairs to the first floor, then into the main area of *Madam Morrigan's Artifices, Tinctures and Ingredients.* The shop is a quiet, dusty place this early in the morning, all the jars and platters sitting silently and waiting for people to show up and buy the stuff.

"What are these things for?" you ask as you point to all the shelves. Most are pretty yummy, but something tells you this isn't a market for foods.

"Oh, I guess you wouldn't know," Abigail said. "Um, do you know how circle magic works? Sometimes it's called Alchemy, or Symbiosy?"

"It all sounds silly. Just make the world do the things you want it to," you say. It's an easy concept to grasp. You don't know why your summoner would have a hard time with it, or why she's giving you such a strange look.

"W-well, I want to go to the Academy to learn more, but I can explain the basics," she says after shaking her head. She reaches up and ties her frizzy hair in a bun, then straightens her glasses. "Magic comes in three parts: instruction, material, source. The circle holds the instructions that tell the spell how to act, the materials of the spell need to be in contact with the circle and the source comes from Aether, that's a sort of liquid willpower that everyone makes just by being alive. It's a lot more complicated than that, though."

That all sounds very silly. "Does Aether taste good?" you ask.

"I don't know. Some nobles drink it, or add it to their food. It's kinda hard to get it though. Every month, everyone needs to go to the tax office to pay their Aether tax. They drain you of a bit of Aether. Or you can pay a fine instead. Um, students of the Academy don't need to give as much because you need more of it for lessons."

"They suck your magic juices?" you ask.

"When you hit puberty, yeah. Everyone does it, it's normal. The Aether is bottled for later, sold to nobles and war mages and used for important things."

You're frowning, you realize. If Abigail says it's normal, then maybe it is. Who are you to tell the mortals what to do with their magic juice. But it still sounds wrong. You might need to investigate that later.

Abigail walks to the front of the store and unlocks the door, turning a sign as she does so. "We sell materials here. The things you need to cast different spells. Though Madam Morrigan doesn't sell any of the really exotic stuff."

You nod along as you follow her across the shop. Your tentacles drift around you, nudging things in place, resorting shelves, rubbing away smudges from glass jars, tossing yummy things towards you so that you can snap them out of the air with your mouth, and dusting off the corners of shelves.

Abigail whips around half a second after you slip a few eel eyes into your mouth. You keep your mouth shut and hope that she doesn't notice that your cheeks are full. She eyes you, then your tentacles that have just finished with one shelf.

"O-okay," she says. "No tentacles on the floor. But if you want to help, there's a broom and dustpan in the back. Here, let me show you."

You follow Abigail, chewing on the eyeballs as you go. When you actually manage to squish one without it slipping between your teeth, it makes a great 'splat' feeling in your mouth and releases some juicy goodness all over. Not only yummy, but fun to eat. The perfect snack.

Abigail opens a small cupboard at the back and passes you a broom which you grab with two tentacles. She sighs, then shows you a metal dustpan. "This is a dustpan," she confirms. "See the circle inscribed at the bottom? If you press your thumb on this part of the handle and push some will into it, it turns all the contents of the pan into harmless smoke. Don't put your fingers on the circle and then press it. I don't want to have to bring you to a clinic because you lost a finger."

"Okay," you say as you grab the pan with a tentacle. What, does she think that you can't follow simple instructions? What a silly summoner.

Now, what does this harmless smoke taste like?

And would it work on a tentacle?

As you wonder this, you begin to dust. Dusting is easy. So easy.

It's a wonder mortals have a difficult time with it. You swish-swish the broom across the wooden planks of the floor, sending bits of dust scurrying across the floor in little waves. There's hair too, probably from one of the shelves where bundles of wolf's fur are stacked together. They don't taste very good, but they do have a nice texture to them. They tend to stick to the back of your throat, and when you cough them up you get to eat them all over again.

You start humming, an old song that you had once heard while travelling in the Paths that Lead to Somewhere, just a little ditty that wormed its way into your vast memory.

You stop humming when you notice reality starting to turn green. Annoying, that. With a huff, you tell the world to stop playing silly buggers and go back to being normal… or as normal as it was before. You're here to work as a dutiful shop clerk, not turn the world different colours.

It takes a few minutes to dust the whole store, minutes that Abigail spends flitting all over the place, righting displays, wiping counters and replacing jars onto some shelves that have been emptied a little through no fault of your own.

You pause to chew on some marbles that were neatly stacked on one shelf. Nice and crunchy.

But you're not here to nibble! Your summoner has given you a great quest and it is your duty to carry it out to the best of your ability!

You wield your broom like a lance ready to charge at dust foes and your dustpan is your stalwart shield against their choking assaults on your nose.

The dust bunnies stand no chance against your valiant charge and are soon dispersing like chaff in the wind to escape your mighty grasp.

But they did not expect the assault from the tentacle nation!

You split your tentacles into hundreds of teeny tiny tendrils that spear out and catch the defeated dust bunnies unaware. Soon they are dangling at the tips of your tentacular grasp, morale broken and dusty blood leaking out.

So you toss them all onto the dustpan like the corpses of enemies being tossed into a ditch.

Leaning forwards a little, you inspect the circle carved into the metal of the pan. It looks like it was stamped on by a big press. There's the name of a company there, and a copyright number again, just like the lights. Strange.

You press your thumb to the place Abigail showed you and wait... and wait some more.

It's not working.

"Abigail!" you yell. "Your pan's broken."

She looks up from where she is behind the counter and moves a lock of frizzy hair behind her ear. "Oh? Did the circle get scratched?" she asks as she tosses a pen she was using into a little cup and moves around the counter. Soon she's kneeling by your side and inspecting the dust-filled pan. "You did good," she says before rewarding you with a smile.

You look away. You are an elder, a Great One of unfathomable power. You don't need the praise of some mere mortal to make you blush. It's the stupid heat in this stupid shop. That's why you're so flustered.

"Let's see," Abigail says as she grabs the pan's handle and presses her thumb over the mark on its side.

You stretch your senses, curious as to how this magic stuff works.

There's a spark of something in Abigail, something wet and warm and soothing, like the very essence of life itself that goes from sitting within her like a still pond to rushing to her thumb. The circle on the pan drinks up the essence and then, with a woosh, the dust turns to smoke.

Cute!

The mortals figured out how to disintegrate things.

"Did you see how that worked?" Abigail asks.

"I did," you say. "I can do it now."

She smiles at you again, then like the stupid summoner she is, she pats you on the head before standing up. "Call me if you need help."

You take a moment to recentre yourself.

The door jingles while you're busy touching your head where Abigail just patted you and that, finally, gets you out of your day-dream of a many-armed Abigail pat-patting you all day long.

There's a short, scruffy looking human in the doorway. He's wearing a hood that doesn't do a good job of hiding his pock-marked and scabbed face. "Abigail!" he says as he spots your summoner behind the counter. "The most beautiful Abigail, it's a pleasure to see you again." He makes big motions with his arms that send his hood reeling off his head and reveals a big, goofy smile. "You're just the girl I need."

"Hello, Moriarty," Abigail says and you can feel her discomfort from here.

But that isn't any of your business. Your battle against the dust bunnies might have ended in victory, but the war rages on!

You collect another pile of dust while the man moves around the store. He spots you at some point, but doesn't actually comment except to snort at the way you're holding the broom tucked under your arm like a lance. It's not your fault the thing is so damned long.

Now to use the magic circle to disintegrate the pile of dust. The tricksy bit is using the same life essence that Abigail did. You, of course, aren't mortal, and are therefore not alive enough to have any sort of life juice in you. But there's plenty of life juice in the world at large.

You press a hand to the ground next to the dustpan and grip the handle with your other. You focus, feeling for the same life juice that Abigail used, but instead of looking for the stuff in her mortal body, you stretch out your senses into the ground and to the core of this living planet.

Plenty of life juice there!

You pull, and after just a tiny bit of resistance, a fraction of a fraction of the world's essence is torn out of the ground, through your hand, arm, shoulder and finally into the magical circle.

There's a woosh.

You notice the perfectly circular hole in the ground first, mostly where the dustpan used to be. Then, when you look up, you see the hole in the ceiling that keeps going all the way through Abigail's apartment, the roof, and into the cloudy sky above.

Neat!

And you still have tons of life juice left in you, so much that you're practically glowing with the stuff.

The dustpan's a little broken, but that's a problem for later.

Standing up, you cross the store, stalling Abigail's conversation with the customer as you walk past her glowing as if you'd just nibbled on a billion firefly butts.

"What?" she asked.

"Getting a jar," you tell her as you walk into the backroom.

It's not hard to find an empty jar. There are plenty of them laying around, waiting to be filled with all sorts of yummy things.

You take a few out of their boxes and push your life juices in them. It feels a little bit like when two tentacles rub together, but in the place your soul would be if you had one.

Grinning, you raise up a jar filled with glowing juices. Perfect! Abigail will be able to use this to fill up her soul's life juice swamp.

Now you just need to give it to her and reap the headpats.

You wiggle the jar filled with life juice around, the contents stirring with big gloops and glops like pudding with too much milk added in. If pudding glowed and was made of life energy.

You realize that you might be hungry.

Either way, Abigail said that some people took her juices out of her every month as a sort of tax, which means that if you give her this she won't have to do that, and will therefore be happy with you. And if she's happy with you, she will give you headpats and cuddles. Not that you want those things, of course.

After a bit of thinking, you realize that the gift doesn't really come from you. It's technically the world's life juice that you sucked out.

Abigail might be miffed if she learns that you stole something to give it to her.

Silly summoner and her silly morality.

Getting onto your knees, you pat the ground. "Thank you, little planet. I will cherish your juice," you say. "But if you tell Abigail I will eat you."

There, now everything is safe.

You rub the dust off your knees, clap your hands together to clean them, then grab your jar again before moving to the front of the shop. Moriarty, that weirdo, is still there. He's leaning way over the counter, his weight on his elbows as he talks to Abigail. "Oh, my sweet Abigail, you poor thing, working here all day. Tell you what. Next time I'll send my Familiar with an order, and when you come to deliver it, we can spend some… quality time talking in my workshop. I know how interested you are in the finer arts. I'm sure I could teach you plenty."

Is this man trying to convince Abigail to mate with him? The fool! If she spends time with him, it'll mean less time with you, which is unforgivable.

You walk up to the man and poke him in the thigh hard enough that he hisses and jumps back. When he looks down, you meet his eyes with your own. "Mine," you say while pointing right at Abigail. "You will not mate her without my permission, mortal."

"I what?" he asked. "I was trying to do no such thing," he says.

"Are you done buying stuff?" you ask.

"I think he was," Abigail is quick to add. She has a bunch of jars and boxes piled up next to her on the counter, most of them already in a pair of cardboard boxes. She quickly puts the rest of them into a box and shoves it towards Moriarty. "Thank you for shopping at Madam Morrigan's."

"Yeah, now leave," you tell him.

"Why, I never! Who is this rude child?" he asks Abigail as if you're not there.

He's the rude one! You reach out with a pair of tentacles and grab his boxes, then wrap your hand around his wrist. He's sputtering a lot, and staring at your tentacles as if he's never seen any before as you drag him to the door. "Bye now," you say as you shove his stuff into his chest and push him out the door.

When you turn around, you find that Abigail is hiding her mouth behind both hands, but the way her eyes are crinkled in the corners suggests that she's smiling. "You can't do that, Dreamer," she says.

"He was rude," you say.

"Well, yeah, but that's just Moriarty. He's always been that way. I think he's mostly harmless, just really full of himself."

"He wanted to mate with you."

Abigail might have contracted some filthy mortal sickness because her skin turns very red in the time it takes you to blink twice. "N-no, that's not, I'm sure you're wrong."

Her denial changes nothing. "I obtained a gift for you. I made it myself." Well, you didn't make the jar, or the juice, but you put the juice in the jar, so that counts as making something, probably. You walk past a confused and still red Abigail to the back where your glowing jar is still waiting and pick it up. "Here, this will make you better," you say as you place the jar onto the table.

Abigail looks at it for just a moment before gasping. The redness is gone now, but your silly summoner went too far in the other direction and is now too pale. "Dreamer, no," she whispers before snatching the jar off the table. She looks towards the door, then grabs you by the hand and drags you into the backstore, jar tucked up against her chest. "Where did you get this?" she asks.

"I made it."

"Dreamer, this is Aether," Abigail says as she shakes the jar. "This much… Dreamer, this is more than a person can make in a year. And it looks pure."

"Yes?" you ask. She's being very silly.

"This is worth more than gold," she says. "You, you could buy the shop with this much."

You fail to see the problem, but Abigail looks scared. She's shaking, shivering and holding the jar as if it might explode at any moment. "The planet helped a little," you admit. "But I paid it in pats. Which you're supposed to do for me since I gave you a gift."

"The planet?" she repeats.

You nod. "I used a sucky tentacle and pulled the life juice out of the core. It still has lots."

"I..." Abigail swallows and gently places the jar on a nearby workbench. "Dreamer, first the apartment, now this... what are you?"

You stare at your summoner, at Abigail, for a few long moments.

She wants to know what you are. That's rather simple, isn't it. You're you. You're the only you around and there aren't any other yous that you know of. If there were other yous, you'd have eaten them already.

"I'm me," you tell her. "I'm the Dream That Rests Eternal In The Spaces Between Spaces, In The Moments Between Times. I like taking naps where I can't be bothered." The last part you add to explain because Abigail is starting to look even more confused.

She kneels down so that she's at the same height as you. "You're not just some magical creature, are you? You're not a mimic."

You don't know what a mimic is, but you doubt any could mimic you. "I'm me. I told you that already."

She laughs, once. It sounds wrong, not like a happy laugh at all. "Yeah, you're you," she agrees to the obvious. "But what are you? You're not human, you're not the sort of creature I've read about in my bestiaries. Daphne didn't recognize you. Familiars are supposed to compliment the summoner, so I want to know—have to know—what you are."

"That's silly," you tell her. If you could distill the essence of what you are and what you're able to do in a few words you would, but people are more than just a race and some attributes, and you're more people than most. "But I can tell you, if you want. I just need to give you the knowledge."

"Give me the knowledge?" Abigail repeats.

You nod. "Yup. It's easy. I just need to put it in your head. But I won't do it for free," you warn her while waving a finger between the two of you. "It's a lot of work, and I guess I should make sure you stay mostly sane because you wouldn't like it otherwise. So I need to be paid for it."

"Paid," she repeats. She looks over her shoulder towards the counter where the cash machine sits. "I have some money," she says.

"I don't care about that stuff," you tell her. Money is for trading for services and stuff. You can do everything already, and if you want to eat something no one will stop you. No, what you want is a whole lot less tangible. "I want cuddles and headpats and love."

Abigail blinks slowly, then her lips curve up and she presses a hand over her mouth to hide a giggle.

"It's not funny!" you say.

She just giggles harder. "Oh, Dreamer. I might not know what you are, but you're not a bad person. I'm happy that you're my Familiar. You're so much better than a cat or an owl."

Well, yes, you are in fact better than either of those. "Obviously," you say. "So, one cuddle for one knowledge. But not just a small cuddle, a good one."

"Alright," Abigail says as she gets her giggles under control. "One cuddle for one knowledge." She reaches her arms out and waits in the optimal hugging position.

You grin as you collapse against her chest and wrap your own arms around her. Abigail 'oofs' at the impact, but she grips you right back. Then she starts rubbing a hand up and down your back, sending warm tingles up your spine.

"You know," she says. "I never really thanked you for being my Familiar. So, thanks, I guess. It's a little weird. I don't think most mages bother, but you're more... you than other Familiars, so I guess it's only fair."

Oh yeah, this is the good stuff. Coming to this mortal realm was obviously the right decision if this was the kind of reward you'd be getting. Hugs and compliments and snacks within tentacle grasping range. There was little more you could ask for.

You reach a hand up and press it to the back of Abigail's head. "Close your eyes," you tell her.

The eyes are the windows to one's soul. It's why you have tentacles to feel things instead of eyes all over. Windows go both ways, after all. "Mmm, okay," Abigail says into your shoulder.

She's ready then. You pat-pat the back of her head.

The human brain is a squishy thing. It's very fragile and kinda poorly made. You need to be very careful as you slip your tentacles through her skull and into the meaty bits.

You root around for a bit and find the metaphorical off switch. With a flick, Abigail goes loose in your grasp, her breathing stops, and her heart beats one last time and shudders to a stop. The hug isn't as nice now that she's dead.

Sighing, you let her down onto the floor, keeping her steady with a whole lot of tentacles while a whole lot more phase into her head. Mortals are so squishy and easy to break, but you're starting to think that they're fun anyway.

You find the bits of Abigail's mind that deal with remembering things; there are a few of them, and they're kinda small. You compare that to all the knowledge of who you are that you wanted to cram in there, the infinite eons spent in the great darkness, the long naps tucked away in corners where space met time at odd angles. The kerfuffles with Great Old Ones and Elder Gods.

It won't fit.

Shrugging, you get rid of all the boring parts, keeping only the more fun memories of who and what you are, then you trim that back even more. It wouldn't do for your summoner to know everything about you. Plus there are some embarrassing things that even you'd rather not remember.

Once everything is nice and neat, you notice that your brain spike is still bigger than the room you're in. That won't fit in her head, not unless you make her head bigger on the inside… a thought for later.

You cut out all your knowledge of things you can do. She wanted to know about you, not learn how to do the things you can do. Some more trimming and you're left with a bundle of fleshy nerves that should fit in her head just like a tiny, cute little tumour.

You pat it into place, tongue stuck between your teeth as you focus.

And done!

You poke her brain so that it starts up again, then zap her heart back into beating. She was only dead for a minute, so she's probably fine.

Abigail gasps and sits up straight. Her apron squishes against her knees as she brings them up to her chest and starts to breathe really fast.

"Are you okay?" you ask.

Her head whips around towards you. "You're a god," she whispers.

You blink. That's silly. She's being silly.

"But… you can't be. There aren't any gods," she says next. "The inquisition, if they find out—"

You roll your eyes. "Of course there are gods. Don't go telling the Elder Gods that they don't exist, or they'll make you stop existing. But I'm not one of them. I'm Dreamer."

She wipes away the drops of blood pouring out of her nose with the back of one hand. She doesn't seem to notice, which is handy because you're pretty sure that's not supposed to be happening.

"I gave canned food to a god."

You sigh. She's being extra silly. Clearly this didn't work out the way you wanted.

The rest of the workday passes in a strange sort of quiet. Abigail returns to her work as if nothing happened, except she keeps looking at you when she thinks you're not paying attention.

Joke's on her, you're always paying attention.

Still, as you sweep the last of the shop and push the remaining dust under a shelf, you're left with enough quiet time to think things through. Abigail is really nice. She gives good hugs, is fun to cuddle, and is kind enough to share her food with you. That's more than you can say about literally any creature you met in any other realm. You don't know if it's because she's a frail mortal, or if it's a quirk that's unique to her.

In the end it doesn't matter, she must be protected.

Abigail's going to get old, and frailer, and then she's going to die.

The wooden handle of your broom cracks as your fists tighten around it. No more hugs. No more cuddles.

Unacceptable!

No, from here on out, you decide that since you're Abigail's Familiar you're going to be the best Familiar ever. You're going to teach her how to be like a god compared to all the other mortals, and if she wants to go to some magic school then you're going to make sure she learns all of the magic and is the biggest boss of that school even if it means having to eat the headmaster.

You're brought out of your reverie about delicious school staff when Abigail trudges to the front of the shop and flips the little Open/Closed board over the front door." That's it for today," she says aloud.

"That was kind of fun," you say as you move to the back and lean the broom against the counter. The floor is super clean thanks to your efforts. And so are some of the shelves because those efforts made you peckish.

"Yeah, I'm… glad you helped," Abigail says. Her smile feels a little strained.

Your eyes narrow as you cross the room and come to stand on your tentacles so that you're at her head's height. Abigail tries to back away, but your tentacuddlers grab her and keep her in place. "You're hurt!" you accuse after a bit of inspecting.

"I'm fine," Abigail lies like a big fat liar.

You harrumph quite strongly and shake your head at how silly your summoner is being. Obviously she somehow got hurt while you weren't paying attention. It's definitely not because you killed her and brought her back from the dead, because that would just be silly. "Stay still," you order her, not that she can really uncuddle herself from your grasp.

"Dreamer," she complains.

You ignore her protests and inspect her properly. Some of her fleshy bits seem damaged, mostly around her head. Maybe you patted too much into her brain and it's trying to fix itself? You're not quite sure. The problem is that you're not a fleshcrafter. This isn't your area of expertise. "You're a little hurt," you tell her. "You need a person that can fix mortals to make you better. Or… I could improve you."

"I think I'll be fine," she protests even more. "I'll get better, and if I don't I'll ask a physician. I know a few from working here, they can help."

You haven't decided what to do when the doorbell jingles as it opens.

Releasing Abigail, you plop onto your feet and lean to the side to see past Abigail and to the front. There's a woman there, tall, with severe features and long braided hair. She eyes the shop with a quick glance, then focuses first on Abigail, then on you. "Hello Abigail. I didn't think we still had a customer left in the shop?"

"Ah, hello Madam Morrigan," Abigail says with a quick bow from the hip.

This lady must be important if your summoner is bowing to her. Plus her name is on the front of the shop.

"How was the day?" the lady says as she moves deeper into the shop. You can sense her scanning everything with a gimlet eye. "Productive, I see, judging by the lowered stock. I'll have to send a request to restock the inventory sooner than I had expected."

"It wasn't too busy, actually," Abigail says as she walks over to the lady and follows her. "Oh, by the way, this is Dreamer, she's my Familiar."

"Hello," you say.

The madam stops and eyes you up and down. "Her dress is ill-fitting. You'll need to find something more appropriate for it to wear. A mimic of some sort?"

"Something like that," Abigail says with a nervous chuckle. "She helped around the shop today."

"You sell delicious stuff," you tell the lady.

Abigail starts going very red in the face at that. You're not sure why, it's not like you lied or anything.

The lady looks around again, then faces Abigail properly. "It will be docked from your pay," she says. "Get me a full inventory by the end of the week. I'll see about charging only the supplier rates. Do train your new Familiar better."

"Yes ma'am," Abigail says while staring at the floor.

"Well, the shop's closed. I'm certain you have better things to do. Go, shoo. Have some fun, you're too young to spend the entire day in this dusty store."

"T-thank you, ma'am," Abigail says before turning, grabbing your hand, and moving towards the front.

How very curious.

CHAPTER SIX

"WHERE ARE we going?" you ask Abigail as you look away from where her hand is holding onto yours and up to her back.

You find that you're just a teensy little bit lost as Abigail leads you deeper into the city. There are lots of mortals around, with little hats on their heads and long coats to protect them from the foggy weather.

You don't have a long coat though, you only have one of Abigail's old dresses on, and Abigail herself is still just wearing the dress she worked in without the apron.

"I have a whole list of things I need to buy if I want to make it to the Academy. They expect you to show up on the first day with the equipment for the whole year on hand."

"That's weird," you say.

Abigail nods even though she's not looking at you. "Yeah, well, they want to make sure that every student can prove that they're ready even before they're accepted. It's how they work."

"Okay," you say. "So what are we buying first?"

Abigail's hand tightens around your hand. "You need some clothes first," she says before reaching with her other hand into the big bag she picked up before leaving the shop. It's a sort of purse, you suppose, but it's bulky and made of stained canvas. She searches within it for a moment before pulling out a sheet of paper with a list on the front. Half of the objects on it are crossed out already. "Then I have a few things to grab too. We'll need to be careful with how much we spend."

You try to reach for it, but your little fingers are way too short. Fortunately, Abigail sees your attempt and hands the list over.

Entry Requirements for the Five Peaks Academy of Magic and Magecraft
To be eligible to enter the finest academy one must present themselves with the following equipment on the day of acceptance:
1x Familiar
1x Set of Carving Knives (Types A through D)
1x Scale
1x Set of Circle Crafting Tools (compass, triangles, rulers, tracing papers, chalk)
3x Regulation Uniforms, matching your gender
1x Grade One hat
Notebooks, pens and other note-taking equipment is strongly encouraged.
Also, be aware that all students MUST have the following books for Grade One lessons:
    Crafting the Circle, by Sir Roun D. Cunference
    How to Train Your Familiar, by Raven D. Agger
    The Call of Magecraft, by C. Thulhu
    Alchemy All in One, by Yog S. Othoth
    Inscribing for Beginners, by Clearence Carver

"No food?" you ask as you take in the list.

"There's a cafeteria in the Academy," Abigail says. "But I heard that it's a little expensive to eat there. We'll have to pack sandwiches every day."

Clearly she underestimates your ability to find things to eat in the most unusual of places. You're pondering taking a nibble out of some of the passing mortals when Abigail tugs your hand.

"We'll pick up the uniforms here," she says before gesturing to a shop across the street.

The store is pretty, with big pillars before it and stonework around the windowed front. A few mannequins in black robes are standing behind the glass to one side, and on the other there's a long ball gown that reaches all the way down to the floor.

You let out a low 'ohhh' as the two of you step into the shop. There are lots of people here, most of them around Abigail's age and concentrated around the racks and racks of black robes and hats sitting atop strange boxes.

"The first graders are the ones with the red trim," Abigail explains as she brings you to the back of the store. "Then in second year, it's yellow, then green, and the final years have purple trim. The hats are also different for every year." She gestures to a rack with four hats sitting on it. The first has nearly no brim and a really tall crown that ends in a point. The others all have shorter and shorter crowns and brims that grow longer with every year until the last one is hardly more than a bump with a huge brim.

"Those look silly," you say.

"It's tradition," Abigail says. "Which does tend to be a bit silly, sometimes." She looks around, then spots all the pretty dresses on the other side of the store. "How about you go check out those dresses and find something you like? I, I don't think I can afford anything like that here, but it will give us an idea of what to look for."

You want to stay with Abigail, but she seems busy wincing at the price tags on the ugly robes around her. So you decide to wander off and do as she asks.

The dresses are very pretty here, with ruffles and lace and all sorts of poofness. There are some in pastel blues and bright yellows that stick out a whole lot. They're nice, but they're not very... you.

And then you find it.

Tucked away in a back corner of the shop, left almost abandoned by the staff on a mannequin that looks a little worse for wear, is the perfect dress. It looks a little worn, but that only adds to its charm. There are big lacy petticoats and a floofy skirt and there's even a capelet draped over the shoulders.

You approach it carefully, as if it's a wild animal that might bolt at any moment. A beige tag is dangling from one of the dress's arms so you snatch it and look at the numbers. There are two zeros before the dot, which in mortal number theory means that this is a very expensive dress.

Abigail seemed worried about money, so there's no way she would buy this, not unless it meant not buying all of her other things and you wouldn't test her love for a dress.

You chew on your lip as you think, chew so hard that you don't even notice the girls walking up to you.

"Poor thing, are you lost?"

You look up to see three girls in the ugly uniforms that Abigail was looking at, two of them with tall hats with red trim and one in a slightly shorter cap and with yellow trim around the hems of her dress. "I am not lost," you tell the one in the middle of the pack.

She kneels down, blond hair cascading around her shoulders as she drops to your height. "You're not? Well, you're too young for the Academy," she says, then she looks at the dress you're wearing. "And you're too poor for this shop."

Her friends titter and giggle. You look down at your dress. It's a bit dusty, and it doesn't fit you at all, but Abigail gave it to you, so it's a good dress. Maybe she has another way of knowing that you have no money. "Okay," you tell her. "You're boring now. Go away. I'm getting that dress and you're distracting me."

She's the one giggling now. "Oh, you are?"

"Obviously."

You reach out with tentacles that the girls can't see and grab the dress. You don't grab it here though.

There are an infinite number of universes, each one layered atop the next like the pages in a book. So, just like someone opening a book up and tearing out a page, you reach into one dimension to the left and tear the dress out of it.

Your nose scrunches as there's an explosion of cloth and lace and frills and the corner of the shop you're in is swamped by a thousand near-identical copies of the same dress.

You're bowled over and the girls are buried under a tsunami of frills.

You blink when the tumbling stops, only then realizing that you might have been a little enthusiastic with your cross-dimensional tearing.

Oh well, now you have lots of pretty dresses! You're sure they'll be cheap once the people in the store stop screaming. But just in case, you tuck a few of them away in the dimensions where you store most of your mass.

Your real body deserves a pretty dress too, after all.

You wiggle into one of the dresses, taking your time and some tentacles to figure out the whole petticoat situation. Then, clad in your new dress, you wiggle your way out of the pile you're buried in and stand atop some dressed to find Abigail.

She's at the front of the shop, a receipt in hand and her mouth open as she stares at all the dresses. When you walk over to her, she grabs some dresses from the counter with one arm, and your hand with hers.

"What are we buying next?" you ask Abigail as you hop out of the store. There are still people panicking inside, mostly as they try to unbury the mages that were too close when you copied your new dress.

Not that any of that matters because you are the proud new owner of the prettiest dress. Your entire body is covered in frills and lace except for your head and hands and feet. Even your real body is now protected by an ablative layer made up of billions of petticoats. Anyone trying to hurt you now is in for a lacey surprise!

"I still need a few things," Abigail says. "I can get those at the other end of the market district. Stay close." She wiggled a finger in your direction. "I know that what happened in there was your fault. You're going to have some explaining to do."

Explain what? You wanted a pretty dress, it was too expensive, so you took a free one from elsewhere. You hardly deserve this finger wiggling treatment.

You spin away from Abigail to demonstrate how unamused you are… And pause.

You do that again. Face Abigail, spin away.

Looking down, you repeat the motion, watching as your floofy skirts rise up with the spin. You spin again, and again, each time making the skirts poof out.

This is *spectacular!*

You spin and spin and spin, giggles escaping you as the world wibbles and wobbles and you leave lacey afterimages in the air and your skirts sing as they swoosh around.

Your giggles are soon joined by Abigail's and she presses a hand over her mouth to hide her smile. "Are you having fun?" she asks.

"Yes!" you declare as you stop. "Lots."

"Alright then," she says. "I don't want to cut into you fun, but we do need to get my things." She lifts her bags where she stuffed her school uniform already, the pointy tip of a hat is sticking out the end, red tassles fluttering. "I'm still missing a lot of little things. And I wanted to visit Daphne later. Because what happened in that... I don't know."

"Okay!" You tell her. "But you need to get a fluffier dress too, so that we can spin together."

She rolls her eyes and plants her hand on your head. "It's easy to forget what you are when you act that way," she says.

"But I'm me."

She sighs and rubs your hair. "You certainly are."

Following next to Abigail, you take in the city all around you, eyes looking up into the sky even as grey clouds churn above and the wind that's slipping between the buildings around you turns cold. You see more and more people fixing their hats on their heads and tugging their coats closed, then you feel the first splatter of rain smack you on the head.

"We should hurry or we'll be all wet," Abigail says before she picks up the pace.

You don't mind the wetness, you're a creature of the depth and of tentacles, being wet is an everyday occurrence to you. But this body is a lot drier. You take in all the long coats that the mortals around you are wearing and come to a decision.

You let your tentacles slip out from the bottom of your skirt, then wrap them around your shoulders and arms and waist. It only takes a bit of effort to spawn more tentacles from those tentacles, then to have them change texture to match the canvas-y material you see a lot of coats are made of. Soon enough you have an awesome long coat wrapped snugly around you, only it's better than any normal long coat because it's made of tentacles.

A tentacoat, as it were.

Abigail is eyeing you carefully, but she just shakes her head once your tentacoat is complete. Obviously she is jealous of your waterproofing methods, so you whip out a tentacle towards her and ignore her squeak as it multiplies and covers her from head to toe. In the time it takes her to blink she's covered in her own tentacoat. "T-thanks?" she says.

"Yes," you reply.

It only takes a few minutes to arrive at the shop, but in those minutes the sky opens up to a downpour of rain that pelts down on the city like a deluge. People start running instead of walking and newspapers and umbrellas rise up to keep the rain away. There's steam rising from the circles engraved within the little gutters along the edges of the streets as they make the water evaporate and the strange horseless carts rumbling along skitter as their wooden wheels lose traction around corners.

Abigail pulls you into a shop at a run, doorbell jingling madly to announce your presence and your victory in escaping the rain.

"Hello and welcome," a deep, rumbly voice says.

You spin on the spot to get rid of some of the water, but your dress is all soaked and it isn't nearly as fun even if it sends arcs of water all over.

"Oi, you're getting my wares all wet, little lady."

"I'm terribly sorry, sir," Abigail says before bowing.

The shopkeeper is a huge man, a slab of muscle that's barely contained in a button up shirt with a leather apron before it. He waves the excuses away, then gestures across the shelves of his shop. "Welcome nonetheless. I sell nothing that would be damaged by a bit or rainwater. Only the best in alchemical equipment here."

Scales and alembics and strangely shaped glass tubes are all sitting on soft velvet cushions within display cases on wooden pedestals and there are bright ads plastered on every wall telling you which company has the best equipment that would make even you an excellent alchemist.

You have to shake your head to refocus. You're here to help Abigail, not stare at the pretty things.

"We're here for Academy things," Abigail explains to the large shopkeeper.

"You will find no better equipment for your schooling needs than in my shop, young ladies, for there is no greater expert in the manufacturing of fine equipment than Henri Ford," the man says before sweeping into a bow that has all sorts of little flourishes of his hands. He's surprisingly graceful for such a huge mortal. "I have a package meant just for people looking to enter the academy. It's not my greatest equipment, I'm afraid, but it is everything you'll need in your first grade."

"I think that would do," Abigail says with a smile. "Though I do have some of what I need already. I work at Madam Morrigan's and she has some old gear she doesn't mind me using."

"Madam Morrigan! How is that terrifying old prude doing?" he asks, his over-the-top gestures fading a little as he eases back into a calmer stance. He moves over to the back of the shop and you notice that there's no counters or anything, just a whole lot of pedestals that he dances around without actually looking at them.

It's a weird way to display all the teeny tiny tools and scales and devices that look so fragile, you decide.

Maybe he wants people to break them? What a tricksy man. While he's busy opening up a package and showing its contents to Abigail, the occasional knife and scalpel being pulled out and set aside as she tells him what she doesn't need, you start looking around.

Most of the things for doing alchemy are made of tin, though lots of them have coppery bits hammered over the surfaces that would be in contact with the… stuff.

You realize that you don't actually know all that much about alchemy. It's supposed to be about turning one thing into another thing, which you suppose is kind of neat. Even you would have a moderately difficult time doing that.

Copying things, on the other hand, you can do easily enough. You yoink some of the prettier equipment away with translucent tentacles, stuffing them into the many, many skirts piled on your real body. You'll find them later. Probably.

"Hey, mister Ford," you say to the big shopkeeper who looks up. It seems that Abigail had most of the things she needs already, so he's not going to be selling her all that much stuff. "Do you have a thing for people to learn how to do alchemy?"

His eyes light up. "I do indeed! A set for true beginners, including some books that would teach you the basics. Perfect for your first experiments in the domain of transformative magics and perfectly safe as well." He stands up and practically dances over to a display where a leather satchel is waiting. "Something like this. Only seventeen marks or seventy-two fiats."

"I don't think we need anything like that," Abigail says. She pats your shoulder. "I can show you a few things later, if you want. But we're a little tight on money right now."

"Oh, okay," you say. No point in arguing over something so silly. Henri puts the bag back in place, and you slip it into your realm when he turns around. Abigail's eyes widen and she gives you a look. She must be proud that you figured out a way to get around this whole money business.

"I-I think that's all we need," Abigail says in a hurry. She tosses the remaining stuff laying around her in a box and fishes inside her purse for a moment before returning with a pile of paper bills. "I hope city fiat is good?" she asks.

"Ah, yes, of course," Henri says, seemingly caught flat-footed by the sudden urgency in Abigail's demeanor. You're kind of confused too.

Abigail thanks the shopkeeper profusely, then grabs your hand and practically drags you out of the shop and back into the pouring rain. You're glad that you never took off your tentacoats because if anything the rain is even stronger now.

"You can't do that," Abigail says, eyes desperate as she pulls you into an alleyway and grabs you by both shoulders. Her hair is plastered against her head and her glasses, usually so good at making her eyes look bigger, are all drippy. "You can't just... steal things, Dreamer."

"But," you begin.

"No. No you can't do that. Please. I... the things at Madam Morrigan's, the stuff just now. It's too much. It's not right."

You don't get it. They're just things. Yummy, shiny things, but still just stuff. You're sure people can make more if they want. But Abigail doesn't seem to think that way at all. "Okay?" you say.

"Do you understand why you can't do that?" she asks.

You shake your head. "I don't, but if you don't want me to I can stop." She makes a noise that hurts you in the heart. "I'm sorry?" you try. You have to blink a lot because the rain is splashing on your face.

Abigail wraps you in a hug. It's wet, and not warm at all because of the coats between you, and it's the best thing. "Oh, Dreamer."

You pat her back and hope that she feels better. If it helps, you could give the stuff back to the shopkeeper. And maybe you could barf up some of the stuff you nibbled from the shop later. But those things don't matter that much. You hurt Abigail's feelings, and you don't know how to fix those.

You'll need to find a way to make her feel better, a mortal fixer of sorts. And you think you know just where to look.

At the far end of the alley is a sign hanging from a rusty post. It's made of tubes that glow from within with green light. *Doctor Dietrich Grenzler, Fleshcrafter.*

That looks perfect.

You really want to visit the fleshcrafter person. It sounds like they could make Abigail better and that's the most important thing. Maybe. You're not sure how or why she's making the bad sounds, or why they're bad.

Then again, finding out why shouldn't be too hard.

You bring a hand way up and touch Abigail's cheek. It's very soft and warm, good for snuggling, as is right and proper. "What were those noises?" you ask.

Abigail makes another noise with her nose, a sort of sniffly sound that you also don't like, then she puts on a smile. It's a bad smile, her lips moving up in the corners but her eyes are still sad. "It's nothing," she says.

You shake your head. You're the elder here, you'll be the one to decide if it's nothing or not, and you decided that it's something. Unfortunately, it's not the kind of thing that you can crush with your tentacles or nibble at until it's gone. "You're making sad noises. I want to know why so it doesn't happen again."

Abigail's smile becomes more real. "It's just… I'm worried. You do things that aren't… right, and it might get you in trouble. The inquisition… it might be trouble and I'm afraid that you'll be hurt."

"That's silly," you say. "I'm unhurtable." At least, nothing you've seen these mortals do could hurt you.

"But they might try to hurt you, and that would hurt me," she says.

You'd nibble their souls apart long before they hurt Abigail! No one's going to make your cuddle provider sad except for you. And if you do it's all an accident. "Fine then. You need to tell me the stuff that I shouldn't do so that I don't do them." You frown a little. "And tell me about the Inquisition. You talk about it as if it's scary. Scarier than me."

Abigail makes another sound, but this time it's happier. She grabs you by the shoulders and squishes your face against her chest while patting the back of your head. Mission success!

When the hugging ends, Abigail holds you by the shoulders and takes a deep breath. "The Inquisition is important. They're the ones that secure copy rights on any magic circles that mages invent and who make sure royalties are paid. That's not all they do. They also make sure that there are no cults and things like that."

"Cults?" you ask.

Abigail nods then hugs you again. You're not sure why, but you won't say no to more hugs. "Cults are bad," she tells you. "They worshipped all sorts of things, false gods and evil prophecies and things like that, but the Inquisition came in and disproved everything and broke up all the religions. Since gods aren't real, religion can't be right, so stuff like that is illegal here, and in most places where the Inquisition reaches. They used all the gold and stuff they got to build big schools like the Academy."

You're not sure how you feel about this. On the one tentacle, the only godlike thing these mortals should be worshipping is you. There should be statues of your tentacular glory all over and they should sacrifice valuable time to pat-patting you on the head. On the other tentacle, now the others like you (but probably not as pretty or as awesome) don't have a foothold in the mortal world to steal your precious pat-pats.

"Okay," you say. "Then I'll be sure to not annoy them too much unless they annoy me first."

Abigail makes another choking noise and your attention snaps back to her. "I think just being who you are would annoy them, Dreamer."

"You're making bad sounds again," you tell her. "Do I need to put back all the things I took to fix it?"

Abigail stands a little taller and looks back towards the street. "I guess we should. But I'm not sure how we'll explain you taking the things out of the displays."

You shrug. "I'll just copy all the things first, so that you can have some too." It takes only a passing thought to spin the stuff you're holding in just the right way for them to split apart. Then you take all of the originals and toss them onto a pile of skirts that you use to grab onto the whole lot without needing a dozen tentacles.

"What do you mean, copy?" Abigail asks.

You don't have time to answer.

A hole is shred into reality a few feet above your head and Abigail 'eeps' as she stumbles back. That's good, because now she's outside of the splash radius.

With a grunt of effort, you push your tentacle through the rip in reality and right into and past the shop's brick wall.

Having a tentacle the size of a small tree pierce through a wall is surprisingly loud, you discover as both you and Abigail shield your head from flying bits of masonry.

"Oops?" you say before letting go of the stuff your tentacle is holding onto. You might have dropped them on one of those glass displays, judging by all the glass-breaking noises.

Your tentacle slithers sheepishly back into the hole in reality and closes it on the way back.

"Oh no," Abigail breathes. She grabs your hand and starts dragging you along. "We... we need to run," she says.

"It's okay," you tell Abigail before wrapping her in a whole lot of tentacles and bringing her closer. Hugging fixes all problems. In fact, hugging is almost as good for fixing problems as tentacles are. Maybe there's some long lost link between tentacles and hugs? More food for thought.

"D-Dreamer," Abigail says as she fusses in your embrace. "We don't have time for this, we need to run."

You snort. No time for hugs? What a silly summoner. If being stuck in a fleshy mortal body has taught you anything it's that there's always time for more hugging and cuddling and other tentacle-summoner-based activities.

Still, Abigail looks kind of worried. She's looking past you and towards the exit of the alleyway where the shopkeeper's voice is coming from. He's screaming a lot.

Maybe you can put aside the cuddling.

But only for a bit.

"Okay," you say before you begin to walk deeper into the alley and past the Fleshcrafter's store. You wanted to stop there to see if they could fix Abigail for you, but it's clear that you don't have time. There might be other solutions; better ones, even.

"Can you put me down?" Abigail asks as she pats the tentacles holding you up.

Since she's asking nicely and since she's pat-patting your tentacle, you decide to be nice and deposit her feet-first on the ground next to you. Then, while she's still finding her balance, you strike!

Your soft, meaty hand slips into hers and latches on before she can so much as twitch. You have snared your summoner's hand! A minor but important victory. "Where does Daphne live?" you ask.

"Huh?" she asks. "Oh, she lives… a few blocks down from here, near the base of Academy Hill."

"We should go see her then," you say.

Abigail looks down at you, but another shout from the alley has her making up her mind. She shifts her back on her shoulder and pulls you along by the hand. "Okay, we'll go see Daphne," she says.

You exit onto the street and, after a bit of looking around, Abigail leads you uphill and along a road covered in splashy puddles that you make sure to stomp into whenever you pass near one.

You notice that the shops and stores around you stop between one street and the next and are replaced by big, tall buildings with wrought iron fences around them and stone towers at every corner.

The farther Abigail brings you the fancier and bigger they become, almost as if they're trying very hard to look like teeny tiny castles.

Maybe Abigail would like to live in a small castle. Or a big castle. You could hollow out one of your older tentacles and plant it in the ground somewhere, like a giant fleshy pillar that would reach low orbit. Then all you'd need to do is add windows and some doors and make a crown for Abigail.

Your day dreaming ends when Abigail slows to a stop. "This is it," she says, gesturing with a nod to the building before her.

Daphne's place is a huge stone house. Three stories tall and really boxy except for the patio ringing the top floor and the two stubby towers on either end. Vines have crawled all across the building, hiding the grey stone in a layer of vibrant green that shines in thanks to the abundant rain.

"Pretty," you say.

"Yeah," Abigail agrees. She's not looking at the home.

You turn to follow her gaze.

There's a building on the hill. No, not quite a single building, more like a complex of buildings. All of them huge and castle-like, with crookedy towers that poke into the sky. There are big observatories poking out from the sides of copper-green roofs and bridges that span the length between one building and the next.

You would see more, but the area around the hill is dotted by forests that cling to the sharp hillside. "What's that?"

"That's the Academy," Abigail says. "It's where I want to go someday. Where I will go."

"Oh, okay," you say. Well, if she wants to you can go there after meeting Daphne and after eating something.

But for now the priority is fixing Abigail. You tug her along and skip across the stoney walkway to the massive front doors. "Why is this house so big?" you ask.

"Because Daphne's the daughter of a Duke, and it wouldn't do for her family to let her live in a place like ours," Abigail explains.

That's silly. Abigail is the summoner of a you. By that same logic, it should mean that people are giving her the biggest place.

Abigail knocks on the door, and without even a squeak, it opens to reveal a tall man in a dark suit. "Hello Miss Abigail. A pleasure to see you again," he says with a dull, monotonous voice. "Miss Daphne is in her sitting room. Please do come in."

CHAPTER SEVEN

"RIGHT THIS way, Miss Abigail," the man in the suit says as he moves to the side of the door and holds it open for you and Abigail. You feel him eyeing you up and down, but his face remains completely impassive.

"Oh, Edmund, this is Dreamer, she's my Familiar. Like Daphne's Archie. Um. Sorta." Abigail places a hand on your shoulder and pushes you ahead a little.

"Oh, I doubt she's as difficult to handle as the Lady's Archibald," the man, Edmund says. "Right this way." With sure steps he walks past you and Abigail and deeper into the house, his flashy shoes clicking on the polished wood floor.

You follow along, only pausing a little to look at the pretty vases on pillars and the big paintings of people on the walls. Some of them even look like Daphne but older and less happy. There are also rooms leading off to the sides, like a big dining room containing a huge table with lots of chairs and a door that leads to a kitchen that smells really yummy.

But it's not time for food, even if your tummy rumbles a little at the smell. You notice Edmund eyeing you before he pauses next to a closed door and raps his knuckles against it twice. "Miss Daphne, you have guests. Miss Abigail and Familiar Dreamer."

"Let them in, Ed," Daphne's voice calls out.

With a firm nod, the man opens the door and invites you in with a bow. "I will fetch the tea," he declares before walking off.

"Come in, come in," Daphne says. "Make yourself at home." She gestures to some chairs planted before a desk that's as big as Abigail's entire bed, a huge slab of dark wood on legs carved to look like waves with little fish swimming up the sides. There are two big, plush chairs in front of the desk just waiting for someone to flounce onto them.

Daphne gets up, tossing a pen onto the pile of papers she was writing on. She comes right up to Abigail and gives her a big hug.

You immediately want to spear her through with a tentacle. Abigail's hugs are your hugs! No one else can have them. But you need Daphne to fix Abigail and ripping her apart would make that more complicated.

The hug ends, but not nearly soon enough. Daphne turns to you with a brilliant smile that bounces off your glare. "Hello Dreamer," she says. "Are you okay?" she asks.

"You touched Abigail wrong. I don't like it," you tell her. "Only I'm allowed to do that. And Abigail when she wants to mate with someone to make smaller Abigails." You decide not to explain what you understand about mortal breeding methods to Daphne even if it's obvious that she could stand to learn about them. You wouldn't want to lose your last meal while describing all the icky details.

"D-Dreamer," Abigail says. She shakes her head, sighs and then flops onto one of the plush chairs, her bags dropping to her side. "Please don't talk about that," she asks.

"Yes," you say. "Mortal breeding is disgusting, which is why you should never do it unless I'm there."

She covers her face with her hands so you can't tell how she feels about that. You chose to assume that she's smiling, happy that you're willing to help.

"So that's what you've been dealing with, huh?" Daphne says as she sits down across from Abigail. Then she has the temerity to pat your summoner on the knee.

You huff, then start looking for your own chair. Problem is, the only one around is on the other side of the desk. The solution is, of course, to use more tentacles. You send a few slithering out the bottom of your dress then over the desk to lift the chair.

Both girls watch with mixed emotions as you bring the chair over and plant it between them, then you plop yourself down. Now Daphne can't touch Abigail without going over you. It's a perfect solution. "We came here because Abigail is broken, and as a fellow mortal that's kinda like her, you can fix her," you say.

Daphne blinks at you, then looks over to Abigail. "You know, I was expecting to give you some advice about caring for your Familiar. Archibald defecated on one of my favourite dresses in the first week that I had him, but I'm beginning to think that your issues are greater than that."

"You wouldn't believe it," Abigail says.

You harrumph. It's almost as if you're being ignored here!

The door opens and Edmund comes in with a silver platter covered in stuff. He places it on the desk then pours some smelly water into three cups, puts the cups on tiny little plates, then puts a small cookie on each plate. He hands one to Daphne, then one to Abigail. You're clever enough to know that the third has to be for you, so you grab the cup and tiny plate with a pair of tentacles.

Edmund watches your extra limbs with no change of expression. "Does the Lady need anything else?" he asks.

You sniff at the cup, then pour it down your mouth. It's dirty water. You swallow it anyway, then breathe out a plume of steam. Like a dragon, but less prissy. The cookie tastes better. Then you stare at the empty cup and plate and shove those in your mouth too. They're both very crunchy.

Everyone is watching you as your cheeks puff out to fit the bits of broken porcelain you're nibbling on.

"I shall find the young miss a new cup, perhaps from the servant's tea set," Edmund says before exiting with a bow.

"That was yummy, but now we need to talk," you say. "Abigail has a lot of problems. I tried putting helpful stuff in her head, but she's still all confused and silly. Instead of spending the day cuddling and hugging and patting me, she wants to work and do other things, which is boring. I don't mind that much, because I want my Abigail to be happy, but it's not as fun as it could be. But maybe mortals are just all silly. She does give very good cuddles, so she should focus on the things she does well."

"Um," Daphne says.

You lean onto the edge of your seat and wait for Daphne to tell Abigail that she should listen to you more.

Daphne sighs and gives first Abigail a look, then she turns that same look onto you. "Okay, it's obvious that both of you are in over your heads," she says.

That's stupid, nothing can go over your head without you noticing, there are too many tentacles there.

Still, Abigail nods sharply and you decide that if your Summoner is willing to listen to this girl then you should too. Maybe, just maybe, the mortal has some wise words to spare that you can nibble on.

"Right, so Abi, tell me what you can about Dreamer."

"Ah," Abigail says before hesitating. "She's… not human." You nod, you're obvious way better than that kind of mortal. "She's um, a god."

Daphne somehow exudes an aura of unimpressiveness. "A god?" she asks.

"I'm not," you say to defend yourself. "Abigail is just confused. Gods are puny little things that are all 'whan whan, I'm big and important,' all the time and they taste yummy." You shake your head. "Most of them are just really young and stupid. Not like me."

Abigail swallows. "So, uh, not a god," she confirms. "But she's…" She wiggles her hands in the air as if to outline your real form in all of its tentacular splendour. "She can make rooms bigger, or smaller, and she can duplicate objects, and she can extract pure Aether from the world. She does things that nothing should be able to do."

Daphne raises one eyebrow up.

Abigail sighs and leans to the side to reach into her bag. You watch as she searches within it for a moment, then pulls out the jar of life juice you gave her as a gift earlier. "Look," she says as she passes it to Daphne.

Daphne takes it, then peers into it with widening eyes. "This is Aether?" she asks. "No, don't answer that, I know it is. This is the clearest I've ever seen," she murmurs as she turns the jar up to see through it. "You extracted this from Dreamer?"

"Nu-uh," you deny. "I wanted some, so I pulled it out of the planet. But it's okay, I gave the planet pats in exchange. It's a good trade."

Daphne eyed her some more, then carefully placed the jar onto her desk. "If it's as real as it looks, and I can pull out my alchemy set to test it later, then this jar might be worth a thousand marks or so. Enough to cover your tuition for the next four years and then buy a little house," Daphne said. She shook her head. "Okay, let's pretend that I believe that your Dreamer here is some sort of... not a god but close enough. What now?"

"I, I don't know," Abigail said. "Do you think we could just... go to the Academy and pretend she's a normal Familiar?"

"I am more than normal!" you declare.

"There's no doubting that," Daphne says to acknowledge your superiority to mere normal people and things. "And yes, you might be able to get away with passing Dreamer off as a strange Familiar. It'll raise some suspicions but your background is banal enough that you probably won't get into any trouble."

"That's not important," you say before pointing to Abigail. "We're here because Abigail is broken and you need to fix her."

The girl leans back into her splush chair and lays a hand on its arm. Her nails click-click on the armrest for a moment as she thinks, then her eyes lock onto you and narrow a little. "Dreamer, do you care for Abigail?"

What a silly question. "She's my summoner," you say.

"Yes, she is," Daphne agrees. Her ability to point out the obvious is incredible. You wonder if it's a mortal skill. "But do you care for her beyond that or do you only care because she's your summoner?"

You blink. "Of course I care. She gives hugs and pats."

"Others can give hugs and pats," Daphne says. "I happen to care a lot about Abigail too." There a faint reddish tint to her cheeks as she says that. "She's a very close friend, one of the best. I hope that we're friends until both of us are old decrepit gossips, just like our moms are, and that we always stay close. But she's not just my friend because she gives good hugs."

For some reason, Abigail giggles as if that's funny.

"I could get my hugs from others," you say. "But they're not Abigail."

"They're not," Daphne agrees. "So you care for Abigail more than just because she's your summoner and because she can give hugs."

"And pats."

"And pats." She nods.

You frown as you think on this, then you look over to see Abigail staring at you, her eyes wide behind her thick glasses. There's concern in her eyes, and a bit of a blush that makes all of her freckles stick out from her pale skin.

Why do you care about Abigail? She's just a mortal even if she gives the best cuddles. There has to be a reason. So you decide that it's because she's Abigail. Abigail has an Abigailness that makes her worthy of your caring for her. Just like you have a tentacleness that makes you the most cuddleable.

"I like Abigail because she's Abigail," you tell Daphne.

She grins at you, the smile very unladylike. "I like her for the same reasons. It's a good thing that no one can like Abigail too much. Unless they're icky boys, right?"

You feel as if you and Daphne have just sealed a secret pact, one to protect Abigail's hugs from anyone that isn't one of you. Perfect.

"Yes!" you agree.

"Good, then in that case I'll ask that you always try your best to make our little Abi as happy as she can be."

"Daph," Abigail whines. "That's so embarrassing. Couldn't you say it some other way?"

"Nope!"

Daphne finishes her tea and looks out the window of her study. "It's late," she says.

You suppose that she's right, the sun is setting outside and Abigail has already finished her own tea. You're on your second cup, though this one doesn't taste as good as the first. The first had little bits of gold leaf on the outside that gave it a nice rich texture.

You finish chewing on your cup and look around. "Are we going home?" you ask Abigail.

Abigail nods and stands up before brushing down the front of her skirts. "We probably should," she says. "We're actually pretty far from home, especially if we're walking through the city at night."

Daphne shakes her head. "Nonsense, you'll sleep here for the night. We have plenty of guest bedrooms that are just there to give Edmund and the maids more rooms to dust, it would be a shame if you had to walk back home." She glances at a tall clock that's ticking away in the corner then back at you and Abigail. "Supper ought to be served soon too, though I would appreciate it if you ate what was on your plate without eating the plate itself."

You think about it, but free yummies in exchange of not eating some things is an okay trade. "Alright."

"Are you sure, Daph?" Abigail asks.

"Don't be daft Abi, you know I love having you sleep over," Daphne says as she reaches a hand out and pats Abigail on the arm. "Now come on, we should get cleaned up. I'll tell Edmund to prepare two extra sittings."

The next few minutes are a mess. Abigail forces you, with threats of withholding pats and snuggles, to wash your face and hands and even the ends of your tentacles in a basin full of warm water, then you both shuffle off to the big room with the long table and the straight backed chairs.

Daphne is sitting at the head of the table already, a small book by her side. There's two more places set up with plates and silverware to Daphne's right, and to her left is a perch with a big fat bird.

The bird turns its head way way around to stare at you as you enter. "Who?" he asks.

"I'm Dreamer," you tell it.

"Who?" the birb asks again.

"That Which Dreams Eternal Between Space and Time."

"Who?"

"I'm Hypnos' cousin?" you try.

"Whooo?"

"The Forever Napper. The one which Rests. Cuddler of Causality. Snuggler of Space and Hugger of Tsathoggua."

"Who?"

You glare and turn to Daphne who has a hand pressed over her mouth and who is busy choking while her shoulders shake. "This bird is supper, right?"

"No, no that's Archibald, or Archie for short," Daphne says.

"He's Daphne's Familiar," Abigail says as she sits next to Daphne then pats the spot next to her. "Kind of like how you're my Familiar."

You eye the black and white bird who looks smugly at you with his big eyes and his puffy chest. "I could take him," you say.

Abigail pats your head. "Please don't eat Daphne's Familiar. Archie's actually really nice once you get to know him."

"Nice is one way of putting it," Daphne says. "He thinks he's more clever than he is and spends the whole day sleeping. I loath to imagine that he's a reflection of myself."

You ponder over that. On the one tentacle, it's obvious that the birb thinks too highly of itself. It's a bird after all. No tentacles and all feathers. On the other tentacle, it spends the day sleeping, which is a great way to spend the day. "I won't eat him, for now."

"Who," Archie agrees with a croon. It's probably bird for 'thank you' and 'please be merciful.' Or at least that's how you choose to translate it.

Edmund walks into the room with a tray and lays out three bowls before each of you. It smells savoury, like some of the roots you ate at the shop. "Sweet porridge with basil and pork," he says as he places the last bowl before you. A smaller bowl filled with little grains is placed on a mechanical arm thing tied to the pole Archie is sitting on. "And seed for the avian sir."

"Thanks Edmund," Abigail says as she flashes the man a smile.

You narrow your eyes. This man brought Abigail tea, then he gave you food, and now he's being extra nice in front of her.

He's flirting with your Abigail! If he didn't just bring you snacks you would be piercing him through with your tentacles!

"You are most welcome, Miss Abigail," he says with a perfectly flat expression that probably hides all his devious flirtiness. "May I enquire about any special dietary needs your Familiar may have?"

"Um," Abigail says. She pauses with her spoon hovering before her bowl and turns to you.

Your bowl is already empty except for the tentacle rubbing out the yummy porridge from the bottom. "Hrm?" you ask.

"Uh, do you have any special dietary needs?" she asks you.

"Lots," you tell her.

"You do?" she asks.

You blink at your summoner and she blinks back.

"No?" you try. "I eat lots."

Daphne starts choking again.

"In that case I will be sure to bring the young lady a large helping of tonight's veal." Edmund bows and the waist and walks off. You huff as you watch him go. He might be right that you can be bought off with yummy food, but eventually he'll run out, and then you'll be onto him.

"So, Dreamer, most Familiars are from somewhere, and I do like hearing about their original homes. Faraway lands and so on," Daphne says as she eats her soup really slowly. "Can you tell us about your home?"

You nod, but before you can talk about your home, you start picking away at your meal.

You pick all of it, and put it away in your mouth.

Soon, you're watching as Daphne sets down her fork and knife, picks up a piece of cloth from the table, and dabs at her lips.

It's terribly disappointing, but ever since you finished eating all of your meat you've been staring at Daphne's plate and hoping that she wouldn't be able to finish it all. She is, after all, really thin and doesn't look like she eats that much.

"So," she says and it snaps you out of your daydreams of eating more meat. "You were about to tell us about your home?" Daphne asks.

You nod along. "Yes. I can pat pat the information into your head, that way there's less talking and more time for eating," you say. Hopefully she will reward this ingenuity with more food.

"Um," Abigail says, her fork pausing over her plate. "I don't think that would be a good idea." She's not even halfway through her meal yet, eating it with little nibbles and humming happily over every bite. You don't think she notices that she's doing that, but the smile on Daphne's face tells you that she did.

You would never steal food from your Summoner, of course. She needs it to grow bigger and stronger and even prettier than she already is.

"Has she… done that before?" Daphne asks.

Abigail nods. "Yes, she has. It was… not quite painful, but still a lot to take in."

"And Abigail died too," you say and immediately regret it when Abigail, Daphne and Archie all stare at you. "I made her better."

"In that case, maybe you can tell me with words instead?" Daphne says.

You harrumph. These mortals are always so worried about their mortality that they're forgetting to live a little. It's very silly. "Fine. My home is, uh." you pause. It's only now that you realize that describing your home isn't that easy. "You know how this place is made of things?" you ask as you gesture at the stuff around the dining room. "My home has none of that. It's a lot of nothing."

"Like… space?" Daphne says. "Astrologists say that there's a great void between the planets and stars."

"Kinda, but at least you have stars and planets and other things to eat," you say. "Where I'm from there's none of that, but a lot of nothing that goes on forever."

"That sounds…" Abigail shudders, then pulls you into a hug against her side, hand rubbing up and down your back. "That sounds awful."

"It's not that bad," you say as you burrow into her side. Not literally, more like squishing your face into Abigail's warmth. "There are others there. Like… conceptual things. They make it less lonely. It only takes a few eons to bump into something in the void."

"Right," Daphne says. She shares a glance with Abigail, then looks towards the door just as Edmund comes in.

"Will the ladies be taking dessert before bed?" he asks.

"Not me," Abigail says as she gestures to her plate. "This is too rich for me already."

"I'll skip too," Daphne says, "but bring something for Dreamer. The way she was eyeing my plate…"

Curses! You were spotted.

"Very well. The guest bedroom next to the Lady's is ready, as is the one next to it." Edmund bows. "When you are ready tell me so and I'll find nightclothes for our guests." He steps out of the room and you watch him go for a bit before turning back to the others.

"What's dessert?"

"It's something to eat when you're done with your main meal," Abigail explains before taking a bite and chewing. "Usually it's something sweet, or a pastry."

Food for when you're done eating your food? These mortals are geniuses!

You eagerly await your dessert while Daphne and Abigail start talking about the Academy again. Abigail is very cute when she gets all excited about classes and teachers and lessons. You've eaten none of those, so you're not sure how you feel about it.

Then Edmund arrives with a plate that has a slice of something that smells yummy and a glass of milk. You take one sniff, then chomp down on the triangular thing. It's moist and soft and melty and great.

Edmund is forgiven for flirting with Abigail. If he provides more of this he can flirt all day.

When you're done eating your plate you look up to Abigail and smile. "Done!"

"You're all messy," she whines before taking her napkin and rubbing your cheeks. "We can't have you going to bed with a dirty face."

"Is it time for bed now?" you ask. You can't quite deny the bubble of excitement in your tummy at that. Bedtime is the best time.

"Yes," Daphne says with a laugh. "It's bedtime."

You nod and push away from the table then stand up. Tentacles, the cuddliest sort, spear out from under your dress and wrap around Abigail and then Daphne. She screams a little, so you place one over her mouth. "No screaming," you tell her. "It's bedtime."

Moving out of the room with both girls cocooned behind you, you start searching for the bedrooms when you find Edmund standing in the corridor. "May I enquire as to what is going on?" he asks.

"Yes, where's the beds?"

"Upstairs and to the right," he replies easily. "Will you be putting Miss Daphne and Miss Abigail down?"

"Yes," you tell him. "In bed. It's bedtime."

He nods slowly. "Very well then, I shall lead you to Miss Daphne's chambers."

Daphne makes weird grumbly noises as you follow Edmund upstairs and into a big room. In the centre of it is a huge bed with four posts on each corner and a mattress buried under a layer of blankets.

You nod approvingly. This is a good sleeping place.

"Sleeping clothes are here," Edmund says as he lays out three gowns onto the edge of the bed. Two are long and one is shorter. "I took the opportunity to find one of Miss Daphne's older sleeping gowns for the young miss."

"Thank you," you tell him because being polite is nice. Then you start stripping the girls with your tentacles and, like the okay sort of person he is, Edmund turns around and stares at the wall.

"D-Dreamer!" Daphne screams as you take off the last of her clothes. "What are yo—" she's cut off as you slip her sleeping gown on.

Abigail seems a lot less combative about the whole thing.

Soon, everyone is dressed and, with a tentacle or ten, you pull up the blankets and stuff a protesting Daphne and a sighing Abigail onto the bed and then climb in. You're sure to drape them in as many tentacles as you can so that they're nice and warm.

"G'night," you say before tucking your face in the crook of Abigail's neck.

Abigail sighs. "I'm so sorry Daphne," she says. One hand reaches over and starts running over the back of your head.

Daphne mutters something then squirms a little in your tentacular grasp so that she's closer to Abigail's side. "Good night, I suppose," she says.

CHAPTER EIGHT

YOU WAKE up with a stretch that has your toes curling and your back going snip-snap. It's a good stretch, one that makes all your limbs wiggle in post-nap happiness.

"Finally," says a voice from off to your side.

You blink the evil eye crud away and take in the person tucked up against your side. Daphne is laying there, her black hair which is usually all neat and tidy poking out every which way and her eyes fixed on you in a low simmering glare.

She has Abigail tucked up against her in a hug from behind, and you are pressed up against Abigail's tummy. There are of course tentacuddlers all over because you are the best at hugging. "Hrm?" you ask.

"Can you let me out?" Daphne asks.

She doesn't seem upset about hugging Abigail, which is normal. Hugging Abigail is fun, if you do it hard enough she lets out these little squeaks that make you want to hug her even more.

Daphne sighs. "I really need to use the ladies room."

"But you're a lady, and we're in your room," you say.

Abigail giggles. She was awake the whole time, even though her eyes were closed. Was she stealth napping? All is forgiven when she pulls you closer and into her warm chest and squeezes you tight-tight. "Good morning Dreamer," she says a moment later when she lets go. "Daphne is right, I need to go to the bathroom too."

The next few minutes are a blur. The girls run off to the bath-rooms, because this house has more than one, then Daphne insists that Abigail can't wear the same thing two days in a row and there's a big kerfuffle about finding her a dress that fits and isn't too Daph-ne-ish.

You, of course, have lots of your own dress left around. Actually, you have over nine hundred million to the power of none. You know because you counted all one of them, and they're all the same; brand new and extra swooshy. So you wear one of those and spin-spin a few times to break it in while the girls get dressed and ready.

"Are you having breakfast here?" Daphne asks.

"Ah," Abigail says. "We shouldn't impose. M-maybe we can grab a bite for a street vendor on the way back home?"

"Are you trying to tempt me to come along?" Daphne asks, a sly smile sneaking onto her face.

Abigail laughs again and adjusts her glasses. "No, of course not. But you do like vendor food."

"It's so disgustingly low-class," Daphne says with a harrumph. "It has no business tasting so good."

Now you're hungry again. "Let's go eat these vendors," you de-clare.

The three of you troop out of the house, an impeccable Edmund wishing you a nice day on the way out and warning you that it might rain later even as he pushes an umbrella into Daphne's hands.

The city is alive this early in the morning, people rushing around or just strolling at a leisurely pace. You lead the way, dress flounc-ing around you and hair bouncing on your head with every skip. Hair is nice, it's like having a lot of small, useless tentacles stuck to your head. You see lots of people, especially women, tying their hair in braids and stuff, but you would never do that to one of your tentacles.

"Do we have work today?" you ask Abigail.

"Ah, no," she says. "Today's Lastday."

"What's that?"

Abigail blinks the way she does when you do something awe-some. "Ah, Lastday is what we call… today."

"So yesterday was Lastday and today is Lastday too? Why not just call it today?"

Daphne covers her mouth and coughs again. "We gave names to the days of the week, and they cycle around. The first day is called Firstday, and the last Lastday. Tomorrow will be the start of a new cycle, so Firstday again, then Secondsday, Thirdsday and so on. Lastday is the seventh."

That seems needlessly arbitrary. "Okay?"

"Lots of places are closed for business on Sixday and Lastday," Daphne explains.

Well, if it means more time to spend with Abigail you won't complain. "Neat! So there's more time to play."

"Exactly," Daphne says with a grin. She points to a little stall set out on the side of the street, the man behind it wearing a big apron and smiling as he gives people something that smells really yummy. "Let's grab a bite and I'll explain the weekdays to you."

You do just that. The man is selling little bits of meat that are cooking on a magic circle engraved on a steel plate which he shoves into flatbread and folds in a strange way. There are veggies and things too, like sauces that he can add. Abigail and Daphne each get one, and when you're asked you demand one of each flavour he has.

Abigail negotiates you down to two meat puffs, one with veggies and the other with cheese. It is a good compromise because you earned a headpat from it.

You're munching along and walking towards home when a question comes to mind. "Hey, Daphne?" you ask up at her.

Abigail sighs and pulls out a napkin to rub your face. "Don't talk with your mouth full."

"Yes Dreamer?" she asks, ignoring Abigail's silliness.

"When did you meet my Abigail?"

Daphne humms. "We've known each other... forever?"

"Pretty much," Abigail agrees. She bumps shoulders with Daphne and soon their arms are linked.

You are not jealous. One day you too will be tall enough to link arms with Abigail.

"Our mothers were childhood friends," Daphne explains. "My mother is the Viscountess of Swinehill, which is to the West of here. She married my dad who's a Baron of a neighbouring region." She shakes her head. "That doesn't matter. My mother and Abigail's met at the Academy, they became close friends and when my mother's schooling was completed, Abigail's mother moved close to our estates to work and stay close. They still have tea every evening."

"We were born a few months apart," Abigail says then she puffs up in pride. "I'm older."

"By three months, it hardly counts," Daphne huffs right back. "But yes, we grew up together, like sisters but... closer..."

"Hrm," you say before skipping ahead a little. Things are truly unfair if Daphne got to spend all this time with Abigail without you around.

"What are you missing?" Daphne asks Abigail as the three of you, four if you count the bird, move deeper into the city. You're pretty close to where you'd been shopping the day before you think. It's hard to keep track of places, what with everything being squished together.

"Ah, not too much," Abigail says. "Just the main course books now."

"Oh," Daphne says. "I have all of those. Just one copy of each I'm afraid or I'd let you borrow mine. In the worst case we can share a book in any elective classes we share."

Abigail shakes her head. "They'll be verifying all of my things. I'm not you, so they'll probably be a bit more stringent with the requirements."

"What's that mean?" you ask.

"Ah," Abigail says. "Well, I said that you need all the equipment in order to be allowed into the Academy, right?" You nod and she goes on. "Well, that's true, but there's a certain amount of, uh, leeway when it comes to some students. Especially those with noble titles like Daph."

"Is Daphne a princess?" you ask. You aren't one of those silly lizards that likes collecting princesses, so you really can't tell at a glance.

Daphne laughs into her palm. "I'm not. I'm actually a Baroness, though it's more of a pat on the back sort of title. My mother is the one with all the political clout in my family, when she retires or passes on, which I hope is a long time from now, I will inherit her title of Viscountess."

"That sounds silly," you say. "If I become a queen then no one else will become one because I'll never die. Your mortal system makes no sense."

There's a pause as the two girls look at each other, then Abigail pats your head. "Well then, you'll just have to avoid becoming a queen," she says.

You harrumph. "So I'll make Abigail a queen instead, that way people will… no, she can't be a queen because I won't share her."

Daphne giggles again. "On that we can agree. It would be a shame if our dear Abigail's time was monopolized by politics."

Abigail huffs and crosses her arms, which means that she's not playing with your hair anymore. "Anyway. To return on topic, the Academy isn't supposed to discriminate because it's run in part by the Inquisition which doesn't need to acknowledge most noble titles. But the truth isn't that easy. It's expected that richer students can get away with more, like not bringing all their equipment with them all the time."

"To be fair, there's some logistical reasons for that. My house is quite close to the school, so I hardly need to bring all of my things over every day."

Abigail rolls her eyes. "Your house is a mansion in the richest part of the city, Daphne."

"More of a mansionette."

Abigail frowns and tilts her head to the side, then reaches up to adjust her big glasses. "Is that actually a word?"

"I'm rich, therefore it is."

Abigail pushes Daphne's shoulder and glares at her, but then she breaks out into giggles and Daphne soon follows. You're having a bit of a hard time understanding the joke, but seeing Abigail happy makes you happy too, so it's okay.

"This is the only shop I know that sells course books and is open on Lastday," Daphne says as she points to a tall but narrow shop set in the middle of a busy street. "Inkpot and Scribeswell's Emporium for Literary Works," she reads the sign above the doorway aloud. "We should find everything here."

"Isn't this place a bit expensive?" Abigail asks.

"A little, but don't worry, I have a tab here," Daphne says, waving Abigail's concerns away. She's about to move into the store when she pauses and looks down across the street.

You can't quite see what she's looking for until you climb the first couple of steps leading to the front door. A ways down the road is a Familiar store, the one you and Abigail had visited just yesterday and where you got all that shiny alchemy stuff.

Now the store is closed. There are poles hovering horizontally in the air that prevent people from crowding in too close and men in long black coats with metal plates sewn into them stand behind the line, big rods with fork-like heads held by their sides. They're wearing hats that look like very fancy buckets with bits of fluff on the front and a silver crest that you can't quite figure out with your mortal eyes.

"Inquisitorial guardsmen?" Daphne asks.

"I like their hats," you say.

Abigail joins you and gasps. "What are they doing there?" she asks.

You notice that she's not looking at the big guys in black, but at two people in red robes and even taller bucket hats who are waving brass thingies at the shop.

"We were there yesterday," Abigail says.

"Let's go inside," Daphne says before placing a hand on Abigail's shoulder.

You follow after them, giving the weird people that made the girls so nervous one last look. They don't look so tough. You could take them.

A bell jingles when you enter, causing a tall, skinny man stacking books onto a shelf to turn and look down on you. He stares for a moment, then his expression brightens. "The Honourable Miss Daphne!" he says. "Welcome, welcome! How can I assist?" he hops off his stool with more grace than you'd expect from someone so skinny and bony and moves closer.

"Ah, my friend here needs some assistance finding her first year Academy books," Daphne says. "And my smaller friend here," she places a hand on your head, "will look around and not steal anything because if she wants something she just has to ask me."

The man blinks, then smiles. "Well then, come along, we still have a good stock of Academy texts left."

You watch as the girls move ahead, then turn to the floor-to-ceiling shelves full of books all in neat orderly rows. Shiny lettering sparkles at you from thousands of leather spines and posters about different books are held in neat frames on every wall. It even smells like paper and parchment and books and knowledge.

This place, you decide, is nice.

There are many books here at first glance, thousands and thousands, but when you look more carefully you notice that most of them have two or three copies set next to each other, some have even more than that. It's rare to find a book that's all alone without at least a twin next to it.

This is, after all, a bookstore, so you guess they sell books.

You hum a little song that makes the tallest shelves seem a little less tall as you walk so that you can see what's where. At first you're not sure what you're looking for. Maybe a book about caring for your Summoner? It would be nice to know the optimal way to pet your Abigail, but you don't find anything like that.

Instead, after a few minutes of aimless wandering, you see a book about the Inquisition's impact on some place you don't know about and it gives you an idea.

You skip along with purpose now, skirts bounce-bouncing as your eyes scan the rows of books. It takes a little searching to find what you're looking for, but you eventually find it within tentacle-grabbing range, which is all ranges.

The Inquisition: History, Impact, Creed, by *Judas Fawkes*

Smiling with well-deserved smug satisfaction, you move to a spot near the back of the store where someone left a big fluffy seat right under a window that's allowing fat yellow sunrays to light up the cozy nook.

You place the book on your lap and open it up. The first few pages are all about who made the book and other boring stuff. Then you get to the chapter called Forward and pause a bit to wonder at just how stupid a name that is for a chapter in a book. What's it forwarding?

> "The Inquisition as an organization has defined Humanity's quest to control their own destiny. From its humble birth to now the Inquisition has made great leaps in debunking superstitions and disproving the existence of so-called 'gods' and has stripped corrupt religious officials and vile cultists of the power and riches they stole from the unsuspecting populace. No other group in human history has done as much to promote growth, learning and critical thinking in the face of a world that occasionally seems senseless. While the methodology of the Inquisition might seem excessively complex at first glance, the intricacies of the situations that the Inquisition deals with demand nothing less, as this book will soon show. In the defence of humanity and its interests there is only the shield of reason to keep mankind safe!"

You blink a few times to stop yourself from taking a surprise nap.

This book is boring. No wonder Abigail is so worried about these Inquisition people. Other than their neat hats there's nothing good about them.

Harrumphing mightily, you leave the book on a nearby end table and flounce back into the rows to find something better to read. Maybe they have something about you? You should totally be the subject of many books because you're you.

After searching fruitlessly for a long time, the only thing you find that can sorta-maybe be about you, though, is a big book about squids and cephalopods and other tentacle cousins. It's a pretty book, with lots of hand drawings and sketches within it of different sorts of tentacles.

Some of them have suction-y cups for extra grabbing power, which would make your hugs even harder to get out of, and others are like your hair tentacles, all thin and ropey. These would be handy for tickle-hugging someone. The best are the big bulky tentacles of some distant cousin called an octopus. Its tentacles are few, but they are mighty.

Soon though, you've looked at all the pictures. It's not worth buying or nibbling on this book. You know what tentacles look like already.

"Did you find anything?" Abigail asks as she finds you in a corner. You're about to go put the tentacle book back.

"Not really," you say. "There's nothing about you or me here."

"Ah, that's… okay," Abigail says. "Were there any books you wanted?"

You frown and think about it for a few long seconds. "Are there any books about hats?"

"Um," Abigail says. "Maybe a guide to millinery?"

"What's that?" you ask.

She smiles and pulls you closer so that she can give you a hug. You're not sure why she's feeling huggy, but you're not going to say no. "Millinery is the art of hat-making," she says.

"Ohh." You think about it a little, but dismiss the idea. You don't want to make hats, you want to wear them. You'll just take one of the Inquisitor's hats the next time you see one.

"Are you ready to go? We should be heading home after this. Daphne needs to do things at her place, and we need to prepare for tomorrow morning. We're going to be getting up bright and early."

"Ah, that means we're going to go to sleep again?" you ask, suddenly excited to get back home.

"That's right," Abigail says. "If there's nothing you want, then we should get going."

Daphne's waiting by the door, standing next to a cloth bag with the store's logo filled to the brim with books. She gestures at it. "I'll let you figure this one out, you're the one with the toned arms."

Abigail rolls her eyes. "That's because unlike someone, I actually work for a living."

"Ouch," Daphne says as she slaps a hand over her chest. "That hurt Abi. I'm going to have to take a bath in a tub full of gold to make the pain go away."

"What if you took a bath with Abigail? Would that make her happier too?" you ask.

Daphne chokes again, but this time her whole face goes very red while Abigail giggles. "I don't think anyone wants to share a bath with anyone else here," Abigail says.

You shrug. "I never took a bath before."

Abigail runs her fingers through your hair. "Well, when we get home we can change that," she says before turning to Daphne. "Will we be seeing you tomorrow morning?" she asks.

Daphne nods. "Maybe. If not in the morning then certainly in the afternoon. I can have lunch in the junior's hall with you and maybe show you around. It will be fun."

There's hugging and grabbing bags and a bit more chatting, and then you're all off and on your way home.

You arrive home in record time, a bag filled with books floating behind you, hooked onto a tentacle that's mostly intangible and invisible except for the distortions it leaves in the air. A few mortals stare, but they have floaty things too so it can't be too weird.

Anyway, Abigail doesn't make a fuss, so it's all good.

"It's good to be back," Abigail says as she unlocks the door and steps into her... your home. It's just as you left it, some rooms bigger than others and the dimensions just a little bit weird. You can tell that physics has been trying to make sense of things but, as usual, failed miserably.

Anything with such strict rules is bound to fail when things don't go as it wants. You shake your head at the silliness of physics and put Abigail's books on two corners of the dining room table at the same time.

"Now we go to bed?" you ask.

Abigail shakes her head and bends over closer to you. She sniffs at you.

You don't know what this means.

"Nope, no bed time for you. You need a bath first."

"But I wanna go nap," you protest. But Abigail decides to become Evil Abigail, the Evil tyrant of Evilness and pulls you after her towards the bathroom. Soon she's making you take off your dress while water runs in the bath. It goes way, way down into the bottomless pit of the tub for a moment before Abigail blinks at you. You roll your eyes, a new gesture that you've seen Abigail use a few times already, and make the bath return to how it was before you made it better.

Then you climb into the water and plop yourself down. "Is this enough?" you ask Abigail.

She sighs and shakes her head before giving you a bar of something that smells like flowers and a glass decanter filled with purple-ish liquid.

"That's soap and shampoo," Abigail explains.

You put the bar in your mouth and start chewing. It tastes like it smells, flowery and clean, but it's all gunky and when you try to ask Abigail for another bar, bubbles come out of your mouth.

Abigail swipes the shampoo out of your hand before you can start drinking it and places it next to the bathtub. "You know what, I'll help you."

Abigail gets undressed too and moves behind you in the bath. Soon she uses a second bar of soap to scrub you down. It's like getting pats, but with more rubbing and bubbles. Then she puts some of the shampoo on your head and rubs it in. It's really nice until some of it gets into your eyes.

"Ahh!" you scream as it burns.

"Oh, I'm sorry," Abigail says. "Put some water in your eyes," she says from right behind you.

You reach up and pluck your eyes out, then wiggle them under the water.

When you push them back into your face and turn to see Abigail, she stares at you with her mouth opened and her face very pale. Maybe the hot water isn't for her.

Abigail soon shoos you out of the bath and makes sure you're wrapped in a big towel before telling you to go wait in your room.

You shrug and do as she asks while she finishes her own bath. Bathtime was okay, you decide.

You find a big shirt for sleeping in, like you had at Daphne's place, and slip into it, then you wiggle your head as fast as you can to get the water out. Your hair-tentacles... hairtacles, don't wick off water as well as your normal tentacles.

Abigail returns and finds a nightgown of her own to put on, then sits on the edge of the bed with a big comb.

You hop in behind her and are about to drag her under the blankets with a whole bunch of tentacuddlers when you see what she's doing. Her comb dips into her wet hair, then pulls it down.

"Abigail!" you say.

"Hrm?"

"Your hairtacles have knots in them!" you say. You've gotten some tentacles tied together before. It's awful and painful and very bad. So, seeing as you're obviously the more experienced of the two, you take away Abigail's comb and start brush-brushing her hair.

You lose yourself in the motions, comb moving down her back and flattening her hairtacles only for it to bounce back into Abigail's normal curls. Soon, thanks to your incredible expertise, there are no knots and Abigail's hairtacles are saved!

"Now it's nap time?" you ask.

Abigail chuckles and turns around, one arm wrapping around your waist before she drags you down and squeezes you close. "Yup!" she says.

You make a happy sound and bring the blankets over the two of you for extra cocooning. "Okay. Good night Abigail."

"Good night, Dreamer."

You wrap Abigail in even more tentacuddlers, not enough that you squish her until it hurts or stops her from working, but still very tight, then you tuck your head against the crook between her collar and neck and snuggle in as much as you can.

Abigail makes a happy sound too and wiggles her arms until you loosen them from your grasp. She brings them up and over your back and pulls you even closer in a tight-tight hug. "Thanks, Dreamer," she says.

"Yes," you say. You should be thanked for giving such good cuddles. "Now sleep. Tomorrow we do the Academy stuff to make you happy."

She giggles and the breath coming out of her mouth tickles. "Okay. I'm looking forward to it. Sleep tight, Dreamer."

The last sound you hear before you start dreaming is a happy sound Abigail makes as you squeeze her just a tiny bit closer.

CHAPTER NINE

"**D**REAMER."

You squirm a little, flashes and visions of the great void, of the strange and wondrous things you saw and felt within it, of the eternal quiet between destinations passing through your mind's eye.

"Dreamer, wake up sweetie."

You remember the cold bite of the dark, and the harsher bite of loneliness. Then you'd find someone, a friend, a rival, a snack.

"Dreamer." Something shakes you. "Dreamer, we need to wake up!"

You yawn, jaw cracking as you open it really, really wide. Then your eyes flutter open and you take in Abigail's face only a hair away from yours. Her eyes are wide and she lets out a sigh and a noise that's neither happy nor sad.

"Good, you're up," she says. "We're going to be late, Dreamer, we need to hurry!"

You yawn again and stuff a hand over your mouth like Abigail and Daphne do when they're yawning. "Okay," you agree. Your tentacuddlers unravel a bit, some of them pushing away the corner of the blankets that are left over you and the others lifting Abigail up to place her next to the bed.

You turn around and stuff your face back into a pillow, eyes closing once more.

A shake of your shoulders has you waking up again. "Dreamer, breakfast is ready."

You snap awake and look around. You don't know how, but in the time it took for you to blink Abigail changed out of her sleeping clothes and into the black robes of her school uniform and is holding a tray with a plate covered in chopped potatoes and scrambled eggs.

"You're so fast!" You tell her as you sit up and use a few tentacles to hold up the platter.

"Just going as fast as I can," Abigail says. "I don't want to be late today of all days."

Well, you decide that if Abigail's in a hurry, then you can do things fast too! A tentacle splits apart into hundreds of fine tendrils that spear into your potato wedges and shoves them into your mouth, then you tip the plate back and open wide so that the eggs can flow down your throat.

The glass of milk Abigail brings you goes down just as fast.

"Mmm, okay, I'm ready!" you say as you hop out of bed. A twist in space and a brand new copy of your dress is flung into you and you squirm until you're wearing it properly. "Okay, we can go now!" you say as you pull out a pair of cuffs and slip those on too.

"Ah, well," Abigail says. "I just need to finish packing, it'll only take a minute."

You watch her scurry around the house in a rush, picking up books and papers and stuffing them in a big burlap sack. She even picks up that ugly cone hat she bought and plops it onto her head.

"Abigail, today is important, right?" you ask her.

"Yes, very," Abigail agrees. "It's the first day. It's... the most important day, maybe."

"Oh, okay," you say. "In that case I should make sure you look extra pretty. That way everyone will know that you're really important."

Abigail pauses in her rushing and turns towards you. Her floofy hair is all frazzled and her big glasses are barely hanging onto the tip of her nose. "Look extra pretty?" she repeats.

Of course, Abigail is already very pretty. She has a cute nose, just like yours, and cute freckles just like yours and cute hair, just like yours. But you can make her even more prettier if you try. And that's without giving her her own tentacles.

Nodding, you reach around with a big tentacle and stuff it into the planet's core to siphon off some of that yummy life juice. "Open wide!"

"Wha—"

A tentacle jams itself into Abigail's mouth and spurts life juice down her throat while she's too tired to yank it out. It's a good thing that you only wanted to give her a little because when you pull it out she coughs and sputters a lot.

"Dreamer! Wh-what was that for?" she asks. Then she notices that her skin now has a nice, healthy glow. "Dreamer, what?"

"I made you more magical!" you say before a tentacle removes her ugly hat and a million more, smaller tentacles run through her hair and unmuss it. "You'll be so pretty that all the other Familiars will want you to be their Summoner, but they can't have you because you're mine. And the boys will want to mate with you. But they can't because if they try I'll eat them."

"Dreamer!" Abigail snaps. It's not a happy sound and you notice that her eyes are pinched while looking right at you. "Enough. Please. I know you just want to help, and it's nice, but you need to ask before doing things."

"But—"

"No, no buts Dreamer. I'm not like you, I'm... I'm less strong, okay? I don't want you to hurt me and I don't want to lose you. Please?"

You freeze for a long moment. Abigail is right that she's all squishy and weak, it's part of what makes her so good for cuddling, but if she's too weak. "Ah," you say. "I'm sorry Abigail. I just wanted to help you be super pretty."

Abigail grabs you in a tight hug. "I don't need to be pretty Dreamer, I'm happy as I am, okay?"

"Oh, okay."

"Right," Abigail says. "Let's hope that I stop... glowing before we arrive at the gates. I look like a pompous noble this way. Sheesh."

"Like a princess?" you ask.

Abigail rolls her eyes, picks up her bag with one arm, and reaches out a hand for you to grab. "C'mon Dreamer, we have a full day ahead of us!"

Abigail is super excited. You know this because she's not just walking next to you, she's bouncing, a huge, happy smile on her face and sometimes she lets out these little barks of laughter that make you want to laugh too.

A few people that she knows seem to notice that she's very happy too, because they smile and wave right back when she's going by.

And then, before you realize it, you're in front of the huge gates of the Academy.

"Ohh," you say as you look way, way up at the thin spiral-y towers all around the grounds of the Academy and then at the main building which looks more like a castle than any sort of school.

"That way, I think," Abigail says as she gestures to one side. There's a sign floating in the air with the words 'First Years' and a large arrow painted under it. All the students past that sign are carrying a whole lot of books and bags and trunks and they have big pointy hats just like Abigail's.

"There's a line over there," Abigail says. She pulls her trunk along even though it's mostly empty. Being the best Familiar ever that you are, you tucked most of Abigail's stuff next to your real body. You even put your lunches and other stuff there. And you didn't even eat her portion of it!

You move over to the line, Abigail shuffling nervously as the students in front of her turn to stare then go back to waiting. There's some chatter in the air, but not much. It sounds more like people are nervous or are trying to keep their Familiars in check.

There are big fluffy wolves and squeaky bats and purring cats and a sleepy tapir and a bug-eyed axolotl and an octopus in a tank (but its tentacles aren't nearly as cool as yours) and they all look so delicious that you're starting to drool a little.

Then the line ends and it's your turn to move into a weird lobby place. An old man in a robe just like Abigail's, but with a hat that's basically just a perfect flat square with some tassels tied to it, is standing in the middle of the path. "Hello prospective student," the man says as he smiles at Abigail. "And welcome to Five Peak's

Academy of Magical Arts. If you would, please move to room one to my right and present your equipment, then to room two with your Familiar for a rapid inspection. Once that is complete you may move towards the main auditorium. Our headmaster will be giving a speech quite soon."

"Ah, thank you, sir," Abigail says before pulling you along. Her hands are all sweaty and her happiness seems to have turned into nervousness. "Dreamer, um, I, I don't know what the Familiar inspection is," she says.

"Does it matter?" you ask.

Abigail doesn't answer you since you've made it into room one and there's a pair of students with round bumpy hats on their heads. If you remember from the store correctly, that means they're fourth years.

Abigail lays out all of her books and equipment and stuff, pulling more and more of it out of her bag as you add it back in. One of the students eyes the pile of equipment on the table, then Abigail's small bag, but he doesn't make a fuss.

"You're good to go, Miss Abigail," one of them finally says before giving Abigail a piece of paper.

She thanks him and starts shoving her things back in the bag where your tentacles grab it and place it on your real body atop a pile of fresh dresses.

You're moving on when Abigail starts to whisper again. "Dreamer, you're… not a normal Familiar. What if you don't pass the inspection?"

You snort, of course you're going to pass, you're the best.

As it turns out, room two is a bit smaller and smells kind of strange, like hay and grains and animal poop. Across the room, behind a thick wooden desk is a wrinkly old woman who is glaring at you and Abigail the moment you walk in.

"Come on, get closer," she orders and you both move closer to her desk. "Closer, I don't have all day for you."

"Yes, sorry," Abigail says as she moves even closer. "Um, this is my Familiar, Dreamer," she says, gesturing at you.

You smile at the professor. "Hello old lady!" you say.

The old lady does not look very impressed with you. "Miss... Abigail, is this some sort of joke?"

"Um," Abigail says. "No?"

"Mimics can't speak. Next time you steal an urchin off the streets and try to pass her off as a Familiar perhaps you should spend less time looking for such an ugly dress and more time reading. Though I doubt your ability to do that much."

"I, but Dreamer's really my Familiar. She's not a human," Abigail says.

The old woman snorts. "Get out. You've failed."

You harrumph and make tentacles slither out from under your dress and peel out of your arms. "See, I'm a me."

The woman stops breathing for a moment, eyes narrowing. "What are you?" she asks. "No, don't answer that. I... have a suspicion." She turns towards Abigail, face going red and blotchy. "Do you have any idea how illegal what you've done is?" she hisses. "Once the Inquisition finds out about this you'll be lucky if they only fine you until you're a pauper."

"What?" Abigail squeaks.

The old lady stands up. "Stay here. I need to report th—"

She is cut off, no longer able to talk because you've surrounded her face with a tentacle. Another tentacle, one that's only a little bit in this world slips into her head and roots around until you find what she's talking about.

"Oh, there are tadpoles here!" you say.

"What?" Abigail asks.

"They're like, uh, ideas that don't last very long, but that a lot of you humans have, like daydreams that all gather together and then become a thing."

"Like you?" Abigail asks.

You harrumph and give her a glare. "Tadpoles are small and weak and they hardly taste like anything and they're only a few million years old. When they grow really old and big and strong, then they taste way better."

"Uh," Abigail says. "What about, um, her?" she asks.

You roll your eyes and fix a few things in the old lady's head, then push her back into her seat and remove the tentacle around her mouth. "And you… you… are the most beautiful Familiar I have ever seen. You are so pretty and nice. I… I should hug you. And pat you."

"No thank you old lady," you tell her. "I only want pats and hugs from Abigail."

"Ah, yes, of course. You pass, obviously." the old lady says as she pushes a paper towards Abigail. "Next!" she calls out of the room.

Abigail grabs your hand and drags you away and past the next student who's standing proud next to a big tall wolf. You're moving fast, but not fast enough that you miss what's being said in the room.

"And what's that?"

"Uh, it's Wuffles, my wolf Familiar?" a boy says.

"Yes, and where are its tentacles?"

"What?"

"Failed! Next!"

You run to catch up to Abigail and slip your hand into hers. "So, what's next."

"Ah," Abigail says. "Well there's that speech." You make a huffy noise at that. "But I'm sure we could skip it if you want. Did you want to explore a little? Maybe we'll run into Daphne?"

"Dreamer, you can't…" Abigail sighed and pressed her face into her hands.

You shuffle a little and look back into the corridor you two just exited. You can still hear the boy with the pet wolf protesting at the old lady with increasing desperation, and Wuffles' whine can be heard quite clearly even over that.

"Okay," you tell Abigail. "I'm going to fix everything."

With that, you slip your hand out of Abigail's and move back into the corridor, then into room two. The shouting stops for a moment as everyone looks at you. "Can I help you sweetie?" the old lady asks.

You take in Wuffles, who is a big grey dog but bigger, and Wuffles' master who is wearing the same thing as Abigail, but instead of being cute like Abigail he's a lanky boy with acne. "Hey," you say. "So, old lady, you should accept Wuffles as a Familiar even if he's not a very good one."

"I should?" she asks. "But he's so… untentacular."

"That's true," you agree. "But he has hair, which is kind of like tentacles."

"Ah," she says and nods.

"Uh," Wuffles' master says. "What?"

You smile at him. "You're welcome. I'm going to pat Wuffles now, okay?" You move over to the big wolf who eyes you really suspiciously and reach out a hand to pat his head.

Wuffles bites your hand, teeth sinking into your skin before he tries to wiggle you from side to side like a big Dreamer-shaped dog toy. You, of course, aren't fond of that idea so your tentacles grab onto your momentum and tell it to go away. You only moved a tiny bit, which is okay you guess.

"Wuffles, no!" Wuffles' master says before he tries to free you hand.

"It's okay," you say. "Wuffles was just afraid." You wrap Wuffles in a reassuring amount of tentacles and pry your hand from out of his teeth. "It's okay, Wuffles. I'll pat you later, when you're more ready for it," you say before wiping the blood and a few fingers off on your skirts. "Anyway, I need to go now. Bye."

"Good bye!" the old lady says.

You return to Abigail and slip most of your hand in hers. "I'm back," you say.

She smiles down at you. "Good! I was just rea—" she lowers the pamphlet she's holding and raises her hand. Her face goes really white, which makes her freckles stand out a bunch. "What happened to your hand?" she squeaks.

"Wuffles."

"We need to find the nurse's office," Abigail says.

You roll your eyes, just like she taught you, and tear your hand off with some tentacles to fling it into a nearby trash bin. Pinching your brow a little you focus and grow a new hand from some spare flesh you have laying around. "New hand!" You exclaim. "Never held before." You wiggle it at Abigail and she grabs it to see if it's hurt, which is silly. If you made a mistake you'd just grow another.

Then Abigail wraps you in a surprise hug and you hum in happy victory. You must be doing a really good job as a Familiar to be getting surprise hugs.

"Let's clean your dress up as best we can before the assembly," Abigail says when she lets you go.

"I have new ones I can change into," you tell her. Still, she drags you into a ladies room and insists on wiping all the blood and extra fingers off. She doesn't even let you nibble on them before tossing them away.

Five minutes later you and Abigail are all freshened up and walking into a big room with lots of chairs and a stage at the far end. A few people with the flat hats of professors are on the stage, as well as a man with a hat that looks like a sideways boat with lots of tassels on it. His robes are really pretty, with lots of little stars sown in and a bunch of different layers.

He looks like a cake.

"That's the headmaster," Abigail says when she sees where you're looking. She pulls you into one of the rearmost rows of seats and sits next to a girl with hair that's just a shade away from pink who's petting a white thing on her lap. "I heard that he was a warlock before becoming headmaster."

"He was," the girl next to Abigail says. "Warlock of the first rank for nearly ten years. He has an impressive academic pedigree too." She smiles. "Ah, sorry. My name is Maddie. This is Cutebee." She lifts her cat, revealing that it has beady red eyes and big floppy ears.

"Oh, hi Maddie," Abigail says. You can feel the shyness trying to cling to her. "Ah, I'm Abigail, this is Dreamer, and it's a pleasure to meet you and… Cutebee."

"My brother named him," the girl says as she hugs the cat thing closer. It's still eyeing you.

You decide that you don't trust this cat and will eat it as soon as you can.

There's a sudden influx of students and you need to get up from your uncomfortable chair to let some pass. By the time the rush is over the hall is filled with Familiars making unFamiliar noises and a sea of pointed hats that bob and wobble along with their owner's heads.

The headmaster walks to the centre of the stage and reaches a hand into his robes. He comes out with a pinch of dust and a thing that looks like a stopwatch. With quick, sure gestures, he does something magical, then spreads the dust in the air in a magic circle, the grains hanging there immobile until he channels through them.

He clears his throat and his voice is loud and clear across the entire room.

"I am not one for speeches," he declares. "Welcome to Five Peaks Magical Academy. You will learn magic and science and the finer arts here. If you fail to learn you will be rejected. Learn well and you shall pass. Surpass our expectations and you will be richly rewarded with opportunities that you would never find elsewhere. Fail to behave and you will meet with harsh punishments. That is all."

He spins on his heel and walks to the side of the platform, arms crossed before his chest as a second, much nicer looking professor steps up where he was. She has a flat-topped hat like the others, but it's tipped way back to show off her soft features. "Hello everyone, I'm Professor Clearwater, I will be teaching your very first class this year, Magical Preparations and Rituals, which will begin in approximately two hours. Until that time you are encouraged to explore the Academy grounds and partake in some lunch. If you find yourself lost, ask a member of staff or a senior for direction. Maps are provided at the back as well. Failing to attend would be hugely disappointing." She smiled. "Before I let you go, I want to wish you all a wonderful time in our school."

CHAPTER TEN

"U M."

She frets a bit to the left, then a bit more to the right. "Ah."

Watching Abigail move around nervously is kind of funny, in the same way as watching a tentacle having a hard time opening a jar is amusing for a few moments. It quickly stops being funny when Abigail turns big, brown eyes onto you and practically begs for help.

"What's wrong?" you ask.

Just to make sure you take a look around the cafeteria. It's a rather large room, with rows and rows of rectangular tables all surrounded by chairs. Students with all sorts of hats are sitting and eating, though most put their headgear aside for the meal. The air is filled with enticing smells from different foods, but mostly from the line at the far end where people are getting meals from a serving place and walking away with trays full of food.

"Ah, nothing's wrong," Abigail lies before taking another bite of her bread.

Lunch for you and Abigail is bread with some cheese and a bit of juice in a glass bottle. All kept fresh and cool in the vacuum of space around your bigger body.

"It's just that," she says after she finishes chewing. "I kind of wanted to make friends today." With a gesture, she points to all the students and you notice that, for the most part, they're all in groups of two or three, talking and laughing and getting to know each other. Familiars of all sorts are moving around, though most weren't allowed into the room to begin with.

You, of course, refused to wait in the Familiar babysitting area. You took one look at the room filled with hay and cushions and all sorts of potential snacks and decided that you wouldn't step foot in there unless you were really hungry.

"Oh," you say. "We can make you some friends." You pat-pat Abigail's hand to make her feel better.

"Make, or make," she asks.

It takes you a while to understand what she means by that. "Abigail! I'm too young to be a mommy yet."

Abigail was chewing through another bite of bread, but her eating skills aren't what you thought they were because she chokes on it mid-bite.

"Anyway, I meant finding you some mortals to keep you company. It's important that you learn how to boss around your lessers now while you're still young." You nod at your own wise words.

"Uh-huh," Abigail agrees.

"So, what kind of friends are you looking for?" you ask before looking into the crowd. There are lots of mortals here. You might be able to find one that fits all of Abigail and your criteria.

"What kind of friend?" Abigail wonders. "Someone nice. That's important. I don't care about their class or riches. I'd like them to be close to my age and it would be nice if they shared some of my hobbies."

"Hobbies?" You didn't know that she had hobbies other than napping with you, and patting your head, and sometimes sleeping with Daphne.

"I like reading, and learning new things and spending time with Daphne. I suppose those aren't really the best hobbies, but they're mine. Oh, and a friend would have to want to graduate from the Academy, like I want to. Shared dreams are important."

You're eagerly nodding as she speaks. Sharing dreams is the most important. Or one of the most important. You would know, dreams are yours. "Is that all?"

"I, I guess?" Abigail says. "I don't really have much experience with friends, other than Daphne, and you."

You nod. It's okay, Abigail will have lots of friends and lots of time to make experiences with them, you'll make sure of it.

That's why you stand up from your chair, climb onto it, then onto the table where you and Abigail ate her lunch. You clear your throat and ignore Abigail's pleas for you to come down. Unfortunately, only a few people are looking your way. This small body of yours isn't attention grabbing.

"Hey!" you call out across the room.

A few more people look your way, but they ignore you really quickly.

"W-what are you doing, Dreamer?"

You huff and with some tentacles, grab all the sounds in the room. It goes really quiet and people start looking around to find where their noise went, but the joke's on them because you have it all. "Hey!" you say and throw all the noise into the word. This time it's super loud, even if you let go of the sound while speaking. "I need your attention now."

Just about everyone is staring at you from your place on the table. "This is Abigail," you say as you point down towards Abigail. Her face is very red, and she looks a little faint, but she smiles and waves so she must be okay. "Abigail is my Summoner and she's the best. She wants to make friends. So, if you're close to her age, nice, like reading, learning, spending time with rich people and patting cute things on the head, then please come here and make a line so that I can decide if you're good enough for her."

Abigail has both hands pressed over her face and is making weird noises when you hop off the edge of the table.

"What's wrong?" you ask her.

She just shakes her head. "Nothing Dreamer, nothing at all," she lies.

You're kind of hurt that she would keep the truth from you. It's not very nice to do that, especially after you went through all that trouble to make her friends.

"I think we should go to class now," Abigail says. She's packing up your lunches as she speaks.

"What? But the mortals haven't even started forming a line yet!"

The class Abigail leads you to is a few corridors down from the cafeteria, which Abigail seems to think is a good thing, even if that means missing out on the opportunity to make friends.

Still, if she wants to be all dutiful and get to Professor Clearwater's class early, then that's fine by you.

You're the first ones there except for the professor. The woman looks up as you enter and gestures at all of the desks laid out in neat rows with a pen. "Pick any seat," she says before returning to her work. The professor's desk is the biggest and neatest one, but you're pretty sure that 'any seat' doesn't include the one she's sitting at.

Abigail pulls you to a desk at the far back and plops you down on the seat nearest the wall before taking the one next to you. It's not the nicest place. From where you are no one in class will be able to see you.

"Just, ah, please be quiet during class, okay Dreamer?" Abigail asks. She smiles wobbly at you and places her hand on your head. "Please?"

Well, if she's going to ask like that. "Okay, I can do that," you agree.

You grip the edges of your seat and begin kicking out your legs in time with the music in your head while hoping that it won't take too long for class to start.

Fortunately, a distraction happens!

A girl walks into the class, bundle of books under one arm and pen tucked over her ear. She scans the room until her bright green eyes lock onto Abigail and you, then turns to walk your way. "Is this seat taken?" she asks as she gestures at the chair next to Abigail.

Your summoner looks at all of the other empty seats, then up to the still-smiling girl. "Uh, no, it isn't," Abigail says.

"Brilliant. I'm Pembrooke, Charlotte Pembrooke." She runs her fingers through thick blond hair, then settles down next to Abigail and extends a hand to her. "I heard what your Familiar said in the lunchroom."

"Oh no," Abigail says.

Charlotte's smile doesn't change at all. "I thought it was a wonderful approach. I was never one for beating around the bush. If you want something, ask for it. And if that thing is friends, then why not ask for those too."

You nod. This Charlotte girl is very wise.

"It was mortifying," Abigail says.

"Perhaps, but it worked," Charlotte says. "I'll be your friend if you'll have me. Or at least… hmm, let's call it a probationary friendship until we see if we get along."

"Oh… oh." Abigail says. "Um, I mean, sure."

Charlotte's smile widens just a little. "Brilliant. So, probationary friend, what's your name?"

"I'm being so impolite," Abigail says before hiding her face in her hands again. "I'm sorry. I'm Abigail, Abigail Normal."

You blink and spin to stare at Abigail. "Your name is Abigail Normal? Like what we are?"

Abigail gestures at you. "This is my Familiar, Dreamer."

"Dreamer Normal!" you say.

Abigail smiles a little and pats you on the head. "I guess so," she says.

"You're very articulate, Dreamer," Charlotte says. "There are few Familiars who can speak so clearly, though most can communicate to some degree. Abigail must be very proud of you."

You decide that Charlotte is good friend material.

Professor Clearwater stands up at the front of the class and you notice that just about every seat is filled already. She moves to the large blackboard that takes up one wall and begins drawing circles, triangles and other shapes into it with quick swipes of her hand.

The class fills up just a little more and then a bell rings.

The professor turns to see her class and nods. "Greetings every-one. Before I begin, can everyone hear me clearly?" There's a chorus of 'yeses' and lots of cone hats bobbing forwards and back. "Good. Then we shall begin this lesson the way most of your lessons start. By immediately getting to the meat."

She gestures to the symbols and glyphs behind her.

"These are the basic circle forms used in the modern day, though there are many, many more. You'll want to take notes from here on out."

With that hint dropped, all the students that don't have notebooks out already start scrounging around for one. Abigail of course has you, and you have Abigail's stuff, so you poke a hole in the world under the desk and plop her notebook and pen onto your lap then tentacle them over.

"Good. This class will teach you the basic inscription forms that nearly all magical circles use, but more importantly it will teach you the steps needed to describe those forms. We will also touch on the history of ritualistic magic and how to prepare for different sorts of rituals. By mid year you will be tested on your ability to prepare different materials for inscription, how familiar you are with various forms and their uses, and how prepared you are to conduct a basic ritual.

"This is the class that will teach you how to prepare to do magic, not the one that will teach you the magic itself. If you think for a moment that this knowledge is not as important then I would direct you to the magical anomalies ward of the Inquisition.

"A misplaced grain of sand. Poorly diluted ink. A crack in a piece of wood. A catalyst that escapes its containment. The tiniest variable can change a simple spell into an undirected weapon, one that can and will take your head off your shoulders, age you prematurely, or liquify your bones." The Professor stares across the room, her hands folded at the small of her back.

"Magic is the manipulation of the building blocks of reality in order to accomplish a task. Without care and precision the same blocks that allow humanity to stand head and shoulders above other creatures crumble. I intend to teach you how not to end your own lives." She smiles wider. "Do try to pay attention."

CHAPTER ELEVEN

C LASS ENDS when Professor Clearwater is interrupted by a loud ringing bell. The professor smiles as she turns away from a blackboard covered in notes and things. "I won't be holding anyone back during our first day together. Go on, have a good evening!"

You help Abigail by stuffing her things away in one of your dresses and then push your chair back behind your desk.

"No homework tonight," Charlotte says and she sounds disappointed. "Did you think of joining any clubs yet, Abigail?"

"Ah, not really," your summoner says as she removes her silly hat and runs a hand through her hair. "Are there any good ones?"

"There are!" Charlotte says. "Though the most interesting ones, the Spell Creation Club and Adventurer's Club both require that you be in your second year. Though I think you can join the latter if you have a group already."

"Okay," Abigail says. "What about clubs we can join?"

"I intend to join the athletics club," Charlotte says. "A keen mind requires a keen body. And keeping in shape is just a good idea besides. There are others of course. We could pick up a pamphlet."

"Sure, that would be nice," Abigail says. "If we have no homework then I don't really have any reason to go home early."

"You live in Five Peaks?" Charlotte asks as the three of you move towards the door. "The city proper I mean. Off-campus."

"I do. I have a small apartment."

Charlotte's eyebrows rise up to her hair. "You live alone?"

"With Dreamer," Abigail says. "It's right next to where I work."

"Oh my, how independent," Charlotte says. "I envy you a little. I stay in the school dorms here. It's practical, but the price is exorbitant and there are so many rules."

Abigail nods along as you move into the corridor. There's a bit of a pause as you all wait to see who will pick which direction you walk in, but then Charlotte starts moving towards the front of the school with a confident step.

"It would be great fun if you were to join the same club. We could help each other out."

"That does sound nice," Abigail says. "But I'm not very athletic."

"Hmm, unfortunate. There's the library exploration club? That one doesn't leave us much opportunity to talk though. Well, we'll see if we can't find something we both like."

Abigail and Charlotte start talking about their hobbies, which Charlotte already knows since you're such a good Familiar and announced it to everyone already. You're walking down a fairly quiet corridor when something screams from behind you.

"Wait!"

All three of you stop and turn at the same time to take in the boy jogging towards you. He's followed by a big, Familiar wolf.

"Hello Wuffles!" you say.

The wolf growls and lunges towards your face teeth-first, but his master yanks him back by the collar. "Wuffles! Down!" he says.

The wolf eyes first you, then his master, but after a bit he sits down with a wolf-y huff. He's still growling, but it's not as loud, just a low bassy rumble that fades in the background.

"Can we help you?" Charlotte asks. She's eyeing Wuffles as if she's a bit afraid of the wolf, which is silly, you wouldn't let Wuffles tear her apart by accident, she's Abigail's probationary friend and you don't let probationary friends eat other probationary friends.

"Yes, yes you can," the boy says as he comes to a panting halt. He presses his hands against his knees for a moment, then stands up. Wuffles' master is a tall boy, a whole head taller than Abigail and with shoulders twice as wide. His robes are almost straining across his chest. He's not fat or anything, just really big.

The poor boy. He's too big to ride his Familiar around. No wonder Wuffles is all angry all the time. He's a useless Familiar. Only good for giving pats and snuggles. Which while important don't provide much needed utility like you, a superior Familiar, can do.

But then, is that really Wuffles' fault? "Hey mister," You say, cutting off what the others were going to say. It doesn't matter, those you cut off weren't Abigail. "You should lose weight. You're too heavy for Wuffles to carry you."

The boy blinks at you, then looks to the two girls. "I'm not fat," he says.

"I didn't say you were fat," you reply. "Just that you're too heavy."

"Putting aside what our dear Dreamer has just said," Charlotte says. "Why did you wish to speak to us, mister?"

"Everette," the boy says. "I'm sorry for disturbing you ladies, but I had some questions and I hoped you could help me?" He looks at Abigail really quick, then lets his attention linger on Charlotte for a while, first on her face, then on her chest before his cheeks go rosey.

"What sort of questions?" Charlotte asks as she crosses her arms.

"Ah, right, it's about what happened at the Familiar testing this morning. Something didn't seem right."

"I'm sure it was just a strange series of coincidences," Abigail says quickly.

"Yeah, maybe," Everette says. "But they were strange and I was hoping you could help me get to the bottom of it."

"We are busy, Mister Everette," Charlotte said. "Maybe some other time."

"I'm really, really sorry to bother you," he says. "But I really want to talk. Please?" he begs.

Abigail is a little flushed when she turns to Charlotte. "Um, maybe we can talk, just for a moment?"

Charlotte eyes Everette for a moment more, then shrugs one shoulder. "Very well."

"I can make it up for you. There's a nice place to eat right next to the Academy. The food is great!" Everette says.

Abigail frets a little, and her hand wiggles for you to grab onto it. She doesn't seem to know what to do.

You tug at Abigail's sleeve. "I think that while that boy might be okay, and Wuffles is nice, we should spend more time with New Friend Charlotte first. She's already a friend so she's more important than some boy."

"Hey!" Everette says.

"I, um, I think Dreamer is right. N-not that you're bad or anything, Mister Everette," Abigail says, her arms waving around in negation. "It's just that I don't think we can really help you much with your problem."

"But I just have a few questions. It won't take much of your time," Everette begins.

The three of them, Everette, Charlotte and Abigail, start talking, but it's boring so you stop listening. Instead you step over to Wuffles who growls at your approach. "No biting now, Wuffles. Your master would be sad at you if you did that," you tell him.

He stops, but still doesn't look very happy.

Reaching up, you begin to sing a little song to make him more happy, because Abigail sings sometimes and that makes you happy.

"This is your snooter," you sing as you pat the top of Wuffles' nose. It makes a hollow fump-fump noise. "It is good for snooting. This is your booper," you continue to sing as you boop Wuffles' booper. "It is good for boo—" Wuffles growls and bites your hand again. Blood starts pouring down his mouth as he chews. "Wuffles, no! I wasn't done with my song!"

You hear gasps from behind you and the next thing you know Everette is prying Wuffles' mouth open and Abigail is pulling you back. "Dreamer, you got bitten!" she says.

You both know that it doesn't really matter, but she still fusses over your hand. You're not even missing any fingers this time.

"I'm so, so sorry," Everette says.

"You ought to be," New Friend Charlotte says as she waggles a finger under his nose. "This kind of behaviour from a Familiar reflects quite poorly on its Summoner. Do you want to make us think that you're little more than a rabid dog yourself?" she asked.

"No, no, I'm sorry," Everette backs away from Charlotte even though she's two heads shorter than him. Maybe it's the big cone hat that's making her look imposing?

"Hmph," Charlotte says before spinning around with a swish of robes. "Abigail, I wouldn't want to impose, but I believe leaving now would be for the best."

"Ah, yes, yes of course. Goodbye, Mister Everette," Abigail says as she pulls you along and down the corridor again, Charlotte by your side.

"Are you well, Dreamer?" Charlotte asks. "If someone were to bite my Web I would be inconsolable."

"Your Web?" Abigail asks as you keep moving.

Charlotte points to a small room with a plaque before it that reads 'Infirmary.' She pushes the door open and looks around, but it's unoccupied. "I think we can take some bandages. If anyone complains... well, this is what the infirmary is for," she says as she moves around to some cabinets and starts looking for things. She eventually pulls out some white cottony things with magic circles sewn into them and little pouches on the sides. "Web is my Familiar. She's been with me this whole time."

"Is she invisible?" you ask.

Charlotte smiles. "Nope, just sneaky. Place your hand here." she says, patting the bed.

A bit of moving around later and Charlotte has wiped the bite marks clean and presses a bandage over them. She activates the circle woven into it and with a flash and a sizzle you feel the flesh around your hands knit back together.

"That was warm," you say.

Charlotte pats your head. "You were very brave," she says. "And Abigail too. I thought you would faint for a moment there," she says as she tucks away the equipment into a bin near the door. "It shouldn't take more than a day or two for that to stop feeling warm. Give it a week and you won't even be able to tell that you were hurt at all."

"Thank you so much, Charlotte," Abigail says.

"Nonsense!" Charlotte says. "What are probationary friends for?"

For some reason Abigail thinks that that is very funny. You don't understand. Of course friends are just servants that Abigail gets along with, that's the entire reason you let them stay near her.

"Should we go see those club listings again?" she asks.

"If you want," Abigail says. "I feel like I've been a very poor probationary friend so far."

"Well then you can make it up to me by helping find a club we'll both enjoy!"

In no time at all all three of you are by the front lobby of the Academy, a huge room with a big marble staircase and a long, long desk at the front manned by an entire team of secretaries who wear little bonnets. There are rotating displays with colourful pamphlets that Charlotte eyes for a moment before picking a few and moving outside.

It's warmer out here than inside the Academy, and you soon find yourselves moving to a nearby hill that's deserted except for a bunch of yummy-looking pigeons and a lone picnic table. Abigail and Charlotte sit next to each other, so you climb onto the table and sit on it with your legs between the two.

Charlotte lays out the list of clubs flat on her lap. "There are quite a few. Some are for men or women only, unfortunately."

"That's okay," Abigail says. She points to one on the list. "My best friend Daphne is in the Gardening Club. she's a year ahead of us."

Charlotte places a hand over her mouth. "Oh my. I didn't think you... well, nevermind. I'm not inclined that way, I'm afraid."

"I don't like gardening either. My job gets my hands dirty enough without me sticking my fingers in the mud. I wouldn't mind trying it out though. Maybe it's less of a chore here than it is back home."

Charlotte is blushing faintly as she looks away and pulls out pen and paper from her purse. "We can draw up a list of those clubs that interest us, then pick out those that we're both interested in. From there we can pick out a final result we'll both be happy with, or maybe a shortlist of clubs to visit."

"That's very... methodical."

"Best to do things right the first time," Charlotte says. A few moments of scribbling later and she has an entire list drawn up, two columns with Abigail's choices on the one side and her own on the other. A bit of reorganizing leaves them with a smaller list.

You, of course, yoink it away. "I get to pick?" you ask as you look over the choices.

The girls look at each other and shrug as one. "Might as well," Charlotte says. "At least we can go see what they're like."

"That sounds fair," Abigail says.

You grin as you set out to make your choice.

"It says the Gardening Club is near here," Charlotte says as she holds up a little map. There are grey squares that you guess are buildings and little black lines for the paths around the school. A bunch of those buildings have numbers on them that Charlotte keeps comparing to a legend. The one you're moving towards is at the far end of the Academy, on the opposite side of the big hill the school is on.

The Gardening Club, as it turns out, is housed in a big greenhouse, the building made of a pretty latticework of wrought iron with glass panels all over it. There's a lot of things within, like big bushes and vines covered in teeny tiny flowers that are really tasty-looking in the sunlight.

Charlotte lowers her map when you come around the building and see a group of five or so other girls all by the doorway. None of them are wearing cone hats, so they have to be upper years.

"I'm not too sure I approve of this entire club," Charlotte admits.

"Why not?" Abigail asks.

You look up to see a bunch of weird expressions crossing Charlotte's face. "Well, I can't say I approve of proper young women doing... that sort of thing together."

"Gardening?" you ask.

Abigail looks just as confused.

It's too late to start asking though because the girls at the entrance to the greenhouse notice you and stop talking right away. They form a sort of half-circle and one of them, the oldest by the looks of her, steps up to your group. "Hello, may we help you?" she asks.

"Ah, hello," Abigail says. "I'm Abigail, and this is Charlotte, and this is Dreamer." You wave. "We were looking for the, um, Gardening Club?"

The girl presses a hand to her mouth. "Coming in a trio. Oh my. Well, you're at the right place, but at the wrong time. I'm Amara, the club president this year."

"Oh, should we have come sooner?" Abigail asks.

Amara shakes her head. "No no," she says while waving away Abigail's concerns. "I mean, clubs only officially open as of tomorrow. You're a bit early. But there's no harm in giving you a tour now!"

"That would be nice," Abigail says.

Amara smiles and moves back towards the doors leading into the greenhouse, soon you're all moving into the big, hot building, the smell of flowers almost suffocatingly strong. "As you might have guessed, we at the Gardening Club try to make flowers stand out as the prettiest things in the world. We also do a bit of gardening on the side."

Amara's friends giggle a little at that. You move deeper into the gardens. Past the open area at the front are a bunch of paths that are cut off from each other by big trellises and climbing vines. The rap-tap-tap of water dripping out of little hoses along the ceiling to platters next to the flowers is actually pretty loud in the muffled space.

"Um, I have a friend that comes to this club," Abigail says.

Amara turns to her, interest clear in her eyes. "You do?" she asks.

Abigail nods. "Daphne, she's been coming here since last year."

All of the Gardening Club girls gasp. "You're that Abigail?" Amara asks.

Your summoner is famous? This is as it should be, of course, but it's a bit strange. Two of the Gardening Club girls are fanning themselves at the back and all five of them are inspecting Abigail very carefully.

"Well, you certainly have the 'girl next door' look pinned down," Amara says as she taps her chin. "You grew up with Daphne, right?"

"Oh, yeah, we've been friends since… well, since we were really small. Our mothers both went to the Academy together, they were even in this club together!"

One of the girls gasps, a hand over her mouth. "How romantic!"

"Abigail, dear," Charlotte says. "I think you're sending mixed messages to these poor girls."

"Oh no, don't tell me that you and, I'm sorry, I didn't ask for your name," Amara says as she turns to Charlotte.

"Charlotte."

"Don't tell me that you and Charlotte are a thing. Poor Daphne's heart will crack."

Abigail looks down at you as if you can help her, but you're just as confused as she is. "Um. Charlotte is a friend? I can have more than one friend, right?"

"Oh, wow," one of the girls says.

"O-of course you can," Amara replies, her face goes very red. "We, we wouldn't get in the way of any burgeoning flowers, even if they—" She pauses to wave at her face. "Even if they're wild blossoms." Amara swallows and moves along the path a little ways. "We have areas like this for tea and scones and gossip," she says as she gestures to an area with little sofas and a glass table with a bouquet in the middle.

"Um, okay," Abigail says.

"Abigail," you ask as you pull at her sleeve. "These mortals are weird."

She nods, but doesn't explain anything.

"We have lots of little paths like these for members to walk down," Amara says as she leads you down a meandering path. It's just barely wide enough for two people to walk side by side. "And there are… areas for other activities," Amara says. She gestures to an alcove set aside where there's a bed covered in fluffy blankets. There are walls of flowers around it, so thick that if you were resting there, no one would be able to see you.

"That's a good napping place," you say. "Abigail, we should nap there together."

Amara and the others gasp. "So young." She coughs into a closed fist. "If you wish, my friends and I can… let you sample the greenhouse. We were just preparing to leave, but we tend to leave the doors unlocked. In fact, that might be for the best." Amara gestures towards her friends, and with a whole lot of tittering and giggling, they move back towards the front of the greenhouse.

"Young?" Abigail asks, her head tilting to the side in confusion and her glasses dipping to the very end of her nose. She's looking at Charlotte as if your new friend can explain better.

"They're implying that you and Dreamer share a relationship that's... more than just Summoner and Familiar," Charlotte says. She might be catching what the others have because her face is looking very warm.

"Of course there's more than that," you say. "I'm going to make Abigail the most happiest."

Abigail frowns a little, looks at the departing Gardening Club girls, the bed, then you, then back again. "Are they, is the whole Gardening Club... girls who are... *that* way?" she squeaks.

Charlotte presses a hand to her face. "You only caught on just now?"

"Oh, oh my," Abigail says.

"What are you talking about?" you ask.

Charlotte looks away, but she answers anyway. "Certain young women have the... perhaps unhealthy habit of... falling in love with other young women."

You think about this for a moment. "That just means that if Abigail mates she won't be making yucky babies that will steal my rightful headpats. There's nothing wrong with that."

Abigail wraps a hand around yours. "I-I think I should be going now. *Thank-you-very-much-good-bye!*"

Abigail is very silent as you move through the school.

"Do you want to talk about it?" Charlotte asks with the tone of someone that most emphatically does not want to talk about it.

"No, no it's okay," Abigail says. "It's just..." her free hand, the one you're not holding onto, wiggles in the air. You're not sure what that's supposed to mean, or if it even means anything.

"You're feeling betrayed?" Charlotte guesses.

"A little, yeah. Daphne… I didn't know she was that way, that she felt that way about, about me." Now Abigail's face is all red again. She's being very silly.

"Daphne loves you lots," you tell her. "Which is okay, because you're Abigail and that makes you the best, so she should."

Now her face is even redder. What is wrong with your summoner?

"Let's just move on," Abigail says. "I think we were going to visit the Cannonry Club next?"

Charlotte nods along and checks her map. "We are. Though they might be closed too." As you move out from one of the rear-most parts of the school, you're greeted by the distant thud-boom of an explosion going off in the middle distance. "Or maybe they aren't."

The Cannonry Club is hosted in a small series of shacks around an open area, all of them facing a large cannon mounted on a platform that allows it to turn. The cannon is aimed way off into the distance, over a small part of the town that's mostly occupied by docks by the churning rapids of the river that snakes through Five Peaks.

You imagine that housing prices are a bit lower downhill.

"Hello!" a young man greets you as he steps out of one of the shacks. He has a wide-brimmed hat with a slightly spiky top, so he's not in his last year but near it. He's also missing most of his facial hair and all of his eyebrows. "Ah, are you fresh meat?"

"Abigail is not for eating," you warn him.

The boy smiles sheepishly and laughs. It's a weird laugh, too high-pitched and a bit off. "Of course, of course, fresh meat is tomorrow! How can I help you ladies?"

"We, ah, we just wanted to see what the Cannonry Club was all about," Abigail says.

He blinks some more and then giggles. "So you *are* fresh meat!" Clapping his hands, the boy twirls around and skips over towards the shacks. "Well, come along then! Always willing to give a tour."

"Ah, sure," Abigail says. She and Charlotte glance at each other for a long time before following. "Um, my name's Abigail, this is Dreamer and Charlotte," she says.

"Hrm? Oh, yeah, names don't matter here. I'm Joe though," the boy says. He gestures to the shacks one after the other. "We have a few… sub-clubs here. More like specialities and fields of interest within the gamut of cannonry. That's the Traditional Firearms group." He points to one shack with a musket sign hanging above its door. "That's the Arcane Artillery group."

The next building in the circle has a bunch of complicated circles drawn next to its door. "Then we have the Mage Cannon group." Joe points to another shack, this one with a staff hanging above its front. "And finally the Demolitions group." The last shack is missing, there's only a crater and a few beams sticking out of the ground where it should be. "The Demolitions group is looking for new members actually, after their losses last semester."

"Losses?" Abigail asks as she eyes the burnt hole in the ground.

"Half of them graduated and one of the members that was supposed to take the lead has a new girlfriend that monopolizes all his time."

"I thought, with the explosion," Charlotte says.

Joe waves it off. "No no, we get blown up all the time here. It's a part of pride that you can tell who is or isn't a member of our club by the number of limbs they have left! It's great fun!"

"It, uh, sure sounds like it, Mister Joe," Abigail says. You nod, because it does sound like fun. "But seeing as how you're not officially open yet, maybe we should come back tomorrow?"

"Oh, yes, of course, that makes perfect sense. Would you like a grenade for the road?" he asks.

"Yes," you say.

"No," Charlotte and Abigail echo each other.

"A young fan!" Joe says. He roots around under his robes for a bit, which requires that he pulls them way up to reveal the pocket lined shorts he's wearing underneath as well as his hair legs, before he finds what he's looking for. "Here you go sweetie. It's nitroglycerine mixed with some clay and a few other agents. It makes it mostly stable unless you smack it hard enough, then it goes off like a bomb. Good, safe fun!"

Abigail and Charlotte's escape is done with a lot more speed than you think is necessary. Joe was really nice after all.

"So," Abigail says after you've retreated a ways and are walking along the outer edge of the campus. "Do you think we should meet up again tomorrow. For lunch, maybe?" she asks.

"To continue our provisional friendship?" Charlotte asks. She smiles and rubs your head. "Sure, it has been fun so far!"

"Brilliant!"

You finish chewing on the last bites of your grenade and grin up at them both. "It's going to be ever more fun tomorrow!" you say.

Abigail is acting strange. More strange than usual, that is. After leaving Charlotte at the school gates her mood went from sorta-normal to… whatever it is now.

You can't help but look up to her and try to see what's wrong. She's walking with her head low, lips occasionally moving and eyes scanning something that isn't there. Her hand keeps squeezing really hard then letting go, and you can tell that she's shivering a little even though it's not that cold.

"What's wrong?" you ask her for maybe the third time.

"Nothing," she lies again.

You stop walking while Abigail continues. She only makes it one step before your linked hands stop her. She turns to you, then looks around a bit. You're both in a quiet part of Five Peaks, the roads here all on a slope that makes it so that the houses on either side of the street all look uneven.

"I don't like it when you're like this," you tell Abigail. "What's wrong?"

"Noth—"

You do the thing where your cheeks puff out and your brows get drawn together. "Don't. Don't say 'nothing' when it's something."

Abigail just breathes for a moment and she wiggles her fingers until you let go. Carefully, she adjusts her glasses and crosses her arms. "It's that whole Gardening Club thing," she says.

"They were nice," you say.

Abigail nods. "Yeah, they were. But Daphne goes there. And it's a place for… for girls who like other girls."

"I'm wearing a girl body and I like you. That's okay, right?"

"It's not the same kind of like," Abigail says.

"There's more than one sort?" Maybe you can like Abigail in *all* the ways.

Abigail nods, her cheeks reddening again. "They like other girls in an… intimate way. A way that I… don't know if I do. Not that… not that I mind that Daphne is that way. I wish she had told me earlier."

"Like how you didn't want to tell me what was wrong?" you ask.

Abigail smiles, it's sheepish and a little embarrassed. "Kind of like that, yeah. But over… years, I guess. And for me. Me. I'm just… me."

"You're Abigail. The prettiest and nicest Summoner ever, and you give the best pats and the best cuddles," you say. To prove the point, you step up to her and wrap your hands around her legs and tuck the side of your head against her tummy. It's nice and warm and good.

Abigail chuckles and you can feel the rumble of it. "Yeah, I guess. But, I… I don't know if I'm like Daphne, if I can… reciprocate."

You look up, then pull away and grab her hands. "Let's go," you say as you start dragging her after you. You know where you're going because you never forget a place where you've slept. Abigail protests a bunch, but she's still a small mortal and there's no way she could stop you.

It takes a few minutes, but you arrive in front of Daphne's place and walk up to the door. A tentacle wraps around the knocker and thump-thumps it against the wood.

The door opens a moment later to reveal Edmund in his suit, one arm folded before his chest with a towel wrapped over it. "Hello Miss Abigail, Miss Dreamer," he says. "How may I assist you this afternoon?"

"We need to talk to Daphne about how much she loves Abigail," you say.

Abigail makes a squeaky noise, but when Edmund moves out of the way she follows after you without protest. "Miss Daphne is in her office," Edmund says as he closes the door behind you.

You nod and pull Abigail over to the little office where you'd talked to Daphne the last time you were here. She's sitting behind the same desk, her school robes discarded over a chair and her hat on the same perch as Archibald. "Daphne," you say. "Archibald."

"Who," says Archibald.

Daphne stares. "Dreamer? Abigail?"

"Yes," you confirm in case she wasn't sure it was you. "Abigail needs to talk to you about feelings."

"Oh no," Abigail says as she tries to hide her face. It's useless, of course, you all know what she looks like.

"Her… feelings?" Daphne asks.

"Yes," you say. "We went to the Gardening Club and we learned that you love Abigail and now Abigail is being silly."

Daphne makes a noise. It's a sort of squeak, like when you squish something alive between two tentacles and all the air inside of it squeals out. Her mouth is also moving a lot. She stops, takes a deep breath, then another, and recentres herself. "I see."

Abigail lowers her hand. "Were you… were you ever going to tell me?" she asks. "That you're, ah, more interested in women?"

"I—" Daphne swallows. "I was going to tell you. You're my best friend. Of course I would tell you. I'd tell you anything. But every time I was going to… I am something of a coward. The longer I went without telling you the harder it became to do so. As you can guess, this is not how I imagined things going."

"How did you imagine things going?" Abigail asks. There's a bit of anger there, so you grab her hand to sooth it out and remind her that you're there.

Daphne closes her eyes. "Well, in the best case scenario you would… reciprocate."

"That's not the case." Abigail says. She's shaking, and her eyes wont meet Daphne's. "I don't… I don't think. I don't know."

Daphne flinches back. "Ah, well, I was hoping to tell you a little after our wedding, maybe?" she smiles, but Abigail doesn't laugh, and you're not sure if it was a joke or not. She deflates. "That fell flat. I'm sorry."

"Dreamer, I think we should go home," Abigail says as she starts towards the door. "I need, I need time, to think."

"No, wait," Daphne says.

"What?" Abigail says. There are tears in her eyes, not happy ones. You're not sure how to fix this. Usually problems just need tentacles to fix them, but they might make things worse here, and more tentacles isn't a solution.

"Can we, can we talk? Maybe tomorrow? Please?" Daphne asks before sniffing. It sounds all wet and disgusting.

Abigail shifts a little, looks down at you, then back to Daphne. You don't know what her expression means. "Tomorrow," she agrees before pulling you to the door. You're almost out when she stops again. "I… you're still my best friend, okay Daph?"

"O-okay," Daphne says. It's choked. "Dreamer, dear, could you close the door?"

You nod and pull the door shut behind you.

There's sad noises from the office after the door clicks shut, but they fade as you walk out of Daphne's place.

CHAPTER TWELVE

YOU WAKE up a bit earlier than you thought you would. It doesn't take much effort to figure out why. Abigail is tucked up against you, using your tummy as a pillow. Usually you're the one using Abigail as a pillow, but sometimes things move around while naps are happening and this isn't so bad. Your tummy is a very good pillow after all.

Still, you didn't wake up just because of that. Abigail is mumbling in her sleep, indistinct words that you can't quite make out that tickle you with each breath. Her eyes are shut really firmly and there's a teeny tiny frown creasing her forehead.

You're pretty sure you know why Abigail is like this, you just don't know why.

You bask in the confusion of that statement for a while.

On the one tentacle, Abigail is worried about Daphne because Daphne likes her. Which is really strange. Daphne liking her isn't a bad thing. On the other tentacle, Abigail probably likes Daphne back, but she's not sure if she likes Daphne in the same way, which is also confusing and silly.

You would go on, but Abigail only has so many limbs and therefore can't juggle as many problems as you can.

No wonder she's having such a hard time sleeping, the poor silly mortal.

You run your stubby little fingers through Abigail's hair and try to let her sleep a little more. The sun isn't up yet, so it's not school time. Still, you're awake now, and as much as you adore napping it's not time for that, not when you need to figure out how to help Abigail.

Fortunately, Abigail has a bunch of books in your little apartment, and they all have knowledge in them. You pop an eye out and fling it over to a tentacle that grabs it out of midair. Now you can scan her library for books about fixing humans.

It only takes a few minutes to discover that Abigail, the silly summoner, has *no* books on that subject. Not a single one. Plenty of books on boring things like physics and magic and Familiars, but not a single good book about Daphne's or love or cuddling.

At least, that's what you think at first!

Some creative searching and you find a pile of books neatly tucked inside the heating vent right next to the bed. Of course Abigail would hide her best books! Just like how you hide all the smart things you know so deep in your own mind that sometimes you forget how smart you are. You pry the metal grate off the front of the vent with a plop and set it aside.

The books within all have images of male humans wearing very little on their covers, sometimes with girls next to them who are usually only wearing sheets. You make a happy noise, push your eye back in place, and with a few tentacles start reading.

You're halfway through the first book when Abigail stirs, looks around with big blinky eyes and sees what you're reading.

Usually Abigail is very cute when she wakes up. There's lots of yawning and stretching and other post-wake-up adorableness. But this morning she's up as if someone just doused her in water. She squawks and swipes the book out of your tentacles. The little jump sends her tumbling off the side of the bed and onto the ground with a thud.

You poke your head over the edge. "Good morning!"

"Good morning, Dreamer," Abigail says. She raises the book up a bit. "Where did you find this?"

A tentacle points off to the side where the grate is sitting next to a hole in the wall. The other books are all just sitting there.

"Ah," she says. "Can you please… not read these books?"

"But it was interesting," you say. "I was learning! If I study hard I can be like the heroes in that story."

Abigail's face is starting to go red. "Please, please don't read these books," she says.

You huff, but it's a small thing to ask. "Okay. I wanted to learn how you fix you and Daphne."

Abigail rolls around and stands up, then adjusts her nightshift so that it falls around her legs instead of riding up around her waist. "We don't need fixing," she says as she places the book back in its place. "We're both just… taking some time to think." She rubs at her face and looks out the window. "And it's early. Urgh, I won't be able to sleep. Do you want breakfast?"

Is she asking you if you want to eat? What a silly summoner. "Yes." You nod your head and begin climbing out of bed too. "But I also want more cuddles because we have more time."

Abigail laughs, and you're happy to hear it. Her laugh is the best happy sound. She sets some water to boil and breaks a pair of eggs on a pan, then turns with her arms raised for hugging.

You collide into her and use your arms and a small portion of your tentacuddlers to squeeze her close while the eggs sizzle and make the room smell yummy.

When hugging time is—temporarily—over because otherwise the food would burn, you move to the table and sit down on your chair while Abigail puts slices of bread into a magical device that burns and magics the bread into toast. "So, how are we going to make Daphne more happy again?"

Abigail sighs and moves the pan around. "You're still going on about that?" she asks.

"It's important."

She scrapes the eggs onto a plate, pours the hot water into a mug and pulls two toast from her little contraption and butters it up. All of that is placed right in front of you with a fork and knife and a little tea bag that you plop into your mouth and swallow. She returns to make her own breakfast while you start devouring yours.

"I… I." Abigail shifts a little. "I love Daphne. She's like a sister. More even, a best friend."

"And she loves you too," you say as you poke at the yellow egg juice with a corner of a toast.

"I know," Abigail says.

"Is it because you don't think she's pretty?" you ask. "The book talked a lot about curves. Do you not like Daphne's curves?"

Abigail goes red again and rubs at her face. "Dreamer, please don't... don't mention that part of a girl's body."

"What about her—"

"Don't mention busts either. Please." Abigail cuts you off.

You harrumph and go back to eating slowly. You were going to mention wonderful personalities, but now you're not sure if that's okay too. Abigail is being very unreasonable with her list of things you can't do and people you can't eat, you find.

She sits across from you and takes a sip from her mug of tea. "Do you think I should try?" she asks.

"Try what?" you ask right back. You're not a mind reader—most of the time—you can't expect to know what she's talking about.

"With Daphne? Maybe just, just one date? Maybe? It would make her happy. And I don't want to lose her because of this."

"But do you think she's pretty?" The book stressed that prettiness was the most important thing about a girl. You're not sure about that. Huggability and cuddliness were never even mentioned.

Abigail goes very red and tries to hide behind her mug. It's, of course, too small to hide her face. "A little?" she squeaks. "But I like boys."

Your eyes narrow. "Which boys?" you demand.

"No boy in particular," Abigail says. "Just... boys."

You don't understand this whole thing about picking people based on such tiny differences. You have a hard enough time telling one mortal apart from the other as is. "So you never look at girls and think they're pretty?" you ask.

Abigail is blushing a lot again.

You sigh. This whole situation is just one big mess. Your summoner is lucky to have such a kind and compassionate and understanding Familiar.

You skip to class, because skipping makes your dress go *floosh floosh* with every step and it feels good. Lots of mortals laugh when they see you skipping, and some of the girls clutch their hands together and make little cooing sounds before they try to pat you. Obviously, skipping does something to the brains of mortals, but it's a good thing because it leads to patting.

Abigail, of course, isn't far behind you. She has a big book tucked up against her chest and is walking with a bit of a skip in her step. Not a proper skip though, just some bounciness. Clearly she's missing out.

"Which class are we going to?" you ask her.

"Ah, this morning is one long class until lunch," Abigail says. "It's an obligatory first year only class called Familiar Care and Training."

You stop mid-skip, spin around, then let gravity do the thing where it pulls you down. "You have classes that teach you how to cuddle?" You ask. This school is clearly the best school.

Abigail pats your head a little as she walks by. "Not quite. Come on, you'll be able to see what I'm talking about in a few minutes." She leads you past a few empty classrooms and a bunch more where students are gathering and chit-chatting. You find it all quite silly how these mortals are all gathered here in their black robes and silly hats, especially the first years with their long cone hats. They have to bend over double just to enter a room without losing their headgear.

Then Abigail brings you to a classroom that's way bigger than the rest. There's a big man at the very front, a professor you'd guess, but his hat is on the desk next to the blackboard. Half his hair is missing, and one of his eyebrows. You suspect that he's a member of the Cannonry Club because he's also missing a hand.

You're not super early, but you're early enough to see a free spot next to Charlotte where only her bag is waiting. There are a few boys talking to her, but she dismisses them with a shooing gesture when she sees you and Abigail walking into the room.

"Hello, probationary friends," Charlotte says. "I saved you some seats."

You grin up at her and plot yourself down between her and Abigail. "Hi," you say.

She chuckles and looks past you to Abigail. "Hello Abigail. You seem to be doing better this morning."

"Ah," Abigail says. She takes a deep breath and nods. "I think I am, yes. How about you?"

"Still on the lookout for a club to join," Charlotte admits. "We're looking into the Old Faith's Club this afternoon?"

Abigail nods and wiggles into her seat. "We are, if you're up for it. I'm afraid I can't stay as long tonight, I do have work to do."

Charlotte waves it off. "That's fine. It even works out for me. The Athletics Club is meeting this evening, and I intend to be there for their first official gathering."

Class fills up as more students move in. You notice Everette sitting in the row behind you, Wuffles right by his side and eyeing you with his big doggy eyes, and next to him is Maddie with her weird white cat-thing Cutebee. You and Cutebee stare at each other, but he never blinks and you can't just pull your eyes out to keep staring at him when facing the front of the class or Abigail would make a fuss.

You content yourself with hiding a bunch of tentacles around the cat-thing in case it gets any clever ideas. Sharp tentacles.

The big man at the front bangs his fist on his desk for attention a moment after the bell rings. "Everyone. This class is meant to teach you how to care for your Familiars. Familiars—as you ought to know, but a few fail to every year—are not merely some animal handed to you for fun. They are linked to you, part of you. You had to give of your blood and will to bring them to you, and in doing so have bonded with them soul-to-soul. Familiars may die, and with them part of you will go."

He begins pacing. "It is possible to have more than one Familiar, or to summon a second Familiar after the passing of your first. Some of the more experienced professors have lost their companions. You'll note that few of them have a second Familiar. The tearing of that bond is one of the leading causes of suicide amongst accredited mages and for good reason."

There's a bit of murmuring in the class, and lots of the students are hugging their Familiars close. You lean over towards Abigail. "You won't summon another Familiar, right?" you ask her.

She smiles and pulls you into a sidelong hug. "The mere idea that there are two of you terrifies me," she says.

Good. You're unique and special. It's good that Abigail knows this.

Of course, if there was a second Dreamer you would eat her.

The rest of the lesson is about caring for different sorts of Familiars, but the big professor man soon breaks the class up and tells the students to form groups of four to discuss their experiences so far and to give each other advice about Familiar handling.

Of course, Abigail teams up with friend Charlotte right away, but that leaves you two people short.

And then Everette shows up with Maddie. "Do you guys mind if we form a team?" he asks.

"Of course not," Charlotte says.

You glare at Cutebee, but you've been outplayed already. There's nothing to do about it.

The four Summoners form a sort of circle in a corner of the classroom, desks pushed aside and chairs moved so that everyone can face everyone else. You're sitting between Abigail and Charlotte, of course, and across from you is Wuffles and Cutebee. Charlotte's own Familiar is still being sneaky-like.

"So," Everette says. "We're supposed to talk about how we care for our Familiars, right? Maybe Wuffles and I can go first?"

"I for one would love to know where you came up with that name," Charlotte says with one of her friendly smiles. "It's very unique."

Everette's face does some weird things, but he ends up smiling a little. "Ah, well. It's partially Wuffles' own fault. I wanted to name her Brutus, or Charger or something, well, ah."

"Manly?" Abigail says.

Maggie and Charlotte both giggle into their hands. Cutebee stares at you.

"Yeah. Then I discovered that Wuffles is a girl and I made a joke about 'well I can't call you Wuffles.' Of course, that's the name she chose. So I have a Direwolf called Wuffles now."

"A Direwolf, truly?" Charlotte asks as she inspects Wuffles. She brings a hand up and Wuffles scoots over to be within optimal pat-patting range.

You reach out to pat Wuffles too. She eyes you carefully, but doesn't stop you from running your hand through her thick, soft fur. It's very nice. You wish Abigail's species had fur in more than just two places so that you could pat-pat Abigail this way too.

"She's very nice," Charlotte says. "Yes she is," she repeats, this time in a strange, squeaky voice directed right at Wuffles. The Direwolf gives her a sloppy puppy smile and drools a bit on your arm.

You, of course, lick it off. You're the best Familiar, which means you're also self-cleaning.

"I guess caring for Wuffles is just like caring for a dog, but more?" Abigail says. Her hand is straying towards Wuffles, but you grab it and guide it carefully towards your head. Obviously your Summoner wanted to pat you and her horrible mortal eyesight led you astray for a moment there. Abigail sighs, probably in happiness and begins playing with your hair.

"Yeah, pretty much. I brought her to a veterinarian for a check up already and found a few different sorts of foods she likes. Mostly her favourite food is anything I happen to be eating at any given moment."

Wuffles makes an agreeing sound and the girls giggle a bit. You don't understand. Eating what your Summoner is eating is perfectly natural.

"What about you, Maggie?" Abigail asks.

"Oh me? Um, yes. This is Cutebee," she says as she picks up the cat-looking-creature and holds him up. "I don't know what he is yet, but he's very friendly and nice. He doesn't emote a lot, but sometimes I swear he knows what I'm thinking."

Cutebee stares at you some more.

"Can I pat him?" you ask while making grabby grabby gestures towards the little monster.

"Of course!" Maggie says. She hands Cutebee over, the cat-thing flopping around with all of the energy of a sack of rice. You grab him carefully under each foreleg and hold him up to your face. "He's really nice," Maggie says.

"Yes, I'm sure he is," you agree as you refuse to blink.

"W-what about caring for Cutebee?" Abigail says. "Anything special to do?"

"Not really? Cutebee likes to go off on his own sometimes. Usually he hangs around the middle school near my house. He's very popular with the girls there. But other than feeding him a bit three times a day there's not much to do. He grooms himself and he never used the litter I got for him." Maggie's smile is very bright. "He's a very good Familiar."

"Yes," you say. "He looks very good." Your eyes are starting to burn. You refuse to lose the staring contest.

"Charlotte, we never saw your Familiar. Is it too big to bring into the class?" Abigail asks.

"Web is always a little shy. Which I find strange since I'm quite the opposite," Charlotte says. She reaches under her robes and you notice Everette snapping his head around not to look as she searches and then removes something. It's small and black and very furry. "This is Web. say 'hi' Web."

The spider poised on her hand spins around and wiggles its butt at you. Glowing lines of butt stuff come out of it like ropes and it manipulates them with its rearmost legs. Within seconds there's a tiny banner stretched between two legs in the air with the word 'HELLO!' on it.

"Thash verhay preeshy," you say around the pair of legs kicking at your face. The long fluffy tail whipping around makes it hard to see, but you notice that Abigail is looking at you with wide eyes.

"Dreamer, no!" she says.

"Cutebee!" Maggie cries as she jumps towards you.

Abigail wraps a hand around Cutebee's tail, by now the only bit of him you haven't eaten yet, and yanks it out. "No, Dreamer, no."

The cat-thing comes sploorping out of your mouth and hangs limply in Abigail's grasp.

"Oh no, no, no," Maggie says, tears streaming down her face as she grabs Cutebee's saliva covered form and hugs him close. He, of course, is still alive, but his head turns your way and his eyes narrow.

You'll get him next time.

Then a rolled up piece of paper baps you on the head. "No. Dreamer, no. You can't eat people's Familiars."

"What?" you ask as you turn to Abigail. She baps you again. "Stop bapping me."

"Stop eating everything." She punctuates this with another bap. "I'm, I'm so sorry everyone," she says.

"It's okay," Charlotte replies. "No one was hurt... too badly. I don't think. Is Cutebee well?"

Maggie nods super fast. "He is," she says before turning her big soulful eyes at you. "Why did you try to eat him?"

"He looked at me funny," you say.

There's a whistle through the air and a sharp bap behind your head again.

"I suppose it's our turn," Abigail says. "This is my Familiar Dreamer. She's a real sweetie." You smile. "Sometimes." You pout.

Abigail is being very unfair to claim you're not the best Familiar ever. Clearly you need to step up your game.

After class, the girls, that is, Charlotte and Abigail, decide to eat outside. Both of them brought their own lunches so they don't need to wait in line in the food selling place and can just go out right away.

You're okay with this. The weather outside is nice and warm and it's sunny. There's a lot of room with trees and things for Familiars that are dumber than you to run around in and even tables where you can eat. A few other students are there too, some in groups of friends, some in couples that are being all disgusting with each other and a few lone ones that are sitting by the shade of trees and writing or reading.

It's a very nice place, you decide, for a big lunch.

"Time for food," you declare as you maneuver your skirts into the optimal sitting position. You don't know how mortal girls do it without the help of a bunch of tentacles.

"Patience," Abigail says, but it's not with an angry tone or anything, she just needs to sit herself down too.

Charlotte sits across from you and Web sneaks out from the neck of her robes and jumps onto the table where she pit-patters around.

Web isn't a friend yet, but Web is Friend Charlotte's Familiar, so she's your friend by association, and you don't eat friends unless you're really hungry.

"What did you guys bring for lunch?" Charlotte asks as she brings out a tin box and sets it on the table. She opens it up to reveal a sandwich, which looks yummy, an apple, which looks yummy, and a dead mouse, which also looks yummy. She smiles across at you. "If I have any leftovers I'll give them to you, alright?" she says.

"Dreamer, stop eyeing Charlotte's food as if I never feed you," Abigail says, but there's a smile when she says it. "And could you pass me the lunches?"

Oh yes, in your efforts to be the best Familiar you volunteered to carry all the things.

With some tentacle trickiness you open a rift in space above the table and let all the food drop down. There's a clatter as the lunch basket Abigail packed thumps onto the table.

"That's… an impressive skill," Charlotte says.

"It's nothing," you reply because that's what it is. A hole filled with so much nothing that something from elsewhere fills it in. You just made sure it was the elsewhere where you are.

Abigail searches through the basket for a bit, then lays down a plate before each of you, some utensils and then two sandwiches covered in tinfoil.

You start munching on yours right away, the tinfoil making it all crackly as you bite through the metal. Near the far end of the table, Web is eating through her mouse with gusto. Abigail sets out a few more things and is about to eat when a voice cuts through the silence of your meals.

"A-Abigail?"

Abigail stiffens and turns at the same time as you do.

Daphne is standing behind you, a small basket clutched to her chest which she is looking at really hard. Her hair is pulled up to hide her face a bit and Archibald is resting on her shoulder, his head rubbing against hers in a weird bird-y hug.

"Daphne," Abigail says. She stands up awkwardly, then moves to the side of the table. "Daph, I—"

"Please," Daphne interrupts. "I... I understand if you don't want to see me anymore." She takes a small step back.

"No, no it's, it's okay." Abigail is being really weird again. She raises her arms then lets them drop by her side. "You're having lunch?" she asks.

"I was just moving by," Daphne says. "I don't want to bother you, but I saw you and—"

"Join us," Abigail says and it's the first thing that makes sense. If Daphne joins your table you can share her lunch with yourself. "There's room, and you should meet Charlotte. She's nice. And Web too, and Dreamer likes you. Please?"

"I can?" Daphne asks. It sounds really confused, like the words are trying to come out but don't know how to. Like Abigail when she was pooping and you walked into the bathroom and she tried to scream but was so red that it didn't come out right.

Abigail nods. "Of course you can. Um. Can I hug you?"

Daphne places her basket on the table as if it's about to burst into flames, then steps up to Abigail who grabs her close.

This is good, now they're friends again and friends share their lunches with their friend's Familiars.

"We have to... we should talk about things later. Because you're my best friend and, and that's what friends do, they talk, and I don't want to lose you and I, I think I might." Abigail flushes, shakes her hand and pulls out of the hug. "Let's have lunch."

Daphne deflates and a small laugh escapes her. "Okay."

There's a bit of shuffling around, and Daphne and Charlotte introducing themselves. Charlotte looks curious about Daphne but Daphne is practically floating so she doesn't seem to notice.

You reach out and grab the skull of the mouse Web was eating and pop it into your mouth.

"Dreamer, no," Abigail says.

You huff. "How am I supposed to know what to eat?" you ask.

Abigail rolls her eyes. "You can eat everything that's on your plate." She of course points to your very empty plate.

Charlotte giggles and puts a corner of her sandwich on it, but that's only enough for one bite. You're still happy about it, but it's not enough.

Then it clicks.

Everything that's… Oh, you *get* it now. This must be one of those weird mortal things, like how they all think they shouldn't hit each other or how they all wear clothes under their clothes and are very private about their underclothes. It's all nonsensical, of course, but mortals will mortal.

You place the salt shaker and pepper grinder from Daphne's basket on your plate. Then you put them into your mouth and start chewing through the glass and the yummy powder within. "What?" you ask Abigail after you notice her staring. "It was on my plate."

CHAPTER THIRTEEN

ABIGAIL STRETCHES her arms way, way up until her back goes crack-pop and she lets out a happy sigh. Class is over and now it's time for more fun stuff, not that playing with Web wasn't fun.

You stretch too, stubby arms reaching up towards the ceiling, and wiggle your body from side to side a little. Some of the girls nearby giggle and there's a big smile on Charlotte's face as she pats your head. "That was a big stretch," she says.

You nod. It was.

Charlotte, still smiling, brings her own arms way up, then bounces on the balls of her feet. You notice a lot of the boys nearby stopping their conversations mid-word to stare at her really good stretching form, especially when she bends over double and presses her hands to the ground without bending her knees. She pulls up, then with both hands on her hips, sways from side to side. "Ah, that feels good."

You're impressed. For a creature with so many hard bony things in her, Charlotte can bend very well. Abigail's face is very red after she watched Charlotte. You think that it's the jealousy of not being quite that flexible. "It's okay," you say as you pat her hand.

That snaps Abigail out of her jealous funk. "We're heading to the Old Faith's club today, right?" she says after clearing her throat.

"We are," Charlotte says with a firm nod.

Everyone tucks their stuff in their bags and you toss Abigail's things into the shadows where your tentacles are waiting to sort them for the next class. Then you're all off to the next club!

Or you would be, if Abigail doesn't stop a few steps out of the class, bringing your entire group to a stop.

"H-hello Abigail," Daphne says. "And Dreamer, and Charlotte," she adds a moment later. She doesn't look nearly as nervous as she was over lunch time, but she's still a little fretful. Really, she needs to get over her whole thing with liking Abigail. It's natural to like Abigail, everyone should do it. You liked Daphne more when she was all tough and assertive.

"Hello Daphne," Abigail says. "Ah, you wanted to... Right now." She goes red again and looks around for a bit. "We were going to visit a club, did you want to come?"

Daphne took in a deep breath of air and straightened herself back up. When she was done her smile was a lot more Daphne-like. "I would love to," she said.

You skipped ahead of the others on the way to the mysterious Old Faith's club, Web riding on your head and grabbing on to your hairtacles for dear life.

"You didn't actually say which club we're visiting next," Daphne says.

"Ah, it's the Old Faith's club," Abigail says.

"Really? Of all the clubs... well, I suppose it's not so bad, though they have something of a reputation."

"What sort of reputation?"

"They're considered, honestly, it wouldn't be polite to say in public. I suppose you'll just have to find out," Daphne says.

You'll find out really soon because you arrive before a classroom in one of the quieter corners of the school that has a black sign with big fancy letters on it that reads 'Old Faiths' on the door. You rap your knuckles on the closed door and bounce while you wait. Web is tap-tapping a beat on your head in time with your bouncing because Web is just neat like that.

The door opens to reveal a person that you think might be a human. He's tall, but really skinny, and instead of wearing the school's normal robes he's wearing a white blouse that's very tight and much tighter black leather pants. He sighs. "More lambs to the slaughter?" he asks, his voice sounds like Abigail when she wakes up in the middle of the night to go pee.

"Hi," you say.

"Hello," Abigail says. "We wished to visit the Old Faith's club?"

"Ugh," he says before eyeing them all for a long time, then he moves back from the door. "Come in, I guess. I'm Lewis."

The four of you step into a dark room. There are drapes over the windows and lots of black leather couches against the walls where people who are all wearing black or red or sometimes white are lounging around as if they're really sleepy. But this doesn't feel like a sleeping place.

"Hey everyone," Lewis says in a voice barely louder than normal talking. "We have new people here to find enlightenment and truth by peeling back the evil and sordid lies of the Inquisition. Let us all guide them to the truth."

You expected a cheer, or some clapping, but there's a lot more sighing and low moaning. You then notice that all the boys and girls have very pale, powdery faces and lots of makeup on. You don't know what this means.

"So, um, Lewis," Abigail asks. "What does your club... do?"

"Ugh," Lewis says. "Like I said, we know that there are things underneath the Underneath, and we want to, like, peel off the coverings and expose the dark, bleeding heart of this decrepit world."

"Can you explain... more?" Abigail tries.

Lewis sighs as if she just asked him something really stupid. He is being very dismissive of Abigail and that isn't okay. "You." He pauses and makes a wavy motion towards your group. "Sheep are all the same. Can't you see that there's more to this world than what's on the surface? There are things lurking in the dark, and we ought to bring them to their rightful place above us."

You think you might maybe know what he's talking about. There are lots of things that like dark hidey places. Like the Abyss and tadpoles and cthulians and sometimes some of your kinda-cousins.

"And so you're trying to... summon those things to our world?" Abigail asks.

"We try, but as with all things, the only result in the end… is failure." Lewis turns around and kinda waddles over to a corner of the room where a girl is inscribing a circle on the ground.

There are all sorts of things around the circle, you notice. Yummy looking fruit, and jars of pixie dust, and a few bowls with some juice, and other snacks.

"Everyone, my dark brothers and black sisters," Lewis says. "Gather 'round, if you please. The time is nearing when we must begin our ritual and call up on the great dark one."

Nearly half of the people move towards Lewis and his ritual circle, most of them looking a bit older than the others. You suppose that the spikiness of their hair and the amount of tears in their clothes is some sort of indication of rank.

"I forgot about our guests," Lewis says. "If you want to see us attempt to commune with the great darkness beyond, feel free to stay. But if you're too much of a sheep, you know where the door is. Summoning the great Pou-tine is not a feat for the weak of heart."

There's some hustling and bustling and suddenly you and Abigail and the others are all moved off to the side of the room farthest from the ritual area. "This is very dangerous," a girl says with a flat, bored tone. "One mistake and we could lose the black pits that are our souls. Stay away, sheep." The girl stays next to you and crosses her arms. "Can't believe I have to babysit."

The rest of the club members gather around a circle with the same energy you have when you're woken up mid-nap.

Lewis leaves for a little bit to a small room at the back, but he comes back soon enough wearing a big robe with a bunch of skulls tied to it. "Are those, are those real skulls?" Abigail asks.

That would be awful. Someone ate those people but didn't eat their yummy yummy head bones. That's such a waste.

"Nah, they're made of plaster. We're not barbarians," the girl says. She eyes your group for a bit. "Are any of you virgins? We might need some blood or stuff later."

Abigail and Daphne squawk and make noises while Charlotte shakes her head.

You don't know what's going on, really, so you sit back and watch the ritual unfold.

Lewis circles around the group with a metal thing on the end of a chain. There's smoke coming out of it that smells like flowers. Then he moves to the front of the circle and gestures to someone who brings him a big book that's already opened. "Step the first. In order to call upon the great Pou-tine we must bring into the circle the ingredients of Pou-tine's making."

You nod. That makes sense. If someone who wasn't Abigail wanted your attention, then putting lots of naps in a circle would probably do it, maybe some pillows and happy dreams and bedtime snacks too. You're not sure how the mortals would figure out how to make liquid nap time, but they're clever sometimes.

If they want to summon Pou-tine, then you know they'll need lots of cheese, and gravy, and fries.

"Bring the blood!" Lewis says.

You blink at that then look up to Abigail for an explanation. She just looks a little worried. "Why are they getting blood?" you ask.

"Ah, I don't know," Abigail says.

"It's not actually blood," the girl says. "We're not allowed to use blood in rituals, it's against the rules, so we use pudding with red dye."

"Oh," Abigail says.

That doesn't seem like it would work, but you're not the expert here.

"Step the second," Lewis says. "Like calls upon like, the Great Pou-tine is a creature of the dark. His call must reflect this."

The lights go out and soon only a single red-flamed candle illuminates the room. That might be a good thing because you're pretty sure you're wearing a weird expression right now. Pou-tine isn't a creature of the dark. And she's a she. Sorta. Mortal genders are strange, but you're pretty sure Pou-tine would be a girl if she was around.

Maybe.

"Step the third!" Lewis says with more fervor. "We chant!"

The students in the circle begin to sway from side to side, all of them slowly humming something. "Om nom nom. Om nom nom."

"Oh great Pou-tine, master of the great dark, heed our call and come unto this mortal realm," Lewis says.

"He's so dark and mysterious," the girl sighs. She's paying more attention to Lewis than anything else.

"He's a dummy," you say. The girl glares at you but Charlotte and Daphne both slap their hands over their mouths. "He's doing it all wrong. That's not how you summon anyone."

If they really wanted to summon Pou-tine then they would need a lot more than what they have here. They have no symbols, nothing that Pou-tine would want, and their chant is all wrong. You're beginning to think that someone taught these students wrong on purpose.

Shaking your head, you split your attention between your small mostly-mortal body and your real big body. A call goes out across the void, not a ritual but a proper message sent between two very old things.

Your message is quite simple: "Hey, Pou-tine, some mortals want to talk." And then you attach the proper place and time to the message. Hopefully the Old Faiths club will appreciate your help.

The room starts to smell like fried potatoes.

Curious, you take a peak on the Other Side only to find Pou-tine's gravy-like tentacles and curds of madness swamping around the void. Its fri-eyes lock onto you and it waves a hello.

You wave back because you're a good neighbour. You only try to eat Pou-tine when you're really hungry or in the mood.

Reaching up with your mortal body's hand, you grab onto Abigail. "It's time to go now," you say.

"W-what?" she squeaks.

"Pou-tine is coming. It's time to go." You accentuate that by pulling her towards the door.

The other girls hesitate a little, but they follow after you.

You only just close the door when the chanting turns to screaming, and you need to step fast to avoid the splat of gravy leaking out from under the door.

"Okay, that was fun," you say. "Where do we go now?"

"Actually," Charlotte says. "Today's the first meeting of the Athletic Club. I came along for this, but I do need to head out." Web jumps off your head and swings over to Charlotte, landing on the top of her chest since it's the most platform-like thing on her.

"Bye!" You say to Charlotte. The taller girl beams down at you and pats your head and ruffles your hair.

"Goodbye Dreamer," she says before pointing to Web who is riding on her shoulder. "Web says bye too."

The spider wiggles one of its tiny limbs in the air before it and if you're not mistaken its big furry mandibles are stretched out in a smile.

"Bye Web!" you say to her before waving. Abigail and Daphne say bye too and then your group splits up, Charlotte heading off towards her evening with the Athletics Club and you and Abigail and Daphne heading off to… "Hey, where are we going?" you ask.

Abigail and Daphne both jump at your question and pause to stare at each other, then they look away. "W-we should talk," Abigail says.

"I agree." Daphne crosses her arms. "Though the Academy is a bit public for that kind of discussion."

"Maybe we could wait until tomorrow?" Abigail says and Daphne nods.

You narrow your eyes. You don't know exactly what's going on between the two. It's all some mortal stuff that's beneath your notice and that you would usually ignore. If it wasn't for Abigail being involved then you would definitely not care one bit. But she is, and Abigail is important.

"No," you say and both girls jump. "You two should talk until you find out what's wrong with each other, then fix it."

"Dreamer," Abigail whines.

"No," you say with a shake of your head. "Talking first. Whining after." Reaching up, you grab both girls by one hand each and start walking. You were already on the edge of the campus, so it doesn't take long for you to reach the streets beyond where there are a bunch of small shops.

"Where are you leading us, Dreamer?" Daphne asks. She sounds calm, but her hand is all sweaty.

"There," you say before nodding to a place across the street. There's a big cafe nestled between an alchemy shop and a small office building, the sign out front calls it the Garden of Lilies. There are snacks at those places, and snacks make things better.

"Oh my," Daphne says as you drag her into the store. It smells like coffee and cake and pastries and other yummy stuff inside. There are quite a few people too, mostly girls but some boys, nearly all of them sitting at little tables for two here and there.

"Hello," says a rotund lady with an apron and a smile on. "May I help you?"

"Yes," you say. "We need yummies and a place to talk."

Daphne coughs to clear her throat and takes a small step forward. "If I recall, this establishment has a… private room, where we can discuss things in confidence?"

The lady's eyebrows rise. "I see. We do have a room available at the back, though it's for, well…"

"I," Daphne looks away. "I'm a member of the Gardening Club."

The lady looks at her, then at you, then at Abigail. "Oh my. In that case, follow me."

The room you're brought to is very small. There a pair of chairs sat next to each other before a small table, and off to the corner is a couch that's just big enough for someone to sleep on if they wanted to. A big urn filled with flowers makes the whole place smell pretty.

"Shall I return to take your orders?" the lady asks.

Daphne rattles off a list of things, then looks at you and adds two cakes to the order. You hope they're for you.

You take over the couch and bounce on it a few times before plopping down and looking at the girls. Abigail sits down on one chair, Daphne on the other. They stare at each other with fleeting glances then look absolutely anywhere else. Sometimes they make noises as if they're going to speak, but then cut themselves off when the other looks at them.

Then the lady returns with a tray. She takes in the room at a glance as she moves to place it on the table. "It works best if you both speak your desires aloud," she says as she places tea on the table. The rest of the tray, cakes and all, is left in the middle. "You have the room for another half hour, miladies," she says before bowing and leaving.

Daphne's cup rattles as she picks it off her saucer. She holds it up for a moment, then lowers it back down. "I… I love you," she says.

Abigail freezes.

"I've loved you since, since I discovered what the word meant. You're, you're Abigail, and that means everything to me. I want you to be happy, to be strong and fierce and a little bit naive and, and to be you. And I want to be near you while you're happy and there when you're sad. Which." Daphne chokes on her own words and takes a gulp of her tea. "If you just want to be friends, then I owe it to you to be just that. The best friend you'll ever have. And no matter what you do, I'll still be there."

Daphne sets her cup down. It's empty now. She stands up.

"I'm, I'm going to go. Don't worry about the bill, it's, I'll cover it. M-maybe we can continue as we did today? It was fun?"

"No."

The word rings through the room and has Daphne stopping mid-motion. She starts to shiver.

Abigail shakes her head, hair bouncing with the motion. "No, that just, that just won't do. You're, you're my sister, my best friend, and even if I'm not sure if I feel *that* way about girls, I know that I love you too. I just don't know if it's the same kind." Abigail takes a deep breath, her brows scrunch up and her hands ball up into tiny fists. "But I'm going to find out."

"What?" Daphne squeaks.

"We're, we're gonna go on a date."

"What?" Daphne squeaks louder.

Abigail is standing up now too, her chair scraping against the floor with the motion. "We're going to go on a date, and m-maybe we'll try… k-kiss." She stops, her face an inferno. "Things. We'll try *things*. And then I'll know if I love you that way too. And if I don't, then we'll have tried, and that'll be enough, and we can still be friends, and I'll help you find someone cute and nice that you can love like, like that."

You take a bite out of your cake.

It's a really good cake.

CHAPTER FOURTEEN

THE PROFESSOR who teaches Eugenics, Etiquette and Ethics is a tall woman in a very tight set of blood-red robes. Instead of having a weird professor hat, she has a sort of wide-brimmed floppy hat that Abigail called a cavalier. You don't know what that means or what it's supposed to tell you about the professor's rank.

Really, if these mortals want to tell rank apart with hats they should put numbers on them, or maybe write the rank on the hat and give friendly people from the void like you a chart to tell them apart. It's quite rude. Maybe you should get your own, better hat, to remind them that you're better than all of them. And you could get one for Abigail too.

Abigail settles into her seat next to you, and as is appropriate Charlotte takes the seat on your other side. This way you're surrounded by friends, even if they're not in a cuddle pile. It will have to do for now.

The professor stands at the front of the class and smiles at everyone. You narrow your eyes. There's something sinister about the lady. "Ethics, the study of what is and isn't morally acceptable. Etiquette, the art of social decorum and societal procedures, and Eugenics, the science of breeding and assisted evolution. Three subjects that are vastly different on the surface but, as you will soon learn, are actually linked at their core."

The professor begins to pace. "Some of you will aim your careers towards the healing arts, others will wish to become tamers and genetic manipulators in the hopes of one day becoming the next inventor of the goblin or orc. Others will wish to join the illustrious Inquisition as I myself have done and will want to know why the many rules and regulations of the Inquisition exist. And all of you who wish to become a proper mage needs to know how to address another mage in society."

She stops at the very front of the class again, and this time you think you're not the only one who noticed that there's something wrong with her smile. "We will begin with the most complex and controversial subject. Eugenics. The art of breeding and creating new species. Starting from human stock has long become both illegal and taboo, but that doesn't prevent the art from thriving. From creatures bred of Familiar stock meant to work in dangerous conditions to warrior species built for combat to new and interesting pet-like creatures. We may be the apex, the greatest species on this Earth, but as we experiment and elevate more creatures we may soon find ourselves with new neighbours and new adversaries."

The professor picks a book from one of the student's desks and gestures at it. "Please open your textbooks to page seven and complete exercise one A."

There's a lot of scrambling for books and such, not that Abigail needs to do that because you're the best and you already slipped her textbook onto her desk before the weird professor lady had finished.

"Abigail," you ask. "You're not going to do breeding stuff, right?"

"What? No, of course not, that's—"

"Miss Abigail Normal," the professor's voice snaps across the room like a whip crack. "I do not recall giving anyone permission to speak. If your Familiar will be a distraction it can be removed from the room."

You glare at the lady but all she does is perk one eyebrow at you. Maybe she'd react more if you smacked her around with some tentacles?

"Am I understood?" she asks.

"You're very mean," you tell the lady. The class goes quiet, people stopping halfway towards getting their books to stare between you and the professor.

"And you are distracting my class," the professor says.

"No, you are by being a big idiot."

There's a gasp and quite a few stifled giggles from all the students and the professor's face begins to match the red of her robes.

"Dreamer, sweetie," Abigail says quickly. "There's a nice room right next to this one where you can wait. It'll be a lot more fun. Don't you want to go wait there? Just for a bit?"

"Miss Normal, control your Familiar or I'll have you suspended!" the professor says over the chuckles and laughs.

You look at Abigail, then at the still red-faced professor. "Fine," you say. "But I'll still be here with you," you say as you get up. Then, in a louder voice so that the professor can hear. "And that old lady is still stupid. She's just what I would expect from a mortal species backsliding into idiocy."

If she suspends Abigail then you'll suspend her.

With a huff you leave the classroom and let the door smack close behind you. It sucks not being near Abigail, but you still have a bunch of tentacles in the room, a whole lot of them with eyes and mouths and ears and other things that let you know what's going on.

The professor doesn't try anything after making a big lecture about proper behaviour, which is good because Abigail would be upset if you broke her teacher.

You cross your arms like Daphne and Abigail do when they're upset and stomp over to the room next to the classroom. It's a small place, meant for Familiars to wait around while their Summoners are in class. It's filled with platforms at different levels, little plush beds, and a corner box filled with sawdust that smells like poop. A huge window at the back lets in a bunch of light that's splashing onto the familiar form of Wuffles who is laying down on a carpet.

You stomp over to the dire wolf. "I'm using you as a pillow," you tell her before letting go of your body and flopping onto Wuffles with a whump.

"Bad day?" someone asks.

You're currently buried in a thick pile of grumbling, growling fur. But Wuffles is being too lazy to bite you out of her sides and you're in too soft a spot to move, so you sprout a tentacle out of your neck and make it grow an eye.

There's a squirrel on a desk nearby, a big one. It's wearing a small blue vest and has a pair of glasses tied to its face by some twine. There's a big book opened below it.

"Who're you?" you ask.

The squirrel chitters a little, then clears its throat. "Sigmund Squirrel, at your service milady. May I ask who, and what, you are?"

"I'm Dreamer, and I'm Abigail's."

Sigmund nods a few times. "Wonderful, truly. What brings you here, Dreamer?"

"The professor's an idiot," you explain.

"Ah, I see," the squirrel says. "How unfortunate. Say, miss Dreamer, if you tell me what happens in greater detail I may be able to trade that knowledge for more knowledge." Sigmund reaches into his vest and pulls out a tiny notebook, no bigger than your thumb, and then a teeny-tiny pen that fits in his little hands. "I'm something of a gossip psychologist, you see."

"Oh, that's neat. I could tell you all sorts of stuff in exchange for other things," you say.

"Excellent. So, please, tell me what happened in class just now." Sigmund pushes his glasses up, the lenses flashing as they reflect the room's light. "And tell me how it made you feel?"

You nod into Wuffles' side then begin to recount your adventures in the Ethics, Eugenics and Etiquette class.

"How awful," Sigmund says. "And how interesting. That's worth some gossip. What do you want to know about?"

"I don't know, what's interesting?"

"Oh my, oh my," Sigmund says. "There's plenty of interesting things going on, but perhaps nothing as interesting as the Old Faith's Club debacle. It seems that something happened, but no one quite knows what. There's lots of speculation. All that is known for certain is that the Inquisition came and when they left it was with most of the students from the club and something else."

"Something?" you ask.

"Something big, in a crate, something that smelled of gravy."

You narrow your eyes. That might need investigating.

Eventually class ends, and Abigail comes back to fetch you and gives you conciliatory hugs in apology for being away for so long.

Lunch is a quick affair that passes in a haze of yummy food and a lot of laughing with your friends, but despite how fun it is you can't quite focus during that time.

The next class is Magical Preparations and Rituals, and Lady Professor Clearwater is talking.

You should be paying attention. What if Abigail misses a bit and asks you a question? But the talk about making sure everything is just right before conducting a ritual and making sure all the ingredients are well prepared is not nearly as interesting as the problem you have.

Someone kidnapped Pou-tine.

Pou-tine is a friend, a sort of pet that you kept around and nibbled at when your paths crossed. The only reason they're here is because you called out across the void and asked them to come. There was no way that weird summoning the Old Faith's Club tried would have worked.

You're beginning to think that you're feeling a little guilty.

"Excuse me," someone says.

The class pauses, every head turning towards the door where a man in a long coat and a bucket hat is standing tall and proud. There's a big badge on his lapel with a lighthouse shaped like a 'I' on it. "May I help you, officer?" Professor Clearwater asks.

"Indeed ma'am, I did not intend to interrupt your class, but I need to speak to some of your students, if you don't mind."

There's a wash of whispers from all the kids in the class at that.

Professor Clearwater nods. "If you could file the proper forms..." she pauses as the man removes an envelope from within his jacket. She nods and turns towards the class. "Very well then, the students won't be penalized for their absence. I don't believe we have any at-home work to assign tonight, so if you are called away today you're quite lucky. I still expect you to inspect the notes of another student so as to avoid falling behind."

The strange man bows to the professor. "May I have the cooperation of Miss Normal and Miss Pembrooke?"

Abigail and Charlotte both jump in their seats, then they stand up and start collecting their things in a hurry. Abigail stuffs all of it in her purse where you grab it for her without really thinking and Charlotte swings her book bag over a shoulder.

Then the three of you are moving after the man with the bucket hat.

"What's all this about?" Charlotte asks.

"In a moment, Miss Pembrooke," he says.

She huffs, but doesn't push for more questions. You, on the other tentacle, aren't so calm. "Where are we going?"

"You'll see in a moment."

"But I want to know now," you say.

"You'll have to wait," he says right back.

"But if you tell me now then I won't," you point out.

You notice his fists tightening and are about to poke him some more when Abigail places a hand on your shoulder and shakes her head. You grumble a bit, but stay quiet until you're brought into a small room with a long table in its middle. You and Abigail and Charlotte are made to sit on one side, all three of you facing a wall with a big mirror.

A mirror with someone standing behind it. There's a circle etched into the other side of the mirror, and the middle part of that circle is completely transparent on the one side.

They might think they're clever hiding behind mirrors, but you've eaten your share of reflections and mirror dimensions and you won't be tricked so easily.

Another man walks into the room with Abigail and Charlotte and you. He's shorter than the first, but his jacket has more badges and his bucket hat has a bunch more feathers and such attached to it. "Miss Normal, Miss Pembrooke, thank you for your time," he says before pulling up a chair across from you and depositing a suitcase on the table. "We're waiting for one last… and here she is."

The door opens up to reveal Daphne who takes in the room at a glance before moving over to sit by Abigail's side. "I trust this is important?" she snaps at the man with all the badges.

"It is, Miss Daphne of Swinehill."

Daphne scoffs. "It's Baroness Daphne of Swinehill, actually."

He nods. "Pardon me, then." The man pulls up the suitcase then makes a big show of opening it up and checking some loose sheets within. "We have questions for you three girls, specifically about your involvement with the Old Faith's club."

This sounds like it might be the kind of thing that Abigail wouldn't want you to talk about, so you decide not to say anything at all. Then again, if these people are wondering about the time when Pou-tine came, then maybe they know something you don't.

The person on the other side of the mirror is a tall, barrel-chested man. His coat hides a suit of armour over cloth and his hat is very tall and covered in sparkly things. He looks very important, and very important people know very important things!

A couple of tentacles sneak sneaky-like into the room from all the darkest corners, then start wiggling through the air towards the big man.

They're almost there when she spins around and slashes out with a sword that you never even noticed her had. A couple of your tentacles lose their end bits and you wince.

"Are you okay, Dreamer?" Abigail asks you in a whisper. It cuts off the conversation for a moment until you nod.

"I banged my toe," you lie, then start rocking from side to side while kicking your feet out under the table. There's a panel there and your feet thump-thump against it with every kick. The girls nod and the man clears his throat before he returns to questioning everyone. Daphne is wearing a smug smile as she answers everything in a way that answers nothing.

The man in the room is having a bit of trouble now. He might have cut a couple of tentacles, but there are billions where those came from and plenty of places where you can open holes in the world to make more pour in.

Soon enough he's cocooned in them. "You won't get away with this!" he screams.

You catch the noises before they have time to leave the room. Tentacles covered in mouths and teeth and other things made for speaking start pouring in. "It's okay, important mister," you say. "You won't remember a thing."

Tentacles dive into his head, slipping past his skull to root around. You're not quite as careful as you were with Abigail, but you try to stop his head from exploding or anything like that while you search for Pou-tine.

It only takes a moment.

Your meat body frowns at what you learn. Pou-tine is being held captive. Not all of Pou-tine, just a small fraction, but it's enough that Pou-tine can't just leave. Like getting a hand caught in a cookie jar that you can't break because if you do Abigail will be disappointed at you.

You're going to need to do something about that. Fortunately, you see what they used to trap Pou-tine and it would be trivially easy to break it.

Maybe after class you can free Pou-tine if you have time between clubs.

The girls decided to stick together after the interview, mostly because they had all been excused from class and didn't really feel like going back, which as far as you're concerned is great. You get to spend more time with your friends!

"So, have you two decided on any clubs?" Daphne finally asks as she guides the group towards the same small park where you ate lunch.

Charlotte nods. "Just one so far. I'm in the Athletics Club already! Need to keep in shape otherwise sitting down all day will lead to me getting all fat and lethargic."

"I should exercise more," Abigail says, but then she makes a face. "But I hate exercising."

For some reason this is funny and the girl's laugh. You don't know why, but you smile anyway because your friends being happy makes you happy.

Charlotte shakes her head, long blonde hair flip-flopping all over. "But really, being at the Academy has been awful for me," she says before reaching over and pulling her robes off. It leaves her dressed in a long skirt and button-up blouse. With a few deft flicks, she undoes some of the buttons over her tummy. "Look, I'm getting handles. It's awful."

Daphne and Abigail are both looking, they're looking really hard at Charlotte's tummy, which is mostly flat as far as you can tell, though when she bends forwards the muscles disappear behind a layer of flabby stuff. It's hard to make out because she has big breasts which the others are also looking at a lot.

"Your tummy doesn't look as comfy to sleep on as Abigail's," you say. "But it's okay. Maybe if you get strong you can give good hugs to make up for it."

Charlotte laughs and pulls you into a hug, confirming that yes, her stronger physique does make the hugging experience somewhat better, but she's not as soft as Abigail. If you had to put numbers to it, which you wouldn't because numbers are yucky, you would rate it as three quarters as good as an Abigail hug. "You're adorable, Dreamer," Charlotte says as she pulls out of the hug, then she pinches your cheek in a way that is most unpleasant. "You make me miss my little siblings."

"Y-you have a lot of siblings?" Abigail squeaks.

"A few."

The conversation turns towards talking about people who are not there while you return to considering your issue with Pou-tine. You're going to have to save them from the machinations of the big mean Inquisition people. The real question isn't how you'll do it. That much is easy. It's how that's tricky.

You've confused yourself again.

"Dreamer?" Abigail asks before patting your head for attention. It works.

"Yes?"

"Daphne and I were talking and, and I think I'll be joining the Gardening Club… t-temporary. Just to see how things, uh, work out there. And to be near Daphne too. B-but mostly, um. Nevermind. I wanted to know if that was okay with you?"

"That's the club in the place with all the flowers?" you ask to which Abigail nods. "The one with the hidden nap time beds? Are we going to sleep together there?"

This makes Abigail look sick and red again and Charlotte covers her mouth with a hand and looks away while Abigail starts speaking. You think it's speaking, but really you don't understand what she's saying and the way she waving her arms around wildly doesn't make things easier to understand.

"Okay," you say to stop her flailing. "I like that club, it was nice." And they had tea sets which meant tea food and tea cups which are all yummy. "Are we going now? Because I had something I needed to do."

That last bit snaps Abigail right back to full attention. Her eyes narrow behind her big glasses. "What sort of things?" she asks.

You decide that it's best if Abigail doesn't know. She still has the bapping paper in her purse and she could remove it to bap you at any moment. "Just things."

"Please elaborate."

You look away, tongue sticking into one cheeks and lips pursing. "Mmm, it's nothing that you need to worry about."

"Dreamer."

You huff. "I'm going to go help Pou-tine."

"The… thing the people at the Old Faith's club tried to… summon?" Charlotte asks. "Is it like, ah, like you."

Abigail shifts and suddenly looks a little nervous. Daphne, who's a lot more composed, places a hand on her shoulder.

You shake your head. "No. I'm way older and much more than Pou-tine. It's more like a, uh." You try to think of the right words but the mortals don't have them. "A greater independent," you decide. "Pou-tine just goes around and does its own thing and tries not to be eaten. Abigail said that boys are the same way."

"Okay then," Charlotte says.

"You're okay with Dreamer?" Abigail asks.

Why would someone not be okay with you? Unless you were trying to eat them or they wanted to interrupt naptime.

Charlotte shrugged one shoulder. "Dreamer seems nice."

You nod. You do seem nice. "Now it's time for saving Pou-tine," you tell them. "I need to do it sneaky-like or else the Inquisition people with the hats will be annoyed and they'll make a fuss."

"Dreamer, no," Abigail says.

152

"But if we don't help, then Pou-tine will stay stuck until all the mortals die and that'll take a whole bunch of years," you say. "If we don't help then it's like…" You pause to think of something they would understand. "It's like not helping someone when their hat is too big to pass through a door."

The girls all stare at each other, then elect Daphne to talk. "What exactly would rescuing Pou-tine involve?" she asks.

You grin. "It's easy. We need to break into that building." A tentacle comes out of your back to point to a building on the next hill over. The Inquisition's castle thing is a big place all made of dark rocks tucked into the side of a big mound of stones, it makes the whole place look smaller than it really is. You know from the memories you took from the important knight man that there are lots of rooms underground. "And once we're there, we need to find the room where they're keeping Pou-tine and break the stuff keeping them in place. It's easy."

"Oh no," Abigail says.

"I can do it all on my own, if you want," you offer.

"That's exactly what I'm afraid of."

There was a big argument. You didn't like it, not one bit, but in the end you won so that's all that matters.

The girls are all gathered in Daphne's house sipping at tea that Edmund delivered while you get ready for your big adventure. An adventure that you're going to do *alone*, because Abigail is fragile and so are your other friends.

You, of course, aren't sitting at the table and having tea. No, instead you're standing across from a very worried Abigail and are trying very hard to pretend that her big wet eyes aren't doing things to your tummy. It's not fair that she can look at you like that.

"You can't come," you tell her again. "You're too squishy."

"I know that, but you might get hurt," she says.

This is not the first time she brings this up and it's not the first time she's wrong about it. "The big mean people can't hurt me. I'm unhurtable. But they could hurt you and that would make me very…" you pause, then realize that you have found the perfect counter. "That would hurt me. Yes. I can be hurt if you're hurt, but they can't hurt me unless they're hurting you." Perfect!

"Abigail," Daphne says as she places her teacup down without so much as a click. "I actually agree with Dreamer. Strange as she might be, she is still more than capable of taking care of herself. If she runs into any trouble or fails to return before nightfall, then we can act on our own. I think Edmund has some old friends who could help mount a rescue. Still, we ought to at least give her a chance."

You nod. Daphne is being very smart.

Then Abigail turns her wet eyes on Daphne and her confidence crumbles. "U-unless, well, maybe we could go," Daphne says.

You huff. This is taking too long. "Fine. I'll stay here and go."

"Oh?" Charlotte asks. She has been looking around ever since she entered Daphne's house but now she's focused on you. "You can split yourself?"

"Oh no," Abigail whispers in horror. You can understand her fear. That would mean having to split her hugs between you and another you, which is only half as many hugs.

You shake your head. "No. I just need to leave some of me here and let this part of me go." To demonstrate you tentacle a hole through the universe and have one of your wigglier tentacles poke out of it in the air behind you. "See, now you'll know that my big body is safe."

"Your big body?" Charlotte asks.

You don't have a lot of time to explain, but it would be rude not to. "This body," you say as you gesture to yourself. "Is my small body. My big body is where I am. This is like a puppet body for hugs and cuddles." Which now that you mention it means Abigail never hugged your big body. It would take many, many hundreds of years for her to hug all of it. You need to hurry up and make her less mortal.

"So, as long as your main body is intact, you can just make a new puppet body?" Charlotte asks.

"Yes," you say.

She shrugs and turns to Abigail. "I say let her try. Though she really ought to wear a disguise."

There's some more arguing after that, but it's about what kind of clothes you should wear and then a long explanation about why your pretty dress, while very pretty (everyone agrees) isn't the best for being sneaky and is recognizable on account of being your pretty dress.

In the end, the sun is well on its way towards the horizon when you step out of Daphne's mansion wearing an all black outfit covered in holes for your tentacles and a lot of black cloth wrapped around your face. Charlotte declares that you look like an adorable ninja.

You don't know what that means, but if it's adorable then it probably does look like you. You are a thing that should be adored.

Walking all the way to the Inquisition's headquarters would take too long, so when you're finally outside you make a big tentacle come out of the ground, wrap your small body around its tip, then fling yourself across the city.

Like throwing a rock only it's you instead.

You cheer as you fly past a bunch of houses and, thanks to your super fast reflexes, snap a pigeon out of the air as an in-flight snack.

You crash into the roof of an apartment building two blocks away from the Inquisition, roll a lot to bleed off your speed, then fall off the edge and crash at the bottom of an alleyway. But you didn't lose your snack and you can fix all the broken bones so it's okay.

Getting up, you dust off your ninja outfit, rub some feathers off your face, then stick your head out of the alley.

There aren't a lot of mortals around at this hour, so hardly anyone notices as you run across the streets towards the big castle and slip through some alleyways and up some walls with your tentacles.

In no time at all you're standing before the Conclave of the Inquisition. The front of the building is large and flat and made of dark stones with little alcoves where statues of people with silly hats holding beakers and rulers and scales are all staring down towards the big doors at the front.

You find a shadowy place next to a newspaper stand across the street, then you grab some more shadows from a few other places and bring them closer so that you're even harder to see.

This is where you'll do all your work.

Reaching out, you send a billion little tentacles that are just on the other side of everything questing within the Conclave to map out every tunnel and passage and room. Some tentacles hit things that shouldn't be and get zapped or eaten, but they're small and don't matter.

You find Pou-tine right where the important man's memories said they would be. It's deep, deep under the building, in a room built with hundreds of circles in the ground and a bunch of obelisks that might be made of bones around. Pou-tine is stuck in the centre with all sorts of equipment being aimed at them.

Nodding, you grab your body with another tentacle and move yourself over to where Pou-tine is.

The room smells like rubbing-alcohol and grease. It's barely lit by a few yellow-ish magic circles on the walls next to rows of metal desks just like in school.

Pou-tine shifts a little, a fri-eye turning in your direction.

"Hello, Pou-tine," you say. "I'm here to free you."

You were originally intending to save Pou-tine and then let them go, but now that you're thinking about it, there might be other uses for something that's kinda sorta like you. If you were way smaller and way weaker and way less smart.

Yes, Pou-tine might be useful to keep around.

"Okay, so I'm going to rescue you now," you tell Pou-tine.

The large pile of stuff wobbles to the far end of the circle, as far from you as it can get without slipping out of the circle. Curious, you look on the Other Side and notice that Pou-tine's main body is just around the corner, but it's stuck.

Kind of like how you and your main body are connected. Which reminds you to check on the tentacle you left with Abigail… and which is currently flopped onto her lap and being pat-patted while Abigail and the others drink more tea.

You bask in the glow of the patting for a moment while considering what to do with Pou-tine, but then the solution is really quite simple. You'll give Pou-tine a body like yours and then you'll have a pet that can do boring things for you so that you don't have to.

It's a brilliant idea!

You just need some materials to build Pou-tine's new body out of.

"Freeze!"

"Stop right there!"

"Raise your hands and back away from the abomination!"

You turn and take in the half dozen Inquisitors in long coats and bucket hats, all of them pointing long rods at you and screaming. You grin.

How convenient!

The return trip is just a bit more eventful then the trip down into the room where Pou-tine was held. Mostly because now everyone in the building is panicking and running around and because you have to carry Pou-tine's new body with you. It's all wrapped up in tentacles to keep it nice and safe.

"Please let me go," Pou-tine asks.

"No," you say. "I need to show you to Abigail."

You arrive at another intersection where a bunch of armed Inquisitors are trying to block your path. You make the corridor way bigger, then pinch up the floor so that it stretched into a wall cutting off the end where they put up a barricade.

Silly Inquisitors, they didn't even try to make it so that their castle was fixed in reality.

"I don't want to go see any Abigails. I don't want to be eaten," Pou-tine says.

"Abigail won't eat you," you say. You've seen the sorts of things Abigail eats. Pou-tine isn't one of them. And if Abigail was hungry enough to eat Pou-tine you'd let her eat you first. But only a nibble.

"How do you know? You could be lying."

"I'm not lying," you say.

The two of you exit the Inquisition building to find a crowd gathering outside of it, but they're just normal boring mortals so you ignore them as a new tentacle comes tearing out of the ground, grabs you, and flings you across the city.

Your aim is a little better this time, even with Pou-tine struggling behind you, but because there are so few lights it's hard to see if there are any snacks available and you land without anything new to eat and with a bunch more broken bones.

Picking yourself off the ground, you look around the garden at the back of Daphne's place. It's quite nice. Well maintained and with lots of pretty flowers and there's a big sofa off to one side of the path. She must have paid lots of attention at the Gardening Club.

Edmund is at the back door, holding it open with one eyebrow raised. "Welcome back Miss Dreamer and… guest. The ladies are in the dining room."

"Thank you Edmund," you say as you squeeze past the butler and cross the house. Pou-tine is still dangling in the air behind you. "I'm back!" you say as you push the door open.

The girls are all still there, though they finished the tea and ate all the crumpets while you were gone. You decide that it's okay and that you'll forgive them. You draw back the tentacle on Abigail's lap, shoving it back onto your real body and closing the rift you made for it, then plop your small body onto Abigail's lap and wrap your hands around her waist.

"Welcome back," Abigail says as she returns the hug. "But, um, who's the boy?"

"You didn't kidnap anyone, right Dreamer?" Charlotte asks as she inspects what little she can see of Pou-tine through your tentacles.

"I didn't," you say.

"She did," Pou-tine lies like a lying liar. He's not a kid so it wasn't kidnapping.

You huff. "This is Pou-tine. I made him a body." That said, you unwrap Pou-tine and let him fall.

The body you made with bits and pieces of the Inquisitors that tried to stop you (you left them alive and better than ever because anything else would make Abigail bap you) is quite nice. It's a bit shorter than yours, and skinnier, and it's a boy body with long, long gravy-brown hair. His eyes are potato-brown and are looking around the room as if to make sure nothing will eat him.

Daphne lunges to the side and slaps a hand over Abigail's eyes. "Edmund!" she calls.

The butler walks in a moment later. "Yes, Miss?"

"Clothes," Daphne says.

Edmund inspects Pou-tine and then nods. "Very well Miss. I will find something suitable for the young master post haste."

Charlotte shakes her head and stands up before kneeling in front of Pou-tine. "Are you okay, sweetie?" she asks.

"Are you going to eat me?" he asks her.

"While you are quite handsome I'm afraid that I'm not inclined to gobble you up. How about we get you some proper clothes, and then a nice warm meal before bed? Do you have a name?"

Pou-tine blinked. "I don't," he says, which is silly because his name is Pou-tine. You think. You're pretty sure it's that.

"Oh my my," Charlotte says. "Well don't worry, big sis Charlotte will take care of everything."

The sun is beginning to set when Edmund slips into the room with an armful of clothes piled up before him. He clears his throat. "Dinner is ready to be served," he says.

You're the first one out of the room.

You plonk yourself down and bounce on the spot until everyone arrives and silently wish they would move along faster so you can get to the eating. In the meanwhile, you tear off your adorable ninja mask and drop it on the floor so that nothing will get in the way of your mouth.

Daphne takes the head of the table, and Abigail sits next to her with Charlotte on the opposite side. Then Pou-tine slowly creeps into the room, eyeing you with every step.

"Don't be afraid," Charlotte says. "No one will hurt you. Come, you can sit next to me." She pats the chair next to her. "Or you can sit on my lap if you want."

Pou-tine slips into the chair next to her, then stares across the table at you. Oh, he's all new to this mortal stuff, so he must need a bunch of help! It's a good thing you're around to make things simple for him. "This is a fork," you say as you raise the fork. "It's for poking food so that your hands don't get messy. And then when you're done you eat it too. This is a spoon. It's like a fork but less good at poking, but there's more of it to eat. And this is a knife. It makes sure you're good at eating because if you're not careful it cuts your tongue out."

Abigail and Daphne start giggling but you were explaining food so you missed the joke.

Next you point at the plate. "This is a plate. Mortals put the things they eat on it because, uh, they like circles and, uh, putting food in the middle of a circle makes it taste better to them." You hope that your explanation is close enough to the truth.

Pou-tine eyes his plate, then pokes it. "They put me in a big circle that I couldn't escape in that weird place," he said.

"So they were going to eat you?" you guess.

Pou-tine's eyes widen. "They were? But I don't want to be eaten."

Charlotte pats him on the back and then starts rubbing circles there when he tenses. "Don't worry. No one will eat you anymore."

"Thank you," Pou-tine says as he ducks his head down.

"Oh, you are adorable."

You glare across the table at Charlotte. You're the adorable one, Abigail said so.

"So, Charlotte, Daphne, what are we going to, ah, do with him?" Abigail asks.

"He can't sleep with us," you declare. "There's not enough room on our bed."

Abigail smiles down at you and begins running her hand through your hair. "There's no need to be jealous," she says. "We can find a way to take care of Pou-tine without forgetting about you. You're my Familiar, I would never abandon you."

You smile the smuggest smile at Pou-tine because he's not anyone's Familiar.

Edmund comes in with a tray and begins placing small bowls of soup before everyone. You notice that the bowls he brings for you and Pou-tine aren't the same as all the others, but that's okay, they still taste nice and crunchy once you drink all the gooey soup within them.

Pou-tine eats a lot slower. He watches Charlotte eating hers, then copies the motions because he's very silly and probably wants to act like the mortals that don't get eaten.

"We still need to find a solution for our new guest," Charlotte says as she wipes her lips with a napkin. "He could stay with me for a little while. The dormitory rooms aren't too large but I have a couch."

That reminds you that there are napkins, so you take one and stuff it in your mouth. It's kind of cloth-y tasting, but the texture is nice.

"I, I would like to stay with Miss Charlotte," Pou-tine says. "If she promises she won't eat me."

Charlotte giggles and pats him on the back again. "I promise. Though you might have to fend off the other girls. I believe they will be quite jealous that I have such a handsome guest over."

"Do you know how to care for something like Pou-tine?" you ask Charlotte. It's important that she does a good job treating your future snack—no, Pou-tine isn't for eating. You stare across the table at him until he starts fidgeting. But then, if he isn't for snacking what *is* he for?

"Is it anything like taking care of a normal young man?" Charlotte asks.

You shake your head. "Nope. Not at all. He's going to need a lot of pats, and cuddles, and you need to hug him really close when you're sleeping."

Pou-tine looks up from his soup, then stares at Charlotte for a moment before he starts reddening like when Abigail says something silly. "That isn't true," he says. "I don't need hugs."

Obviously he never got hugs before. It's kind of sad. Equally sad is how he'll never get Abigail hugs because those are all for you and sometimes Daphne.

Edmund arrives with the main meal, some roasted bird and potatoes and other vegetables and lots of sauce. Abigail hands you her half finished bowl of soup and warns you not to eat the bowl, only the juices, then you're served your portion of dinner and it's eating time, not talking time.

"Abigail," you say between crunches of bird bones. "Are we sleeping with Daphne again?"

Abigail and Daphne stare at each other, both pausing mid-eating and going strange colours.

"Goodness you two," Charlotte says. "I'm certain Miss Daphne has more than one room in her home. There's no need to push your little... relationship too far too quickly."

"So we're sleeping at Daphne's but not with Daphne?" you ask. Strange, but it doesn't matter as long as you don't miss out on naptime. "Oh, Charlotte, you need to remember that naptime is very important for Pou-tine."

"I'll keep it in mind," she says.

You nod. You're truly lucky to have so many good friends and also Pou-tine.

CHAPTER FIFTEEN

"DAPHNE IS looking around at all the other students, a frown making her brow scrunch up. "People are nervous," she says.

You look around too. The people moving around the corridors are mostly in tightly knit groups, with their Familiars close to their sides. Most of them are either looking around as if they expect something to jump at them or are moving a whole lot faster than usual.

You guess they are nervous, like Daphne said. Maybe it's because of all the Inquisitor people running around the city and asking weird questions or the guys in big armour patrolling around the school that Abigail called soldiers.

Something's up, and it's making all the human's be all scared. "Why are they all acting like that?" you ask Abigail. It would be good to be sure that you're right, after all mortals are both unpredictable and silly.

Both she and Charlotte stare at you for a moment, then Abigail pats your head. "People are just afraid. *Someone*—" She gives you a pointed look before continuing. "Broke into the Inquisition's Conclave and stole something. Of course they would react to that. And because they're reacting poorly to it, everyone else is also becoming nervous."

"A few of the second years mentioned house-to-house searches, or perhaps a closing of the city gates to prevent anyone from exiting the city," Daphne says. "It won't come to that, of course. The nobles and merchants need cargo to keep moving and they'll fight against anyone searching their homes lest they learn of their dirty secrets."

Abigail nods along. "M-maybe, ah, we can find something to do outside of the city. For a little while."

"The weekend is coming up, and I don't think we have anything too important in our Firstday classes," Charlotte says. "We could leave as a group, visit one of the little towns nearby."

"Or you could visit my estates," Daphne says. "I would love to show you around, Charlotte and Dreamer. Abigail already knows everything there is to know about my lands, of course."

The girls start talking about boring things and you tune them out as you walk next to Abigail. Leaving the city might be fun, though you've hardly been in it for very long and there's still plenty to explore. But if Abigail wants to go then you'll go with her. As long as you're all together it'll be fun.

You arrive before a huge set of double doors made of thick wood with super detailed carvings etched into them of people and trees and animals and books. It's a sort of landscape with a tree in the middle broken up only by the crack between the doors. 'Librarium' reads a plaque above.

"Oh, you're going to love this, Abi," Daphne says as she pushes the doors open.

The room smells like books. Musty paper and old leather and secrets inked into parchment. You close your eyes to sniff it all, then open them to take in the library.

It's a huge place. The entire room is built like a cross with a large circle in its middle. The circular shaft rises two floors above, with balconies all around, and also descends five more floors below the one you're on. Each level has four big rooms sticking out of it like the spokes of a wheel, and the very bottom has a lot of seating room and desks arranged so that taking one means that others can't see you except from above.

"Ohh," you say as you take it all in.

Abigail claps, then stops as the sound echoes across the library.

"I'll have to ask that you restrain your enthusiasm a little, though it is nice to see people enjoy the mere sight of our library so much." A boy steps up to your group. He's short, barely half a head taller than Pou-tine and all skinny. He's practically swimming in his school robes, but his hat has the wide brim of a third year student. "Welcome to the Librarium," he says in a voice that's just above a whisper.

"I'm so sorry," Abigail says as she bows a little.

The boy waves it off. "Most book lovers have a similar reaction," he says before grinning. "It's usually a good sign."

"This is very impressive," Charlotte says as she takes in the entire room. "Some of the people here aren't students."

You look around and notice that she's right. Some of the people aren't wearing student robes. Others look way older than the average student too. Most of these are nose-deep in a tome or another or are following someone who is wearing the school robes.

"The Five Peak's Academy Librarium is the finest around," the boy says. "Quite a few mages, and some non-mage scholars, come here to satisfy their curiosities. Others to purchase copies of manuscripts or to sell us rare tomes."

"Wow," Abigail says. "Is access free?"

The boy shakes his head. "One fiat an hour. Unless you're a member of the Exploration Club, in which case the fee is waived in exchange for some work every week or month, depending on which part of the group you're in."

"I've heard of that," Daphne says before turning towards Abigail. "The Library Exploration Club has a second club called the Library Expedition Club tied to it."

"That isn't quite accurate, but I suspect it's close enough," the boy says with a grin. "So, were you here for some knowledge in particular, or were you interested in the Club? If it's knowledge you seek, Sandra at the front desk can help. A guide costs extra but it's better than losing time searching, unless the search is what you're here for. You never know what you'll learn."

Abigail shakes her head. "We were looking at various clubs and thinking of maybe joining. If you would have us, and if you could show us to someone that can, ah, show us around."

The boy grinned. "I'd love to. I'm Skinner—or that's what my friends call me—leader of the expedition group of the Exploration Club."

"Ah, so what does that mean?" Abigail asks.

"Come along, and I'll show you," Skinner says as he begins moving off to the side.

Skinner leads you and your friends to a small room off to one side. There are maps on the wall and lots of chairs around a big table and of course plenty of books. A floofy cushion off to one side holds an equally floofy and familiar squirrel.

"Hello, Sigmund," you say.

The squirrel rises his head from where it rested on his tail. "Ah, hello Dreamer," he says before resting his head back down. His belly is nice and plump and you suspect it hides a food baby, which means he's having a post-snack nap, which is one of the greatest sorts of naps.

"So," Skinner says. "I suppose I should sell you on the idea of the main club, which is what most members of the Library Exploration Club join. But I'm the leader of the subgroup called the Library Expedition Club, and I would be a poor leader if I didn't try to at least sell you guys on the idea of joining an expedition."

"What's an expedition?" Abigail asks. "I mean, what's a Library Club Expedition?"

Skinner grins and gestures to the map on the nearest wall. He points to a golden pin right in the middle. "Five Peaks is well situated as a central hub on the peninsula. Lots of traffic coming through, plenty of mages and scholars passing by. The political climate here is also favourable to groups of researchers and the like," Skinner says. "Which means that there's a great need for books and we can purchase them to our heart's content. But books don't always come to us."

Skinner pointed to a bunch of pins across the map, these in bronze or silver.

"We have the locations of abandoned laboratories and research centres where documentation was left behind, the location of towns where some mages and scholars are working on their own manuscripts and the location of books buyers across the region. Most of our work is nice and safe. Leave Five Peaks, find the book or books you're looking for, return. Some of it isn't. That's why we work closely with the Adventure Club and occasionally some mercenary guilds outside of the school."

"It sounds dangerous," Abigail said.

"It sounds fun," Charlotte said right after.

Daphne hummed. "It sounds like it might be an opportunity to leave the city."

You blink. It's your turn to say something, isn't it? "It sounds like supper time. Hey, Mister Skinner, how many of the books can we eat?"

Skinner's smile freezes for a moment. "I'm sorry, what?"

"How many books." You point to a book in case he forgot what those were. "Can we eat?" You point to your mouth.

"None. You can eat none of the books," he says. "Our entire goal is to procure and protect knowledge, not… eat it."

You decide that Skinner is no fun.

Abigail pats you on the head. "It's okay. I'm sure we can find something for you to eat if we do ever go on an expedition. Speaking of which, Mister Skinner. How often do you do these, and are they dangerous?"

"We're leaving for the next one tomorrow. The level of danger we expect is graded before an expedition leaves, though even the lowest tier leaves with an escort. There are bandits and the like out there, though they have rarely been an issue. They want gold, not books, and facing off against three or four mages is usually a bit much for them."

You let the girls talk to Mister Skinner while you look around the room. Then, when you're bored of that, you have tentacles look beyond the room and to the huge library. There are thousands of books, maybe millions of them. Some, very few of them, but some, call out from darkened, unvisited corners with the promise of lore that is ancient and forgotten.

Silly books, being all mysterious and edgy.

One of your tentacles opens one of Abigail's empty notebooks that was placed on your big body and another finds a pen. You begin scritching and scratching some words in a True Tongue into the notebook. Just instructions on how to call you and what sort of food you like best and how to reverse summon the food straight to your belly. You even promise great rewards, which you hope the mortals reading understand means you'll cuddle and hug them for the food. Then you slip the notebook in one of the more commonly used shelves.

There. Now a mortal, no matter what language they speak or read, will be able to contact you to bring you food.

This is an excellent idea. You should do it more often. Maybe start a club that's all about feeding you. A club for everyone in the city. With Abigail as the leader, of course. And statues. Statues of tentacles that make people feel happy when they look at them.

You're brought out of your tentacle-based scheming when Abigail stops patting your head. "We'll need to think about it," she says to Skinner. "But one expedition to try wouldn't hurt, I don't think."

Skinner smiles. "I would be escorting you myself, and the only expedition we have lined up for now is low risk. Just a quick jaunt to a nearby town, then back. It's a day's walk on foot, half that by carriage. And the club would cover the cost of the Inn and transportation as long as you document the voyage properly."

Daphne nods. "I might be interested. I ended up using the club's services quite a bit last year and I find myself with some free time. That and it would be good to explore outside of the city a little."

"I'm just in it for the exercise and the fun," Charlotte says. "But I'll stay back if you guys want."

"We'll think on it," Abigail says.

Skinner grins. "Our next expedition leaves from the front gates of the school an hour past sun-up. Show up dressed for an excursion and you'd be more than welcome to join."

CHAPTER SIXTEEN

YOU'RE ALMOST bouncing off the walls of the houses around you, your excitement too big to fit into your teeny tiny body, so the excess energy is making you all spasm-y and wild. You want to run, and hug Abigail, and skip, and maybe sit down and take a nap, all at the same time.

"Calm down, Dreamer," Abigail says with a laugh.

She's a few steps behind you, wearing a 'sturdy' skirt made of some thick cloth and a blouse under a heavy woolen jacket. A big backpack, mostly filled with light things, is riding on her back and her hair is tied back in a pony-tail to keep it out of her face. She looks ready for adventure.

Unfortunately you don't have any adventuring clothes, just your pretty dress, but you suppose that it's okay for now. You can always just explore new places and eat them while looking pretty.

"I wanna go," you tell Abigail as you spin to face her. Then you spin a few more times because you can. "We're going to go see places and things and it's going to be fun. And you said we might have to sleep in a tent!"

Tents, you discover, are an ingenious mortal device that allows them to sleep wherever and whenever they want. All they need to do is set up the tent and then they can go take a nap. You will acquire one of these tents very soon, and you will use it. Always. In fact, you might make a second body and leave it inside the tent so that you're always napping.

You tent-based daydreams are interrupted when Abigail starts waving ahead of you. "Charlotte!" she called out.

Charlotte is waiting a little ways down the street, standing tall and proud and ignoring all the people looking at her. She's wearing brown shorts and a loose shirt under a leather jacket that has furry ruffles around the cuffs and neck. There's a thick belt around her waist with a short sword hanging from it and she's wearing big, heavy looking boots.

"Hey Charlotte," Abigail says. "Wow, you look." She stares at Charlotte for a while, mouth opening and closing a little. You notice that she's staring a lot at Charlotte's legs, which are very long, and at the spot mid-thigh where her shorts are digging into her muscles. "Ah, I, uh."

"Like it?" Charlotte asks. "It's some old gear, but it might come in handy. You never know when you might need to run when you're out of the city, or if you might need to fight."

"Yes," Abigail says.

"Do we have to run?" you ask. You'd much rather not. Skipping is better.

Charlotte laughs and pats your head, as is only appropriate. "Not if we can stand our ground. So, big pack, and I'm sure Dreamer's carrying some things. Are you both equipped for a two day trek?"

"We are," Abigail confirms.

You don't think you brought enough food, but that's okay, you can find more outside the city where there are apparently entire fields of food.

"Brilliant!" Charlotte says. "I left little Pou with some of the girls. He should be fine. They really took a shine to him, especially Arabel and Arana, the girls with the rooms next to mine." She bends over double to pick up a big canvas bag that was just laying there and then swings it over her back. "Coming?" she asks.

"Yes!" Abigail says

Charlotte makes an agreeable humming noise as she starts walking. "Dreamer, do you want to carry Web?" she asks as she gestures to the spider crawling out of her bag.

"Yes," you say before using a tentacle to carefully place the spider on your head. Its feet are very small, so the headpats it gives you are also small, but Web has eight feet, so it makes up for it.

The four of you climb up the hilly roads until you reach the main gates of the Academy. There, waiting under the huge stone arch, is Daphne and Archibald and Sigmund Squirrel, the three of them having a deep conversation until Archie spots your group and lets out a loud 'Who?'

"Hello Daphne," Abigail says. She moves towards her friend, hesitates, then wraps her in a hug.

You note that Daphne is wearing a split skirt and a thicker coat than usual, but it's all covered in embroidery and lace. Maybe you can get pretty adventuring clothes somewhere. That would be the best of both worlds.

"It's good to see you," Daphne says. "I was starting to worry." She turns to Charlotte and smiles, then looks her up and down too. "And it's a pleasure to see you as well, Charlotte."

Charlotte snorts. "I'm sure it is, Baroness," she says, her voice flat. "Is the expedition ready?"

"Nearly." Daphne leads everyone into the big courtyard in front of the school. There are three wagons with strange machines hitched before them and six other mortals standing around. Four of them look like normal people from off the streets, dressed in plain clothes and focused more on the wagons, but the other two are people you recognize.

Skinner turns away from the wagons and grins at your friends. "We're leaving in ten!" he calls before returning to a checklist.

The other boy is one you know fairly well. "Ah, hello girls," Everette says, one hand falling down to pat Wuffles on the head. He looks different with a thick cloth armour covering most of his body and a helmet tucked under his unoccupied arm. "I guess we'll be moving together today!"

Your group set out on three wagons, each one pulled by a metallic contraption that belches a dark acrid smoke that made the horses on the road whinny and whine. Crossing through the gates leading out of Five Peaks was easy. The guards looked at everyone, you included, and poked at the things carried in the wagons, but since that mostly amounted to a few books in a chest and some coal they didn't make much of a fuss.

And so, just like that, you were let out of the city.

The outside of Five Peaks isn't quite what you expect. There are less trees near the city and a lot more little ranches and farms fairly close to the road, with cows and chickens and other things that Abigail told you you couldn't eat before you even asked.

"Is this going to take long?" you ask.

It's not really uncomfortable. The bench is a little hard and the bouncing will make your butt sore at some point, but it's not all bad. You're squished in between Daphne and Abigail, right where Charlotte told you you should sit to act as chaperon. You don't know what that means, but you suspect it's a type of hat.

"I don't know," Abigail says. She's taking in the sights too. You're not moving fast enough to make your hair flutter with the wind or anything, but it's a near thing. You're certainly moving faster than Abigail and your friends would on foot, especially over the hilly terrain.

"We're heading to a village called Twinforks, it's about two days' walk, a day by carriage," Daphne says. "We didn't leave as early as we could have, so I suspect we might have to stay at an inn for the night."

"The air is a lot fresher out here than in the city," Charlotte says. "You don't really notice the difference until you're out of the walls."

Abigail shrugs, then pulls her jacket on closer. "It's a bit colder too. Nothing to break the wind." She wraps an arm around your shoulder and pulls you closer. This is okay. You can be warm for Abigail, no problem. "I hope we don't run into goblins or anything else."

"No, goblins are territorial," Charlotte says. "They don't usually linger around roads that are travelled on frequently, not for long anyway, the city guard patrols for quite a ways out and each town has its own militia that would tear goblins apart if they blocked a road. Goblins are smart enough to avoid people."

"Good," Abigail says. "I'd really rather not get into any sort of trouble. Though you seem ready for it. Where did you get a sword?"

Charlotte smiles and unclasps the sheath of her sword from her belt. She pulls the handle, revealing a few inches of shiny, sharp-looking steel. "This old thing? I wish I had an interesting story to go with it, but it's just something I bought a while ago to keep safe. Hardly ever used it."

She passes the sword over to Daphne who pulls it out completely and stares at it, obviously not sure of what to do now that she has it in hand. "It's… pointy?" she says.

"Yes, yes it is," Charlotte says before giggling. "Never had to play with a sword before?"

"No, I have guards for that," Daphne says primly.

"Don't have any here," Charlotte says.

"That's true," Daphne agrees. She slides the sword back into its sheath and hands it to Abigail. Your summoner doesn't seem to know what to do with it, so you carefully take it from her. You wouldn't want her to get cut. "I do have these," Daphne says as she lifts her skirt a little and pulls a small cylinder from a sort of belt around her thigh.

"Oh, can I see?" Abigail asks.

"The explosive or her legs?" Charlotte asks.

Daphne passes Abigail the cylinder and tugs her skirt down as if it's on fire. Abigail studies it very carefully, her face flaming.

You, in the meantime, study the blade. It's very hard and sharp. Probably too hard to eat with your mortal teeth. A quick swipe with your hand across the blade has you dropping a few fingers on the ground.

Mortals certainly have interesting ways of defending themselves. You compare the sword to one of your combat tentacles and find the tentacle… wanting. A bit of focus has the tip of the tentacle sharpen, then it hardens and you form an edge just like the sword's. You already have poke-y tentacles for poking holes in things without as much effort. This can be your slice-y tentacle, for slicing things.

It can even cut things without rending the fabric of reality. Useful!

"What's that?" you ask Abigail. This new weaponized tentacle will be fun to play with later, but maybe there are other mortal weapons you can copy.

"It's a spell canister. The circle is folded in a tube, with each re-agent in the centre separated by a thin layer of paper. They're all powdered reagents, so they don't get mixed," Abigail explains as she carefully inspects the device. "See this at the top? It's a time release circle. Fairly simple. You pour aether into it and it delays the time the aether takes to reach the main circle, when it does the circle activities and does... whatever it's meant to do."

"That one is a flash and burn," Daphne says. "A bright burst of light and sound and heat. It's meant as more of a deterrent against wild animals than anything else."

"Hrm," you say as you give Charlotte back her sword. You care-fully take the bomb cylinder, give it a sniff, then toss it into your mouth. It's nice! With a bunch of layers that all crunch differently and powders with different tastes. Some taste like fire, others like hot stuff. "It's good."

The girls stare at you, then Charlotte starts giggling, soon fol-lowed by the others. You don't know why learning that the bomb tastes good would make them laugh, but you smile anyway because it's a happy sound.

"Whoa!" comes a cry from ahead. Wheels squeal and the wagon jutters as you all slow down and come to a rapid stop.

A look ahead reveals why. There's a tree laying across the street and blocking the path.

Skinner is up in a moment. "We need to move that, now!" he says, sounding rather panicked all of a sudden.

Then a bunch of people start moving out of the woods. Not gob-lins, not unless goblins are a sort of human. Big, burly men with clubs and swords who look at the wagons and the girls with looks that you don't like.

"Oh no," Abigail says.

Charlotte is gripping her sword, Daphne has two bombs, one in each hand.

You wonder if this means that lunch will be delayed.

"Now, hand over the goods, and the girls, and no one's gonna get hurt," one of the bandits, the biggest one in the lot, says. You eye him carefully, taking in his scruffy face and dirty clothes, but also the big axe he's holding by his side.

Skinner looks back towards your wagon and winces. "I see," he says. "Do you know who we are?"

"We don't, and we don't care," the bandit says. "Any one of you moves and you're dead."

"But, sir," Abigail says as she sits up straighter. "That's not a good—"

An arrow zips by her face, a thin line cutting into her cheeks. The bandits laugh as she squeaks and falls back.

An arrow almost hit Abigail.

Someone hurt Abigail. You watch as she falls back and slaps a hand over the cut across her face.

That arrow could have killed Abigail.

You can't hear the others, all the noise drowned out by a sound that's like a million waterfalls tumbling past your ears. Numbly, you look up and see the bandits jeering, laughing, some of them making rude gestures. Daphne is trembling as she tries to help Abigail. Charlotte is glaring, her sword out and held by her side.

"**No**," you say.

Tentacles burst out of the ground all around your wagon and in a blink the entire thing is cocooned in walls of your flesh. It's dark within, dark and quiet until you remember that Abigail doesn't like the dark and the inside of your tentacles begin to glow.

"Take care of Abigail," you tell Daphne. There's no smile in your voice. The happy is *gone*. "I'm going to take care of those things out there."

Before she has time to reply you're yanked out of the cocoon. You hover in the air, feet planted on nothing as you tell physics to go eat it's own tail. "I," you say, voice like the birth of stars. "Am Dreamer. But there are no dreams left for you."

A few of the bandits laugh.

Your new combat tentacles lance through them, sprouting branches that sprouted more branches into infinity.

They can't laugh anymore.

The other bandits are beginning to back away, some arrows are shot at you, but you don't care, not even when they hit and make your pretty dress ugly with your black blood. It doesn't matter. You find the one that hurt Abigail and shoot towards him so fast that the air screams at your passing. A glance reveals everything there is to know about him down to the terrors that made him bawl as a infant

You send tentacles into him, tiny ones that look more like writhing noodles than normal tentacles. They each grab a tiny part of him until every cell and atom that makes up the bandit is in your grasp, and then they *pull*.

The bandit is dust.

He doesn't *deserve* to be eaten.

You move onto the next. You had been waiting for an opportunity to try out your newer, sharper tentacles, and this is it. Bandits make loud screaming noises as you break them apart into bite-sized bits that you gobble down while still moving. There are more and more tentacles around, some of them warping the world so that those who run away come running back, others, made from the trees and grass and air, grab onto your lunch and hold it in place.

It takes a minute, maybe two, but in the end you float above what had once been a road cutting through a forest. It is now a twisted landscape of tentacles, warped trees, and holes in space and time that go on forever. Abigail… wouldn't be happy with all of this.

You close up the holes, patch the time warped bits, and yoink the strangest trees back to your real body where they are promptly eaten.

It's better now, much better. The only problem is that your tummy is really full now and every step makes it bounce and gurgle. So you crush it down, making your meal smaller and smaller until it eats itself.

You land with a 'hop' in front of Skinner's wagon where the boy and Everett and Sigmund and Wuffles are all huddled together and looking off into the distance. "It's okay, they're all gone now," you tell them.

"T-thanks," Skinner whispers. It's a very loud whisper in the otherwise silent patch of forest. You suspect that one of your tentacles might have eaten all the sound and maybe also all the birds.

"You're welcome."

The tentacle cocoon around the girl's wagon gets pulled back into the ground and you jump up to check on Abigail. She's dabbing a cloth at her cheek where a line of dried blood formed. "Dreamer!" she says before spreading her arms wide.

You crash into her, ear pressed against her chest as you listen closely to the thump-thump of her heart and make sure she's completely okay. "You're alive," you say.

Abigail laughs and your tummy flips at the happy sound. "I am. Dreamer. What happened to the... what happened?"

You pull back and make a frown settle on your forehead. "There were bad people. They hurt you. I got rid of them."

Abigail and the others take a moment to look at the world beyond the wagons which, despite your efforts to smooth things out, is still a little... crookedy. Skinner jumps out of his wagon a little ways ahead and moves over, making sure to jump over the bits near the side of the roar where things are misshapen. "Ah, we're going to... take a short break. But not here, I think. And while we're taking that break, I would like to talk to you, Abigail." He looks at you, then back to Abigail. "If you wouldn't mind?"

Abigail looks at the others, then at you. "I guess that cat is out of the bag," she says.

Daphne is quick to shake her head. "He's the leader of this expedition, but that hardly gives him much authority over you or your person, and especially not over Dreamer. Hold firm and don't let him walk all over you... actually, do you want me to accompany you?"

Abigail shakes her head. "No, no I'll be fine."

"I'm coming," you say simply.

Abigail looks at you for a moment, then pats your head. "Alright," she says. "You can come."

Of course you can, you already said you would. She's being silly again. You hop off the wagon and help Abigail down with the judicious use of a few tentacles, then the two of you start heading over to where Skinner and Sigmund are standing next to the tree that's still blocking the road.

You notice Wuffles backpedaling away from you inside her wagon until her doggy bum is pressed right up against the opposite side, she even whimpers a little. "It's okay," you tell her. "I'll be back soon and we can cuddle and I'll pat you."

Skinner looks up when Abigail's shoes crunch over the little rocks on the road. "Ah, Abigail, and Dreamer," he says. "Thanks for coming so soon. I wanted to, ah, discuss things with you."

"Yes?" Abigail asks.

Skinner eyes you carefully for a moment, then looks up at Abigail. "Could we talk alone?"

"No," you say with a shake of your head. Your hand snakes up and grabs onto Abigail's. "Abigail was hurt really badly. I'm not letting her out of my sight."

Which leads to a very serious thought. You're here while your friends are way over there in their wagon still. Too far for you to hear them if they need help with something. That's... probably a big oversight on your part. What if a bandit sneaks back?

You make an eyetacle spawn out of the side of the wagon, just a long stalk with an eyeball on the end that blinks a few times before wiggling around to face the girls. They're both staring at it really hard like. Ah, maybe they don't know it's a friendly eyetacle.

You help by pushing out a tentacle whose end bit or just a hole lined with serrated teeth, then you make it squish up on the edges in a sort of smile. There, now the girls know that it's a friendly nomtacle.

A few ears pop out of the sides of the two tentacles so that you can hear and you're done. Now if something happens you'll know right away, and it only took a few seconds to set up.

"Dreamer?" Abigail asks. "Are you okay?"

"Yes," you say. "What does Skinner want?"

The boy takes a deep breath. "I wanted to thank you. You saved us from quite the dangerous situation there. Though I also... question your methods."

You shrug one shoulder the way Daphne does sometimes. "Someone hurt Abigail. They deserved what happened."

"You mean the man you disintegrated?" he asks.

"That's the one, yes. The rest weren't as mean so I only got rid of them." Abigail's hand around yours tightens which might mean you said something wrong. "But don't worry, no one else hurt Abigail so they all get to keep on doing their stuff until they do hurt Abigail."

"Right," Skinner said. "I'll be sure to inform everyone that they ought to be careful." He licks his lips and looks around. "We're going to continue on our mission. If that's okay with you? Though things might be delayed on account of needing to take another road. I don't have the materials or time to move this tree out of the path."

A tentacle wobbles out from the forest and splits at the end with a loud screeching noise. Then, while everyone is watching, it pinches the middle of the tree and flings it out into the woods the same way your small body might pick up a branch and flick it aside.

"Done!" you say. "Do you think we can get to the inn in time? I've never been to a place that's dedicated to making people sleep before."

"We'll see what we can do," Skinner says faintly.

Abigail places a hand on his shoulder. "Just don't think about it too hard. It only makes it worse."

That said, Abigail starts walking back to the wagon with you in tow.

"So?" Daphne asks as you approach and help Abigail climb back to her seat. "Any news?"

"I don't know," Abigail says. "He seems open, and that look in his eyes." Abigail pauses. "I think we can convince him that keeping quiet would be in his best interests, but I'm not good at that sort of thing."

"I'll chat with him later, no worries," Daphne says.

"It ought to help that despite everything, little Dreamer here acted in the best interests of the expedition," Charlotte adds before she boops your nose. "Did you get any loot from the bad men?" she asks.

You shake your head, then pause to consider. "I filled up my tummy, is that loot?"

Abigail and Daphne both blanch, but Charlotte's smile only grows. "It most certainly is. You should have saved one for me. I had my sword ready and everything."

You nod. "Next time."

A moment later Skinner restarts the engine on the first wagon, then the second's roars to life and soon the entire expedition begins to move. The adventure continues, but you think that a nice nap in the back of your wagon would feel nicer than just sitting around.

It would give you time to digest while the sky rolls by.

CHAPTER SEVENTEEN

"DREAMER, WAKE up," Abigail says as she shakes your shoulder.

Wake up. Your two least favourite words being spoken by your most favourite person. You reach up and grab Abigail to pull her close. She squeals as she falls onto you and your arms wrap her in a warm hug. "Five more decades," you protest as you bury your face into her neck and go back to sleep.

Abigail giggles. "Well, if you won't wake up the easy way," she begins. You feel cold fingers pressing up against the material of your pretty dress right over your ribs.

The comfy haze of sleep pulls back a little. "No," you say.

"Hrm," Abigail replies. "Maybe I won't." Then she starts poking your sides and you squirm. "Maybe I won't stop until Dreamer is awake!"

"No!" you protest louder as Abigail begins to torture you, hard mean fingers poking into your ribs and sides. Your feet thump-thump on the wagon's floor as you try to wiggle your way out of Abigail's grasp, the noise is lost under the sounds of Abigail's giggles. Your own laughter joins in a moment later, even though you're telling your small body, quite sternly, not to laugh. It's embarrassing.

"Are you awake now?"

You open your eyes to glare at Abigail. This has become her favourite way of waking you up and it's mean and unfair. There's an unspoken rule to the ritual that says that you're not allowed to just tentacle her away while she tickle tortures you, otherwise you would turn the tables around. "Yes," you say before sitting up and looking around.

You're in a town. There are small homes with thatched roofs with plumes of smoke rising from their chimneys and there are people moving around and doing stuff. The laughter of kids and the bark of dogs competes with the distant birdsong from a nearby forest. Water gurgles and splashes nearby.

The other wagons are a little bit ahead, parked before the biggest building in the entire one-street village. "This is it?" you ask.

"It is!"

You turn to find Charlotte pulling a bag out from the back of the wagon and hoisting it onto her back. "Welcome to Twinforks," she says.

"Like the things for eating?" Actually, now that you think about it, using two forks for eating makes more sense than a fork and a knife.

Charlotte shakes her head. "No, the river that runs through the town forks twice. Silly name, but it works for them."

You release Abigail and stand up, neck craning to take in the big inn building. You know it's an inn because there's a sign that says *The Adventur' Inn Stop* dangling from the front with a shield and sword logo above it.

"Wanna see the inside?" Charlotte asks.

"Yes," you say. This place has piqued your curiosity ever since you heard of it.

"I'll be with Daphne," Abigail says. "We'll pay for the rooms and bring some meals to ours, is that okay?"

You don't like leaving Abigail all alone, but she does need a little bit of room to spread her wings. You've heard this saying a few times already, and you're really looking forward to Abigail sprouting wings. "Be safe," you tell her before jumping out of the wagon. "I'll be with Charlotte, but if you scream I'll be there before you screamed."

"Um, okay?" Abigail says before waving you goodbye. She looks a little confused but that's alright.

"Never been to an inn?" Charlotte asks.

You shake your head and reach up to grab her hand, as you're supposed to do when walking with a bigger girl. Charlotte tightens her grip on your hand and smiles down at you. "You're too cute," she says.

"Yes," you agree.

The inside of the inn is a big place, with plenty of tables and chairs and some people that look like they're relaxing. There's a big fireplace off to one side and the air smells like food and smoke and tobacco from the group of old men with pipes in one corner. A big staircase off to one side leads up to the second floor. "We have rooms three, four, and five," Charlotte says, "For the entire group."

You do some quick math. "So we get to sleep together?" you ask.

"I guess so. Just for tonight." Charlotte nods. "We'll be setting up a watch just in case too."

"A watch?"

Charlotte lets go of your hand, but uses her now-freed limb to pat your head, so it's okay. "One of us will stay awake all night to make sure nothing bad happens while the others sleep."

You freeze halfway up the stairs and turn to face Charlotte. "You're not going to sleep just to make sure that we're okay?" you ask.

She shrugs one shoulder. "I can sleep more later."

You sniffle, holding back the tears that have sprung into your small body's eyes before you crash into Charlotte and give her the best hug you can.

Such a sacrifice! To go without sleep just to keep others safe. Charlotte is one of the best mortals. You would gladly call her a friend.

"Hey there, are you okay?" she asks.

You nod into her chest. "Yes. I have good friends. We need to get you better stuff," you declare. "So that you can keep us safe better."

Charlotte pats you some more because she's the second best. "I don't need anything like that," she says. "Come on, let's check out our room?"

Finding out which room is yours isn't hard. It's the one with all of Daphne's stuff in it. She brought more luggage than you and

Abigail and Charlotte combined so she must be very ready for anything bad that might happen. The room is small, a bit bigger than Daphne's own room, but with four small beds and a few dressers taking up a lot of space, as well as a table with some chairs around it off to the side.

Right away, you begin inspecting the beds and mattresses and frown at their quality. Abigail's stuff is better. But they're bug free and mostly clean.

This whole inn place is rather disappointing. Still, you push all the beds together so that they form one great big sleeping spot and fluff everything up as best you can while thinking about what kind of equipment you could give Charlotte. The best would be combat tentacles, but mortals, especially girl mortals, don't like having tentacles coming out of their bodies because they're silly. The boys are a bit better about it, but they're very particular about the location of their tentacles.

The solution strikes a moment later. A whip! Yes, that's a perfect idea and the perfect weapon.

Now you only need to figure out the specifics of it.

Soon, everyone gathers in the room, and there's much talking and merry making and all that good stuff before finally it's bedtime.

The next morning, someone rude wakes you up and promises you food from the main floor downstairs.

"More please!" you tell the nice lady.

She's big and plump and has brown hair tied up in a bun behind her head so that it doesn't fall into the yummy, yummy food she makes. The woman bends down a little and pinches your cheek. "Oh, aren't you the sweetest thing?" she asks.

You look up to the nice lady and nod. It's a very serious question, even if you think it's not being taken seriously. But you can't fault the nice lady for asking. In only one morning she has climbed from unimportant background mortal to the fifth most important person in your life. You watch her leave with fondness.

"Still not full?" Abigail asks as she blows the steam off of her teacup.

Everyone is gathered at one of the big round tables on the first floor of the inn. The background mortals taking care of the wagons aren't there, but all the fun people are around. Daphne is sitting on Abigail's other side, slowly feeding Archibald bits of bread. Everette and Skinner are at the opposite end of the table. Everette ignoring Wuffles' pleading gaze for more food while Skinner is frowning at a letter.

Charlotte is right next to you, picking at her eggs and ham with a fork. You hope she'll stop and give the leftovers to you, but you're not in a hurry. The nice lady said you could eat as much as you wanted for breakfast at her inn and you intend to make the most of that.

You're about to explain to Abigail that even with nice lady's greatest efforts, you still doubt she'll be able to fill your tummy, not that you don't appreciate the attempt, when Skinner sighs and raps the table with a knuckle. "Everyone," he says. "We have a small problem."

Daphne snorts. "I'm sure."

Ignoring her, Skinner wiggles the letter in the air. "The supplier the Library Expedition club came here to visit doesn't, unfortunately, have all the things we came to get. It seems that the bandits that waylaid us were becoming quite the thorn in the local's side. But, they will have what we need by tonight, tomorrow morning by the latest."

"Which means we're stuck here," Daphne says.

Skinner shakes his head. "Not quite. If you girls wish to leave I would understand. I'll even allow you to return with one of the wagons. We should be able to rent another under these circumstances. Or we could find you a caravan returning to Five Peaks this afternoon. I won't hold you back."

"But we could stick around," Charlotte says.

"You could, yes, and return with us tomorrow. It's up to you," Skinner says.

"What would we do if we just stayed here?" Abigail wonders.

"I'd say shopping," Daphne says. "I doubt anything in this little town couldn't be found in Five Peaks and at better price and quality."

Everyone remains quiet for a moment, Skinner returning to his letters as he begins to write something in a journal of sorts.

Then Everette coughs into a gauntleted fist. "Well, if it's something to do you're looking for, there is a board." He points to the far end of the room where a board is mounted to the wall with bits of paper on it, each one carefully pinned with little ribbons of different colours. "I'm in the Adventuring club, which means I can take bronze ranked tasks without penalty. Depending on the task it might be a bit much for one person alone."

"That sounds interesting," Abigail says.

"No Abigail," Daphne says. "You are not going to do menial labour for a few marks. It's hardly worth the risk."

Abigail smiles at Daphne. "But you don't even know what the tasks are yet."

"No, but I know you. You'll see some pitiful message about a farmer whose flock was stolen by some goblins and will want to help the poor fool."

Abigail sniffs and stands up. "It won't hurt to at least look. And I'm sure with Dreamer and Mister Everette along I would be perfectly safe." Abigail nods firmly, then adjusts her glasses which look ready to fly off her face at any moment.

Daphne presses her hands over her face. "Why, why is she like this?" she asked.

You pat her arm. "Because she's Abigail."

Charlotte stands up and stretches a little. "Well, I'm certainly ready to join on any adventure. It sounds amusing, and a bit of coin wouldn't hurt."

And that reminds you of something you had nearly forgotten. You jump to your feet and grab Charlotte's hand. "Tell the nice lady to put all the food on my plate," you tell the others at the table before you drag Charlotte to a quieter corner. She doesn't resist at all because she's a good friend and good friends allow you to bring them to dark places. "I made you a gift," you tell her.

"Did you now?" she asked.

You nod and reach into another place and pull out the gift you've been working on all night. It was made while most of you was napping, but it's still very pretty. "Here," you hand it to Charlotte.

She stares at the leather-like handle and the metallic, eye-shaped pommel at the bottom. The top part that sticks out of the end is a long coil of thin whippy tentacle and near where the thumb should rest are a few little switches.

"Ah, is this a whip?" Charlotte asks as she turns it this way and that. She lets it uncoil to drape onto the floor.

"Yup!" You say. "It reads your mind to know what to hit, and if you press on the things near your thumb it changes."

Charlotte blinks down at the whip and, carefully, pressed one of the switches. Hundreds of spikes tear out of the ropey length, some of them digging into the floor with next to no resistance. "Oh my," she says. "Not my usual kind of whip, but this might be handy. And it reads my mind, you said?"

The whip coils itself back up into a near bundle which she inspects closer. Then your face is buried in her chest as she hugs you.

"Thanks, Dreamer. I'll be sure to cherish your gift."

You nod and grin and then leave her hug. "Just remember to feed it," you say as you run over to Abigail and Everette who are both looking at all the pages on the board with quests written on them. Obviously they'll need your help picking out the best mission!

Everette explained the way the quest picking system works to you with simple words and big gestures. You suspect it's because he's touched in the head. Poor Wuffles, having such a boring summoner.

"So," you say to recapitulate. "For some reason some metals are more important than others, and so you decided to use that to rank the difficulty of these quest things."

"Uh, yeah, exactly," Everette says. "Bronze, then silver, then gold. Each rank is more dangerous, but also pays better."

"What about the other metals?" you ask.

"Well, they're not part of the ranking."

"Why not?"

"Well, the others aren't as, ah, rare?" Everette says, though it sounds as if he's asking you a question.

You turn to Abigail because she knows lots of things. "What's the rarest metal? And what's the most common one?"

Your Abigail hums a little as she thinks. "Iridium, I think. It's a very rare reagent and it is a metal. As for the most common, that would have to be aluminium, though it is very difficult to work without the right spells. Iron is probably the most commonly used metal."

You nod and spin back to face Everette. "Where are the Iridium level ranks? And why aren't the lowest ranked quests aluminium?"

The boy stutters and gestures a little, then shakes his head. "There aren't any others," he says. "Just bronze, silver and gold. That's it. And of those, we can only take the bronze, which is all they have here anyway."

"I never actually thought about it," Abigail says. "But they really should change the system to some sort of rank that doesn't correspond to a metal. What if large gold deposits are discovered and the value of gold decreases, or a mage finds a gold-substitute for most spellwork. It has happened to some other uncommon reagents before, it could happen to gold. Then the Adventuring Club would be stuck with an antiquated system that no longer makes any sense."

"Yes, well," Everette says. "Be that as it may, gold is worth more than silver right now. And there are neither gold or silver options on this particular board."

You're beginning to suspect that he might be irritated. "Okay, so which quest offers the most to eat?"

"The rewards are all listed at the bottom," he says before pointing to some numbers below the quest details. "They pay in Five Peaks Fiat."

"So the quests that are labelled with gold don't actually pay in gold?" Abigail asks.

Everette presses his face into his hands.

"They pay in money, but I want stuff to eat," you explain.

"You can trade money for food," Everette says and Abigail pats your shoulder which probably means he's right.

So the optimal options, then, are obviously those where you get to eat something, then make lots of money to get to buy even more stuff to eat. Or maybe there are quests where they'll need special sorts of tentacles, or that would allow you to learn new ways to use your tentacles like with Charlotte's sword.

"There are two of them that are right next to each other," Abigail says as she points to two different sheets. "One is to scout out the location of a bandit camp. The other… oh my, there's a wild troll on the loose."

"What's a troll?" you ask.

"It's a fearsome beast," Everette says. "Strong and difficult to fight, with a thick hide and just enough brains to be clever."

You decide that Everette is an idiot and turn to Abigail for a better answer. "It's a very big monster," she says. "They were made by a mad eugenicist hundreds of years ago to fight in a war. They're very strong and quite large."

She said words that mean 'big' twice, which means it must be a good snack. "Okay, let's go eat the troll and then the bandits."

"We only need to scout out the bandit camp," Everette says, then, after seeing your blank look, he explains more. "We just need to know where they are and then report that."

"They'll be in my tummy," you say. A tentacle reaches out and plucks the two notices from the board and then smacks them onto Everette's chest. "Do the thing with the papers. We'll get the others."

You and Abigail move over to the table where Charlotte looks quite satisfied and Daphne is wearing a very flat, very unimpressed look. Next to her is your third portion of breakfast, all piled up in a big mound of eggs and ham and teeny tiny potato cubes that you dig into with two forks.

"You took a quest," Daphne says.

"No," Abigail says, and for a moment Daphne relaxes. "We took two."

"Damn it, Abi," Daphne says. "I can't believe you drag me into these things."

"You could stay at the inn," Abigail says.

"And leave you out there without me to look over you? No way. You might get hurt, or injured or lost," Daphne says. It's a fair point and the same reason you'd never let Abigail go do dangerous things without you there to eat them.

"I'll go get dressed. This sounds like a great excuse to take a nice long walk outdoors and enjoy some sunshine," Charlotte says.

"And we get to eat things," you add after swallowing the last of your eggs.

The girls all look at you, then as one start shaking their heads. They obviously don't know what it's like to go eons without anything new to eat.

"Right. Let's all get our things and meet up outside in a few minutes? I don't think anything is beyond walking distance, but maybe we can find some farmer or something to give us a ride closer so that we can save ourselves some walking."

"That sounds passable," Daphne says. "A gold mark ought to get any one of the locals to drive us anywhere."

"A gold mark would be more than what we'd make on the quest. Before we split the profits," Charlotte says.

"I thought we were doing this to pass the time?" Daphne shoots back.

You roll your eyes and lick your plate clean. For all of their talk about being civilised and such, your mortal friends are big on squabbling about silly things.

CHAPTER EIGHTEEN

"I SEE, THANK you, sir," Everette says to the old man before bowing and rushing back over to the group.

Daphne and you are the only ones really paying attention, Abigail and Charlotte are both too busy snooping around the farm and making cute noises at all the baby cows in the baby cow pens.

You're not sure what you think about farms. On the one tentacle, food, on the other, they smell like poop.

"Alright everyone," Everette says as he returns. "We have a direction." he pointed off towards a big forest past a field where a few big cows were grazing.

"Well then, shall we?" Daphne asked. "Abi, Charlotte, the calves will still be here when we're done," she called.

Abigail pat-patted one of the baby cows while you eyed it suspiciously. You weren't going to eat it because it stole one of your pats. But if you had to eat all the cows, because of some strange and unforeseen circumstance, that one would be first. "I'm coming," she says as she rushes back.

You and the others start trekking over to the place where the farmer said he saw the big ol' troll, you at the front while the others follow behind at a slower pace. You're very excited to see what troll tastes like.

Then again, maybe you fighting the troll all on your own wouldn't be fair. Charlotte has her whip, Everette has a sword. Wuffles has teeth, and Abigail has Daphne. They could all fight for themselves, get some practice in case a troll appears at the academy and assaults them while they're in the bathroom or something.

You slow down a little once you're in the forest. The ground is all uneven and rocky and there are branches and rocks and roots all over, so it's a good thing that you can hang off to the trees with your tentacles.

"Look at this," Charlotte says as she kneels down a little ways into the woods. She points to a smudge on a tree. "Blood. Not troll's blood. Maybe from one of the cows it stole."

"Good eyes," Everette says. "Can you tell where it went?"

Charlotte points ahead. "That way. Look at the way those branches were moved aside. It's not exactly trying to be subtle."

"It is the biggest thing around," Everette said.

"Oh, and there are queen's lilies," Abigail said as she pointed to some flowers off to the other side. "Their roots aren't terribly valuable, but they're a good reagent for some types of spells. They're mostly used as a soporific. And they can be eaten if boiled."

Flowers can be eaten? That gives the Gardening Club a whole lot more value. Next time you'll stop by their clubhouse and tell them that you're there to eat all their lilies. But in the meantime you grab some of the flowers, roots and all, and stuff them into your mouth.

Kinda grassy, but the roots do taste a bit like carrots. Maybe other flowers have different tastes?

The trek continues, mostly in silence except for Daphne's frequent complaints and Abigail's gentle admonishments that everything is alright. The only other noise comes from when you tear flowers out of the ground and chew on them.

And then you stumble into a clearing and lock eyes with a huge monster. It's big, with bulging muscles under dirt-covered skin and has a weird squished face. It looks like a very, very large and very hairy man that got into one fight too many. Its face is covered in blood, but that might be the cow it's in the middle of snacking on.

"Found it!" you tell the others.

"Dreamer, come back," Everette says as he grabs you from behind and flings you back into the woods.

Wait, did he think you would get hurt? What a silly boy.

Everette pulls out his sword and Wuffles starts to growl deep and low.

"Ah, are you going to eat that?" Abigail asks you as she helps you to your feet and brushes the dirt off of your pretty dress. You're going to make Everette pay to clean it.

"Yes," you say. "But you need to kill it yourselves first."

That earns you some looks from Abigail and Daphne. "What do you mean?" Daphne asks. "I thought you were all about the over the top violence and consumption of things."

"Yes, but I want to make sure you can fight too," you say. "Look, it's coming here."

The troll is indeed rushing over, a large tree trunk serving as a club which it swings around and tries to use to squish Everette into the ground. He rolls to the side, neatly avoiding the crushing blow but ending up on his side when he couldn't roll right back to his feet.

That's when Charlotte and Wuffles come in. The girl flicks out her whip, the tip snapping at the air with a crack and cutting a line across the troll's chest while Wuffles circles around the troll and bites into its ankle.

"We need to help them," Daphne says as she starts pulling bombs from under her skirt.

"R-right," Abigail says. She seems a little panicked until she reaches out and grabs one of your tentacles. "Dreamer, I need the end of this to be sharp."

You blink, but that's not hard to do. The tip of the tentacle she's holding grows pointy and hard a moment before Abigail moves closer to the fight, then plants herself before a tree and starts carving into it.

You don't know what she's up to, but you let her play with your tentacle because it feels funny and you like it.

The fight continues, with Everette taunting the monster and Wuffles slowing it down while Charlotte's whip takes slices out of the monster. Daphne, meanwhile, frets and worries and seems reluctant to toss her bombs so close to her friends.

And then Abigail cheers. "I've got it!" she says. "Dreamer, I need aether."

"Life juice?" you wonder. "Okay. I can get some. Where do I put it?"

Abigail points to a deep hole she made in the trunk in the middle of a circle she carved. It looks a little rough, but workable.

"Okay," you say as you poke a small tentacle into the hole, then jam another into the ground.

"Oh shoot," Abigail says. "Everyone, retreat! Now, now, now!"

The others take a moment to move, but they do, leaving the troll looking around all confused.

Then the lifejuice you yoink from the ground fills into the circle Abigail made.

The effect is instantaneous.

Between one blink and the next the entire clearing is filled with a huge tree, one that's growing sideways out of the tree that Abigail carved into and whose branches are shooting off every which way. Including into and through the troll.

"Wow," you say. "Good work Abigail!"

"Wow," Everette says as he gets off his bum and uses a nearby tree to help him stand up. His eyes are fixed on the spot where the troll used to be. Technically it's still there.

For once, you sort of agree with the boy. Abigail really did a number on the troll. You can still see most of its body. The arms and legs aren't too badly mangled. The torso isn't doing so well, though, what with the three new tree trunks growing into and then out of it.

You can't help the wash of pride at the sight. It looks exactly like how you would get rid of the monster with your own tentacles, but this was all, or mostly all, Abigail's work. "Good job!" you tell your summoner.

"Th-thanks," Abigail says. Her eyes are very wide as she stares at the troll that is now part tree.

A treell? Trell? No, that's silly.

"Do you want to eat it?" You ask. It's only fair that she gets the first choice of that yummy looking meat. Of course, Abigail could never eat all of that on her own, and you did help a bit, so you should get a share too. A big share... Most of it.

Daphne steps up next to Abigail, then wraps an arm around her shoulder and steers her away. "Dreamer, can you take care of that for us?" she asks before bringing Abigail away.

Well, if you're being *asked* to eat the troll you won't say no.

"Actually, can I have a bit?" Everette asks. "Just a, ah, haunch or something." He pats Wuffles who has rejoined him on her big furry head. "Wuffles needs something to eat, you know."

You huff. "Fine, I'll share," you say. This will be paying Wuffles back for all the times you napped while hugging her big fluffy sides.

Summoning a bunch of tentacles, you concentrate until their sides are nice and sharp, then begin carving through tree and troll meat. The way bits of troll fly all over and flop against the ground with delicious meaty noises is very fun.

You flick aside one of the trolls thighs, bone and all, for Wuffles who catches it out of the air and growls playfully as she tears into it, both paws working to keep it pinned as she tears chunks of it apart. She's a very messy eater. You take another bit and bring it over to Charlotte who found a place to sit on one of the branches that Abigail made.

"I'm more of a cooked meat sort of girl," Charlotte says.

"It's for your whip," you explain.

She stares with one eyebrow rising, but takes out her whip and pokes the meat with it. A small seam along the whip's side opens up, revealing a bunch of teeth that grab onto the meat and start gnawing away at it. "Well, that's certainly going to handy next time I need to tell a boy to back off," she says.

You shake your head. Any boy that wouldn't be impressed by Charlie's whip probably doesn't deserve her attention in the first place.

Your tentacles set all of the meat aside into a big pile, then, because you're a well mannered familiar and also the best, you pull out your plate and start shovelling the meat onto it while tipping the plate back so that all the giblets fall into your mouth. A couple of small tentacles pat the meat that's going off course back towards your mouth.

Troll tastes a bit like the way farts smell, but more meaty. It's not that bad, but you decide that you like the yummy food at the inn a lot better. You stop eating when you get to the yuckier bits of the troll meat and push those into the ground to feed the planet. You kind of took some of its energy after all, you should repay it at least a little.

"Okay, I'm done," you say as you leave the grove that's still filled with wild branches and go find Abigail who is waiting with Daphne rubbing her back.

"Dreamer," Abigail says. She sighs. "Come here."

You come, and then Abigail whips out a handkerchief and starts rubbing at your face while you make protesting noises. You know that if you don't let her wipe your mouth she gets all huffy and then she'll run after you if you try to avoid her.

"Such a messy eater," she mutters.

"I used the plate," you complain. She has no right to judge your eating habits when you're eating with the same tools as her.

Abigail rolls her eyes, but there's a smile tugging at her lips. "This is the part where I would usually say something like 'don't change' but really, using a fork and knife wouldn't be the end of the world."

"It might be," you sulk.

Daphne shakes her head. "We should head back."

"No," Abigail says right away. "We should keep going. Those bandits, they're, well, they're bandits. If we can do something to help, then it's our responsibility to at least try."

You're pretty sure it's not, but if Abigail says so, who are you to disagree? "Okay. I'll go get the others."

"Oh, I'm ready," Charlotte says as she walks over. She's wiping her hands on a bit of cloth. "I looked in the troll's cave. Turns out my whip can glow, which is handy. Nothing but scraps I'm afraid. Not that I was expecting any great loot."

"We're ready to head out," Everette says as he too comes over, a very full Wuffles by his side. She's panting happy doggy breaths all over, a long troll bone still in her mouth where it's getting covered in a steady stream of drool.

"Do you want to come with us, Daphne?" Abigail asks. "We could bring you back to the farmer's place?"

"No, I'll come with you. I'm an idiot for doing it, but I will," Daphne grumps.

You grin at the lot of your friends, and Everette, then nod. Time for bandits.

It takes quite a bit more trekking through the woods before someone finally says something smart. "I can't see them," Everette says.

You look around but you can't see any signs of the bandits either. The whole group is on a big hill overlooking part of the forest, a nice vantage point to try and spot the hidden bandit camp. Unfortunately it doesn't seem to be working out. Probably because it's a hidden camp, not a visible camp.

Charlotte narrows her eyes and looks farther out. The girl uncoils her whip from her side, then cracks it upwards where it hooks around one of the nicer branches of one of the trees at the top. With a twist, big teeth stick out of her whip which she uses as a sort of ladder to climb up.

"Am I the only one mildly disturbed by how familiar she's becoming with that thing?" Daphne asks.

You shake your head. There's nothing wrong with the love Charlotte is showing for her whip. It's the best whip, it deserves to be cuddled and cooed after and fed a few little treats.

"Just a little?" Abigail says. "Really, glass houses and all, I can't exactly make a fuss." She reaches over and starts patting your head. She must mean that the affection she shows you is similar, of course.

"Nothing!" Charlotte calls down. "The view is pretty though."

"We might have to call this one a failure," Everette says. "We only have a few hours until we have to trek back. If we don't find the bandits soon then we won't have time to do much about them."

"I thought this was a scouting mission?" Daphne asks archly.

"It is, but, well, we have Dreamer. I thought the pay might be better if we ah, took care of the problem, as it were. You know, violence them up a bit."

You harrumph. He thinks that just because you're along you'll do violent stuff? To help him? You only do violent stuff for yourself and Abigail. Maybe Charlotte and Daphne if they ask really nicely.

"I think capturing them would be better," Abigail says. "If we can do that much."

You consider that. Capturing isn't nearly as fun as eating, but you have been eating a whole lot lately. Maybe skipping a meal or two wouldn't be too bad if it's what Abigail wants. "I can go look for them," you say.

Abigail shakes her head. "I don't want you to leave my side. What if something tries to hurt us?"

You smile and pull Abigail into a surprise hug, one that she deserves for being such a clever summoner and for thinking about her own safety like that. "Don't worry," you say. "I can be here and also elsewhere and also elsewhen at the same time. But we only need me to be all over for now."

"Um, what?" Daphne says.

"Look." You gesture to the ground where—with a bit of a rumble—a tentacle the size of your small body pokes out of the ground. Then it shifts and warps, bits pulling in with squelchy noises and other parts poking out like extra tentacles. In moment's there's a new you standing there, all naked and glassy-eyed. Then you give it one of your pretty dresses and no one who doesn't know you would know that it's not your main small body.

"My name is Dreamer and I'm hungry," the new you says. It turns its head to Everette and frowns. "Are you Abigail?"

"No," he says before taking a step back.

New-you frowns harder. "Are you food?"

You shake you main-you's head. "I can't split it without losing some control," you explain. "But it's still me. Now I just need to make enough to find all the bandits…"

Dozens, then hundreds of tentacles break out of the ground all over the hill and soon there are Dreamers all over the place. You, of course, keep on hugging Abigail so that she knows which Dreamer is the best Dreamer and where to direct any patting that she might want to do.

It's not like patting the other yous would be bad, it would still be a pat for you, but not for you-you, which is why you need to defend Abigail from yourself.

"So," Daphne says, sounding sort of faint. "This is how the world ends."

"Abigail, you need to tell the stupid mes to go find the bandits," you tell Abigail.

She opens and closes her mouth a few times. "Can you, ah, take them all back after?" she asks.

"Yeah, probably. Now hurry up, I'm all hungry."

"Right," Abigail says. "Um, everyone, uh, Dreamer!" she says, voice rising until every Dreamer around is looking at her. You all begin to smile because Abigail is paying you all attention. Everette starts saying bad words under his breath. "Right. We need to find the bandits. Can you do that?" she asks.

"Do we get pats?" one of you asks.

The impertinence!

"Um. The one who finds the bandits gets pats, yes," Abigail says.

Nearly a thousand Dreamers scamper away, a sea of pretty purple dresses disappearing into the woods with tentacle-swings that send them from tree to tree.

Soon you can't see a single Dreamer where you are atop the hill. It becomes nice and quiet and peaceful.

"What was that?" Everette says because he can't read the mood. "I, I was willing to overlook a lot, but that wasn't something a familiar should be able to do. That wasn't... that wasn't natural!"

Charlotte swings down from the tree and lands next to the girls before crossing her arms. "Shut up Everette. Dreamer hasn't hurt anyone. At least, no one that didn't deserve it."

"But she, she's... what is she?" he asks.

"I'm me," you tell him, your own glare forming. "And you're you, which makes me way better, so stop judging."

"Dreamer's a good girl," Abigail says. "Please don't do anything to make trouble."

You preen at Everette. Now he can't deny that you're the best because Abigail said so.

You'll have to rub it into the faces of all the other yous out there.

It only takes a few minutes for two of you to find all the bandits in their little camp. It's not a very impressive place. Half a dozen wooden shacks set in a sort of semi-circle around the entrance to a small cave.

Your two clones look at each other, then one of them starts smiling all smug and gloat-y. "I got here first," you say to yourself. "I get the headpats."

"No, you didn't," your other you says right back. "I got here first so *I* get the pats."

You narrow your eyes at yourself.

Then one of you swings a tentacle and the fight is on.

The bandits scream and run out of their huts to watch as two of you spin and roll across the ground of their camp, tentacles spearing out every which way as you try to be the first to grab yourself. One of you gets lucky and manages to poke a tentacle through the other you's chest.

"Got you!" you scream.

"No, I've got you!" you scream right back, revealing that it was a trick to get you to lower your guard. You gasp as you crash into yourself and wrap little hands around your throat to throttle your head into an unlit firepit. Tentacles are wrapping around each other all around you to keep them away from the fight in the centre.

Just as quickly as it begins, the fight ends and only one of you is left standing, bloody and with some broken bits, but still standing proud. "I get the pats!" you declare before your tentacles spear into your dead body and start eating it.

The bandits who have been watching all along don't seem to know what to do about this, but their just stupid mortals who won't get any headpats. "Who the hell are you?" the biggest, burliest bandit asks.

You slap him across the face with a tentacle for interrupting your fantasizing about all the headpats you're going to receive. He flies off, teeth spraying out of his mouth.

The you that's next to Abigail, the best you, according to yourself, turns around to look up to Abigail. "I found them," you say. "Do I eat them now?"

Abigail shakes her head. "No, no just, um, can you keep them from moving?"

You consider this. Movement is a change in location. Moving is the act of doing that change. They can't act if they're not in the same time as you, so all you need to do is tell time not to mess with them for a little bit.

Or maybe they would stay where they are and the planet would keep on moving and that would punch a bunch of holes through it. Which is rude, especially after the planet helped you so much. "I can tie them together with tentacles," you say.

"That would work, yes," Abigail says. "Can you lead us over?"

"Are you going to loot them or will you wait for us to arrive?" Charlotte asks.

"Loot?" you repeat.

Charlotte grins and there is something feral there. "Loot," she repeats. "As in, take everything they have worth taking. It's like stealing, but without the whole moral issues."

You crane your neck back to look at Abigail who sighs. "You can loot them," she says. "But don't hurt them too much and don't eat anything valuable."

"Okay!"

A few more of you arrive at the camp, all of you pouty and miffed that you weren't the one to find the bandits and so won't get to be patted for your efforts. The bandits are starting to look very nervous now that there are a hundred or so of you all around them, pretty dresses writhing as you prepare combat tentacles.

"Okay," the you who won the right to headpats says. You're done eating your own body and fixing all the holes in yours. "All you bandit people get ready to be looted please."

Abigail would be very proud of you, you're being polite and haven't killed any of them yet.

"Who the fuc—" A speartacle pokes through the rude bandit's head. A bunch of you glare at the you who stabbed him, but you just shrug.

Well, Abigail doesn't need to know about that one.

"On the ground now." you chide the others. "I'm going to loot and tie you, and then my friends are going to come here."

The bandits are surprisingly fast to comply. You start looting the whole camp, bursting into their shacks, eating all the food they left behind and taking all the shiny stuff that Abigail and the others might want. You make a big pile in the middle of the area that's full of swords and coins and things.

Looting, as it turns out, is a whole lot of fun! You shove tentacles in all of the bandit's pockets and when they struggle against that, just take all of their clothes. Some of them even have food hidden away in pockets and such.

One of you ends up with your small body very wobbly after drinking a bunch of fruity things in glass bottles and another one of you explodes into giblets when you chew on something you think might be a grenade, but overall it's a net gain.

You wonder what it would be like to loot an entire city.

Abigail arrives and just sort of stares for a while before taking a deep, shuddering breath. Then the you that found the camp rushes over. "Abigail! I'm the one that deserves the pats!" you say.

The other yous cross their arms and pout a bunch, but it's true, you do deserve the pats.

"Ah, well, um, good work," Abigail says as she pats you on the head.

You beam.

Then the best you gets tired of having so many other yous around, especially if you're going to take Abigail's attention away from yourself. Yous start to pop and collapse into heaps only to be picked up by passing tentacles and tossed into holes in reality.

The bandits, all of them naked, stare in mounting horror as all the yous are eliminated.

Then there's only one you. You think.

You're mostly sure that none of the other yous escaped and that's good enough.

"Look," you say as you point to the pile of stuff. "Loot!"

Abigail did the finger-waggle thing at you, so you know she was serious when she said that the bandits should at least have underwear and socks for the trip back to town. That's why the long row of mostly naked men trailing out behind you in single-file are not completely-naked men instead.

You, of course, are in the lead, with Abigail and Wuffles and the others too.

Abigail isn't very good at the whole walking through a forest thing, which is strange. You're better at it than her and you only had legs for a few days now.

The bandits are brought to their feet, and after collecting all the loot, you and your friends set out back to the farm.

"Are you sure they won't try to run away?" Abigail asks as she looks over her shoulder to all the bandits behind.

"Nah," you say. "I'm keeping some eyes on them."

Sometimes when the bandits turn their heads around fast enough they catch a glimpse of your eyetacles before they slink into the shadows. They usually shiver a lot after that, or start muttering things until another bandit tells them to shut up.

For a bunch of ruffians they're very well behaved. They only tried to run away once.

You're thinking of asking Wuffles for a ride when you hear Daphne and Everette talking up ahead just out of Abigail's hearing range. The girl is talking to the boy in quick whispers that sound rather heated and Everette is shrinking back and away from her. Or he's trying, but Daphne has a white-knuckled grip on his arm.

"I don't care. I don't care about the Inquisitors, I don't care about the law, and I certainly don't care about your jumped up sense of self-righteous morality. All I do care about is Abigail and making damned sure that she's happy. Fortunately, Dreamer and I agree on that."

"Yeah, but, you saw it, didn't you?" Everette asks.

"Of course I did. Do you take me for a fool? Dreamer might look like a girl but she's the farthest thing from it. Why do you think the Inquisition outlaws speak of gods and the like?"

"Because that's heresy?" he tries. "There's no such thing?"

Daphne rolls her eyes. "And if there was, what could a god do? You've had the basics of a scientific education drilled into you, haven't you? If a god did exist, what would the signs of its existence be?"

"I, I don't know?" Everette said. "Unexplainable things?"

"Good, now in the context of what you know of magic, could you explain even a tenth of what Dreamer does with no obvious effort?"

"Are you saying she's… it's a god?" he whispers back. A look over his shoulder has him blanching as he catches your eye.

You wave.

"I'm saying that it doesn't matter what she is. She's snuck into the Inquisition's headquarters and there wasn't a damned thing they could do about it just because she felt like it. Dreamer could turn Fivepeaks into a crater at a whim. For some reason she cares about Abigail and listens to her. So right here and right now you are going to listen to me."

"I have to report this," he says.

"If you do that what will they do? Try to separate Dreamer from Abigail? She would tear through the Inquisition like a rabid wolf in a sheep's pen. Would they hurt Abigail? Dreamer can open portals into outer space. I'm quite certain the only reason they don't bleed out our atmosphere is because she knows that Abigail needs to breathe. Dreamer could kill every last human on the continent, I'm certain of it, and she would eat us all if it wasn't for Abigail. So what you're going to do, is shut that stupid mouth of yours before it flaps and we all end up dead because you couldn't keep a secret."

Everette is quiet for a while. "Fine," he finally says. "She hasn't done bad by me yet, nor has Abigail. But if they cross the line I'm doing what I need to do. How are you going to keep the bandits quiet?"

"They're a bunch of peasants, who will believe them? If you hurt Abigail you're a dead man, whether Dreamer gets to you before me is up to blind luck," Daphne growls before slowing down. A moment or two later she's walking next to Abigail who catches up to her. "Hey Abi, how are you?" she asks with a big smile.

"I'm well?" Abigail says.

You grin. Daphne is a good friend, which is good. Abigail needs all the friends she can get. They'll help her do stuff she doesn't feel like doing once you instal her as queen or whatever the highest position is with all the mortals.

Your group travels along with a lot of happy chatter. Not from the bandits though, they mostly complain and grumble about their socks getting wet and how it's not fair that you ate their leader and stuff. It's their fault for being a mild inconvenience to Abigail in the first place, so you don't feel bad about it.

And then you arrive in town and Skinner is waiting for you with Sigmund on one shoulder and a pair of men with weird wide-brimmed hats next to him.

"Welcome back," he says. "It's good to see you're all safe and sound. Did you find some friends in the wilderness?"

"They're bandits," Charlotte says with a big happy smile. She now has some shoulder armour that she got as loot, and a big sack off of other things she thought might be worth selling. The rest of the stuff, of course, is all digesting in your tummy.

"I see," Skinner says. He gestures to the two men who look a bit confused. "I was just talking to the constables here about forming a search party. I'm glad to see that won't be necessary. I trust you can handle all of these fine gentlemanly bandits? We're leaving in an hour."

"Um, yes sir," Abigail says.

CHAPTER NINETEEN

"WE COULD check out the bookstore?" Daphne says as she looks about. The boring people that Skinner brought along are all packing up the wagons you came in and getting ready for the trip back home, but there's still plenty of packing to do and it is kind of boring to watch.

You would help, but Daphne told you to keep a 'low profile' and then Abigail explained what that meant. You shouldn't tentacle things in front of just anybody unless Abigail (or one of your other friends) is in danger.

You think that maybe she should have told you this earlier. How were you supposed to know?

"The inn is nice," Abigail says. "But I agree, we should check out the bookstore, at least for a little bit."

"That sounds more fun," you agree. The inn lady already told you that lunch won't be served for another few hours. That means that you have to wait a bunch before more food is served, but it's okay, you're used to waiting eons between snacks, a few hours… well, okay, maybe you could convince time to hurry up a little, but then that would mean less time with Abigail.

Charlotte makes a humming noise. "I think I'll leave it to you two, Daphne, Abigail. I'm going to go have a sit, isn't that right Everette?"

"Are you sure we should let them walk around toowwww—" Everette's face goes pale and you look down to see that Charlotte's boot is pressing down on his feet.

"You guys have fun~" she says before dragging Everette into the inn.

"Is she okay?" Abigail asks.

You shrug. She's probably fine. Worse case, she has her whip still. Daphne, on the other hand, looks a little reddish herself.

And then it clicks. She's going to be with Abigail all alone, except for you, and she wants to do mating things with Abigail. How very mortal of her. This must be the dating thing you have heard about.

You, of course, will help.

"Okay, let's go to the bookstore," you say as you reach up and grab both Daphne and Abigail by the hands and start dragging them along behind you.

Initially you weren't too sure about the idea of Abigail doing nasty mortal stuff with another mortal, but if you had to choose, Daphne would be at the top of that list. Daphne has a lot of money to buy food for any small Abigails that are made in the mating process (which you're still not sure about, mechanically) and she would go very far to protect Abigail. She could be the royal consort once Abigail is God-Empress of mortal kind.

Which reminds you...

If you're going to get all the mortals to treat Abigail the way they should (that is, with lots of bowing and giving her plenty of stuff) then you'll need to teach them about how great Abigail is.

You spawn another you (with no tentacles because you're keeping a low profile) just around the corner in an alley between two buildings. This you looks around for a bit, then starts wandering towards Abigail until you remind yourself that you're there for something else.

You, that is, the you in the alley, pat-pats the ground a bit, and then you build a small altar out of rocks that you push out of the earth. Some of the rocks deep, deep down are very shiny, so you use those to make a small statue of Abigail smiling, her hair all spread out behind her like billowing tentacles and with a big pair of glasses perched on her little button nose. Then you write some simple instructions in a True Tongue onto the altar.

Very easy! Now, when the conditions are right and/or you're a bit peckish, the altar will appear and anyone that sees it will be able to read and understand that they should put yummy food on the stone slab.

But you'll need some sort of activation thing to tell you when they're done…

You add to the statue of Abigail, giving it a bust and some arms that are raised as if to give a hug, then you add hinges that allow the arm to turn and be lowered. Two more statues appear on either end of the altar that look like you, but smaller.

Now, when they're done putting food on the altar to Abigail they just need to lower the arms so that they're patting the statues of you and you'll know that it's time for a snack.

You guess you can give the people that do that for you something. Maybe some knowledge or some gold or a pet from the void. It doesn't matter. What matters is that they'll know that Abigail is good and that they should give her, and you, all of their stuff.

You really are the best familiar.

The three of you, that is, you and Daphne and Abigail, arrive at the bookstore and slip into it to find a few shelves with some nice-smelling books and an old man snoozing behind a counter. "I'll leave you to your mating ritual," you tell the girls. "I'll be looking at the books on foods I want to try."

Abigail sputters a bit and Daphne does the thing where she makes her face go red. "Wh-what mating rituals?" Abigail asks.

You blink at her. "Aren't you two doing that together?" you ask. "You know, the thing mortals do before mating. Dating and stuff?"

You're never going to admit that you don't actually know exactly how mortals mate. It's beneath you.

Instead, you wander off while Daphne explains that today is not a date (which is silly, there's a calendar on the wall and there's quite obviously a date for today on it) and go check out the food books.

You wonder if you can read anything while riding Wuffles back home. And what kind of convincing Wuffles will need to let you ride her back home.

By the time you and your friends are riding into the gates of Five Peaks the sky is putting on its night time colours and you know that sleep time is coming soon, you can feel it.

The guards at the gate barely poke at the wagons and all the books and shiny loot you're bringing back, not after Skinner shows the guard captain some papers. Your entire group enters Five Peaks with barely a squeak.

"Are we going to bed after?" you ask Abigail. You, Abigail, Daphne and Charlotte all took over the same wagon on the way back so that you could snuggle up against the colder evening air. It's nice and it means that you only need to look up to see Abigail's reaction.

"I think so?" Abigail says. She looks to the others for confirmation.

"No, no," Charlotte says. "We just finished our first adventure together. We should be celebrating."

"Celebrating how?" Daphne asks. She's snuggling against Abigail's other side and you almost think she's enjoying it more than you are.

Charlotte makes a wavy gesture in the air that could mean anything. "You know, go out to eat. Stop by an inn to share some stories and a few drinks."

"I'd rather go to any establishment that doesn't call itself an inn," Daphne says. "There is a nice restaurant a block or two from the Academy. I've enjoyed their service before and they have small private rooms for discerning customers."

You can tell that Charlotte is doing the eye-roll thing, but she isn't saying no. "That sounds nice," Abigail says. "We can use the money we made from those quests!"

"And the marks we looted from the bandits," Charlotte adds.

Soon enough, the wagons bump and rattle all the way to the Academy's front gates and Skinner and the mortals he hired to care for the wagons hop off. The young man moves over to your group of friends, Sigmund draped over his shoulders. "I suspect that that is that for this adventure," he says. "I'd appreciate it if you could stop by the library tomorrow afternoon. We… have things to talk about."

Daphne tenses a little and stands up tall before her seat. "We will do just that," she says. "In the meantime, these last few days have been taxing, I think we're all going to call it a night."

Abigail hops off the wagon and then makes grabby gestures at you. When you come close and prepare for a strange hug, she instead grabs you under the arms and places you on the ground.

"Very well," Skinner says. "I'll see you tomorrow then. Have a good evening, ladies," he says before backing up.

"Bye mortal!" you call out to him politely while Daphne leads the group away.

You walk along down the block, as a small group with Daphne at the head and the rest of you trailing behind like those ducks that you sometimes find in the void. That is, until Daphne stops before a pretty building covered in climbing vines and lit from within by a bunch of candles. There's a small patio that goes around it with couples sitting at tables and enjoying food that smells great.

Daphne waves to a man in a vest by the door. "Are there any private rooms left?" she asks.

"Indeed, ma'am," he says. "Does the lady wish to use one?"

"I would, yes," she says. "Seats for four."

You're all ushered into the pretty building so fast that you hardly get to look at the paintings on the walls or into the vases on marble plinths before you're climbing up a staircase. Then it's into a room that's a bit bigger than your home with Abigail, the only furniture, the table and chairs in the middle and a bench next to a bay window overlooking the streets below.

Four menus are placed on the table by a waitress lady who then scurries off with instructions to ring the bell in the middle of the table when she's wanted.

She's the person bringing food, which means… but then Abigail takes the bell out of your hand and places it at the far end of the table without even looking.

"So, before our drinks arrive," Daphne says. "Should we pick what to toast to?"

"To loot?" Charlotte asks.

Daphne throws a napkin at her which makes them both giggle a moment later.

"Ah, I think we should toast to a weekend spent with good friends," Abigail says.

"And to somehow convince Dreamer not to eat the world like one of those gods in the old stories?" Charlotte asks.

You harrumph. You would never eat the world. Abigail lives on it, and it's been nice so far. The moon, on the other hand… "I'm not a god," you pout.

"Aren't you?" Daphne asks. "I'm not well versed in the myths that existed before the Inquisition came around and swept everything away, but your actions so far…"

"Nuh-huh," you say with a shake of the head. "Gods are little things that bumble around and come from things like mortal imaginations and stuff. They're merely conceptual and can usually only do stuff that has to do with their own… stuff." you frown. The mortal tongue has too many words for some things and none for others. "Like, a time god can only do things with time. Make it go faster, stop, go backwards and stuff like that. It's weak."

"Weak," Abigail says. She sounds a little faint. Maybe she needs to go to sleep sooner.

"Yeah," you say, happy that your friends are so clever. "The bigger gods are better. There's more to chew on."

The door opens and the waitress returns with a tray that has a bottle and some glasses on it next to a pitcher of water.

You only get water, but the others, especially Daphne, fill up their cups to the brim with strange smelling juice. "A toast then, to…" Daphne pauses, then shrugs one shoulder. "To many more drinks to come."

"Aye," The others say before drinking.

You do the same, but all you get is water. Oh well, you have good company to make up for it.

The waitress brings two more bottles before the main course is even served. There's only one left now and it's halfway empty.

You watch Daphne while your fork twirls around and around in a plate full of long stringy noodles (they're like teeny tiny tentacles!) sometimes the twirling noodles grab onto a lump of tomato-covered meat and you like to imagine that the meatballs are tiny planets and that the noodles are some of your many tentacles. Then you plop the whole thing in your mouth and get to slurp in the noodles that stick out.

It's fun food!

Daphne is making it even better.

"I," she begins while pointing a finger at Abigail. "I think that you, you Abigail, are very cute."

Her words are coming out a little slurred and you're beginning to suspect that there's a reason Abigail didn't want you to drink the juice they're drinking.

"Thanks," Abigail says. She's a little wobbly too, with flushed red cheeks and a big smile on. "But you're beautiful. It's not fair being so pretty."

Daphne waves her hands as if in denial and you think that maybe she forgot that she's holding a cup. "No no, see, beauty isn't everything Abi. There are like, a lot of girls that are just so, so pretty. Look at Charlotte. Actually, no, don't look at her. She's too pretty, it's not fair. But you Abi, you're cute, and that's good enough because you've got such nice, nice." Daphne made more gestures. "Traits."

Abigail's cheeks are both very red now, and so are Daphne's. You're not sure what's going on, so you go back to eating your noodles.

Abigail reaches for the bottle in the middle of the table and instead of grabbing it tips it over. It almost crashes into your plate, but thanks to your quick tentacular action you catch it and set it straight.

"Oh, thank you Dreamer," Abigail says. "I'm a little... a little into my cups, I think."

"You're not the only one that thinks so," Charlotte says. She's already done eating and is sitting back, a half full cup in one hand that she's slowly swirling around, the juice twisting in circles within. Unlike the others she seems perfectly normal.

"Maybe a little," Abigail says. She leans to the side and hugs you close. You can't eat like this, so you let go of your fork and nestle into her arms. Also, you wipe your face on her sleeve. "I have the best, best familiar," Abigail says. "I wasn't sure at first, and I was scared, but you're the best Dreamer. So, so nice."

Abigail keeps hugging you, and you shift to the side to make the hug even better.

Then she starts snoring and you feel some wetness slipping into your hair as she drools all over you.

This is wonderful!

You carefully help Abigail sit back up, then lean her down with a few tentacles so that she's resting on your fluffiest tentacles with her head down on the table.

"Shh," Daphne says. "Abi's sleeping."

"Yes," you say.

Now that she's sleeping… you reach over and grab the bottle of juice the girls have been drinking from and give it a sniff. It smells fruity and kind of tangy.

"Oh, I can't imagine this ending well," Charlotte says. She raises her cup to you. "Enjoy."

You shake your head. "I can't drink this. Abigail told me not to," you say before replacing the bottle in the centre of the table. A teeny tiny tentacle slips in and pokes at it, then it touches your cup full of water and turns it into the same stuff.

"I think that might be cheating," Charlotte says.

You roll your eyes. There's no such thing as cheating. Not when it comes to hugs, eating or tentacles.

"Oh, let her have a bit," Daphne says. "It'll loosen her up."

"I'm plenty loose," you say. Tentacles need to be wiggly to work. You ignore Daphne's sudden bout of giggling laughter as you pick up the cup and take a big gulp. It's okay, you guess. Not as good as some other things you've tried. The acids at home tasted better, more of a tingle to them than this has.

Still, you finish your cup, refill it with water, and turn that into more juice. You want to be like your friends.

"I can't wait to tell Abigail in the morning," Charlotte says as she takes the bottle and refills her cup. "To Dreamer! For being herself and not eating us," she raises her cup in the air.

You've seen them do this before and get to your feet so that you can clink your cup against theirs. "And to Abigail," you say. "For inviting me to your planet so that I could taste all the stuff on it and make a bunch of friends."

"To Abigail!" Daphne cheers.

Abigail raises her head and looks around. "Wha?" she asked.

"It's okay," you tell her before gulping down your second cup. "You can go back to napping now." You pat-pat her head. It's not nearly as nice as being the way getting the headpats, but there's a certain satisfaction to being the patter.

"We should get her home," Charlotte says.

"She… she can sleep at my place," Daphne says.

Charlotte eyes her, then shakes her head. "I think Abigail should go to her own home tonight. You too Daphne. Do try to remember to drink some water, we have classes tomorrow morning."

"But I don't wanna," Daphne says.

"Abigail will be there…"

Daphne pouts. "Fine."

Grinning, you begin to move things around so that picking up Abigail will be easier. It's time to go home and to bed.

Abigail needed help getting up the steps, and even more help opening the door to your home. You're a little worried when she flops onto the bed and goes right to sleep without so much as taking off her dirty travel clothes, so you do the nice and responsible thing and undress her and find a sleeping gown in her things for her to wear while sleeping (sleeping gowns are a kind of clothing you very much agree with).

And then you watch Abigail as she snores, a bit of droop slipping out of the corner of her mouth.

She's extra cute while she's napping, but just in case, you push some happy dreams into her mind. And then it's your turn to go to bed… but you're not sure if you feel like it.

Oh, you're always ready for a nap, but your small body is all excited and wants to move, not sleep.

So you come to a simple solution! You'll go around and take a walk. Stretch your tentacles a little, maybe find some nice night-time snacks.

But that would leave Abigail all alone, which is unacceptable.

Two new Dreamers spawn from the abyss in a flurry of flappy-flappy tentacles. You face yourselves and waggle your fingers at you. "Okay. So you and you, you're going to sleep with Abigail."

Both of you look very excited at this.

"No funny business, and while tentacle hugging and tentacle cuddling is okay, Abigail doesn't want anything more than that, okay?" you say.

You both nod, ten there's a mad scramble to get onto the bed and as close to Abigail as possible. Abigail is a very lucky summoner because she's getting hugged from two directions, she even sighs and cuddles closer.

That done, you pat down your pretty dress to make sure it's clean then head out of the door.

The city of Five Peaks stretches out before you as you use a couple of tentacles to fling yourself into the roof. It's quite pretty at night, with the flicking of candles in a thousand windows appearing like blinking eyes in the dark. It's become a sort of home for you, you guess.

You contemplate improving the city while you walk across the rooftops, occasionally using a tentacle bridge to cross the gaps between homes and shops. Eventually you reach the end of the road and the gap between homes is a lot bigger because there's a sort of square around a large fountain. There are stalls all around the area, but they're closed at this hour.

This is your first time in this corner of the city. Most of the time you and Abigail head out the other way, towards the Academy and Daphne's house.

You walk off the edge of the roof and crash into the ground feet-first, knees bending into a courtesy like Daphne does when introducing herself.

There isn't too much to do in the city when everything is closed down, you realize. All the little mortals are asleep, and you can feel plenty of them dipping their toes into the land of dreams. It's kind of nice, like a sort of compliment, you figure.

Skipping ahead (because when you skip your dress floofs and it's the best) you move over to the fountain in the middle of the square and look within. It's just normal water, but it smells a little ickly and it's probably not very good for drinking. At least, not for mortals.

The fountain has a bunch of water spouts hidden in the mouths of monsters and for some reason babies, and above it all are statues of a man and a woman with crowns on their heads. The man has a sword above his head, and the woman is holding a scroll. There's a plaque at the base of the fountain with some words about 'doubting and therefore knowing.'

Very boring.

You want more of that fruity juice that you drank at the restaurant with your friends, so you turn the fountain into a fruit fountain.

Juice gurgles out of the little baby faces and the weird monsters carved into the stone. But soon it turns back into water.

You frown at it.

The water has to come from somewhere. Most things in mortal places come from somewhere.

You frown extra-hard at the fountain and now all the water coming out of it is juice, all the way down to wherever the water used to come from. Then, because you find the monsters and babies ugly, you make them look more like you.

The guy with the sword can become…Charlotte, and the lady can become Daphne. More or less. It's tricky to work with stone.

Then you replace the sword with a whip and the scroll with a tentacle. And the plaque with the date and stuff now says 'Dreamer was here' but in a True Tongue.

Art is fun!

You drink lots and lots of juice, until your little tummy is aching with pleasure, then you waddle off. You're a bit more tired now, more than ready for naptime.

As you walk back towards home and Abigail, you cross over a nice little river that smells like grapes and then you splash into a few purple puddles alongside the road.

You can't wait for tomorrow when everyone discovers your art. They're going to be so proud!

CHAPTER TWENTY

YOU DON'T want to wake up. Waking up in the morning is just not the way things are meant to be. Everyone, mortal or otherwise, should get used to the idea that the perfect time to wake up is somewhere around night time. That way you can hop out of bed, eat a bunch, then jump right back in.

But no, mortals are all busy bodies that want to do stuff right away because they know that they might die at any moment. Even Abigail, who will never die because dying is for other people, is up at the crack of dawn and shaking your shoulder for you to get up.

You consider pushing the sun away. Or maybe spinning the planet in the other direction to make the night last longer, but Abigail would get all huffy and you're pretty sure you already considered and dismissed that plan once before.

"Okay, okay," you mutter and you push the blankets covering you away. Abigail is standing on the side of the bed. She managed to escape your cuddles at some point and even had time to get dressed.

Was she trying to give you as much sleep time as possible?

This is why Abigail is the best Summoner.

She raises a hand, and presents a clear glass cup to you filled with sloshing juice. "Explain," she says.

"Juice?"

"No. Wine," she says. "Wine that I got from the tap when I went to get some water."

"Okay," you say.

She makes a little spinny gesture with her hand that means 'get on with it' in mortal. "Well, how did this happen?"

Sitting up on the side of the bed you rub your eyes to get rid of the eye crud you accumulated (one of the best parts of the morning!) and then yawn really big. "Oh, I think that comes from my art project."

"Your art project?" Abigail asks. "I'm... too hungover to deal with that."

"But it's really pretty," you say.

Abigail looks at you for a bit, then takes a long swallow from her cup. "Go on."

"I found an ugly fountain down the road," you say while pointing a tentacle more or less in the right direction. "It was very ugly."

"You mean the statue of the king and queen of Five Peaks? The one with the fountain?"

You shrug. "The ugly one. I made it better. Now there's a Daphne and a Charlotte and they look really cool. And also there's my face and I replaced all the water with juice."

"All the water?" Abigail asks.

"All the water going to the fountain," you say.

"Which is fed by either the river or the city reservoir. Brilliant."

"It isn't brilliant. I didn't think of making it glow, but I can change that."

"Please don't," Abigail says. She looks around, then with a shrug of her own finishes her cup. "We should head out."

"Breakfast?" You wonder.

"I have some change, we can pick something from a street vendor. If they're not too drunk."

You hop off the bed and are dressed so fast that even time doesn't know when you went from wearing nothing but a nightgown to one of your pretty dresses. "Let's go!"

Upon stepping out onto the street, you notice that things are a bit different in Five Peaks this morning. There are a whole lot more people on the roads, and a lot of them seem to be in a very good mood. There are wagons rolling past with barrels behind them and people are singing and dancing, though they don't seem to be very good at it.

Abigail, who knows where all the best foods are, leads you to another street that you never visited. This one is much wider, and the sides of the street are lined with carts and stands where people that smell like those cows you saw once are crying out the prices of the stuff on their tables.

Abigail doesn't even pause as she passes all of them by and walks in a straight line towards a stand where an older, matronly woman is stroking some coals over which some sticks with yummy-smelling meat are roasting. Every time a glob of fat rolls off the meat, it falls into the coals with a satisfying sizzle.

Abigail waves to the woman and gestures with her hands while she speaks. "One for me, two for Dreamer here," she says.

"Coming right up, dearies."

You watch the woman work with rapt attention for a bit, but soon you find that you need to distract yourself or else a tentacle might accidentally slip over to grab one of the meat sticks.

Your art last night was a lot of fun. Maybe you should consider adding more art. Like shrines and altars around the school so that the students can bring you nice things. And in exchange you'll reward them with a good night's rest and pretty dreams filled with fun things and tentacles.

It'll be like having a business. You'll trade your services to the mortals in exchange for goods. Mortals do that a lot. You follow Abigail's motions as she pays the woman with some papery bills, then she hands you two meat sticks.

Yes, this day will be a very productive one!

"Is it good?" Abigail asks as you both start walking back in the general direction of the Academy.

You need to chew a bunch before you can answer because you stuck an entire stick in your mouth and the long wooden bit is pushing against your cheeks when you try to chomp on the meat. A bit of tricksiness with your mouth-tentacle and it all goes down. "Yes!" you declare.

"Good, glad you like it," Abigail says. "Now let's go find out how Daphne is handling her morning."

"She was very strange last night," you say.

"Oh, I have no doubt," Abigail says.

As you nibble on your second meat stick and eye the remains of Abigail's you contemplate just how productive you should be now that the day has begun.

"Abigail," you ask as you're walking over to the Academy. You're almost by the main gate already, and you can see a bunch of students all over, some of them walking in really silly ways, others laughing as they drink from big mugs. The party made it all the way here.

"Hrm?" Abigail says.

That's one of those not-quite-a-words that means 'yeah, go on' in mortal. "Is there a word for when a bunch of mortals all start doing things to help one person?"

Abigail frowns a bit and seems to think about it. "That depends, how are they helping?"

"By doing things like sacrificing stuff, and they do that thing where they worship that person because they're the best, and they listen really hard to what they say?"

"I... Dreamer, I think you're describing a cult," Abigail says.

It's your turn to frown. "What are cults?"

"They're when a lot of people start to follow one person, really fanatically. They usually have their own beliefs and such, and can be a little crazy." She's eyeing you now. "Why are you asking?"

"Just needed to know the name of something," you say.

So... you're going to start a cult. It's good to know what it's called, that way the future members won't be confused.

"Dreamer," Abigail says and you snap your head back to look at her. "What are you thinking about?"

"I'm thinking about all sorts of stuff, but mostly I think I'm going to stay with the familiars today. I'm still sleepy."

"Ah, okay," she says with a nod and a relieved sigh. You don't know what she's relieved about, but she does give you a head pat so it's okay either way.

There's a bit of hustle and bustle by the school entrance, with some teacher telling the students that they can't come in if they're inebriated, but they're overruled by someone that looks like they took a bath in your fountain.

And then it's off to class!

You're not sure which class Abigail has this morning, but it sounds like one of the boring ones.

It doesn't matter!

You stand in the familiar babysitting room, hands on your hips and eyes roving across a sea... or well, about twenty, familiars. There are cats and mice and something that looks like a small dragon, and they're all looking at you.

"Okay," you begin. "So, we're gonna start a cult. It's gonna be really great. All you need to do is be nice to Abigail, and put some of your food on her shrine. Even if it's animal food."

The familiars eye each other, and you can tell that some of them aren't convinced. It makes sense, after all, you would have a hard time just parting with your food unless it was for a good cause... or a great cause. You need to convince them even more!

"You get stuff for being in the cult," you say. "The person who leads the cult gets... uh, headpats. And the others will get the satisfaction of knowing that Abigail is happy, which is really nice and makes your tummy feel warm. Also, people don't think you're important, because you're all just familiars, but that's not true. You can be important, by bringing food to the Abigail shrines for m— for her to eat later."

They still don't look convinced.

You hum like Abigail does and tap your chin as you ponder how to convince all the familiars to join your cult. How did those hokey religions do it?

There was this thing about making all the people that aren't a member look bad, and then... group activities? Singing? Who knew starting a cult was so much work.

"Okay, so, you like your masters, right?" you ask.

The familiars all seem to agree that their masters are pretty swell.

"Well, your masters are all gonna die from being mortal, right?"

There's a lot of unease at the idea, and you can sympathize, Abigail was totally able to die before you came around. Now she's not allowed. If one of those conceptual death gods tries something you're going to have words.

"Right, so if you give stuff to the Abigail shrines, then, if you give enough, I'll maybe make it so that your masters don't die. And I can give them other things, like tentacle bits to make them better." Charlotte seemed to love her tentacle whip, so maybe others would too?

The animals now seem a whole lot keener on the idea of joining.

Now you need to find a common enemy. That one's easy.

"Now, since you've joined the Abigail is Cool Cult, you're basically enemies of the Inquisition. They're really mean, and they don't like you. And if they find out that you're in the cult they'll be extra mean to you and your summoners. So we all have to silently agree that we don't like them."

There, that ought to work.

With a satisfied nod, you use some tentacles on the surface of the planet's moon to carve out a nice big shrine to Abigail, then you teleport it over to the corner of the room. "Please put some of your yummy, yummy food on there, please," you say.

As the familiars shuffle about, you consider just how awesome you are and whether having a big throne for yourself would be over the top or not.

Either way, Abigail is going to be so proud!

But you can't tell her right away. The familiars still need to practice chanting her name in low humming tones at night. That's an important part of the aesthetic.

"Hey girls, hey Dreamer," Charlotte says as she meets you and Abigail and Daphne in the corridor. Class finished some minutes ago, so you got to drop all of your culty activities for a few minutes and rejoin Abigail.

She had asked you how things went, and when you told her that you had done good and then taken a nap she was so proud that she gave you a pat. Doing good things really did give good rewards!

"You're excited to see us," Daphne says to Charlotte.

The taller girl shrugs, her smile still firmly in place. "You know what they say. Distance makes the heart grow fonder."

You blink at this and try to process it. Does being far from something actually make that thing better? No, of course not. She must mean that being separated from something for some time makes rejoining it much better. That kind of makes sense.

Abigail has been going on about something called the 'Scientific Method' whereby any new idea needs to be tested, even if it makes sense; and this idea is easily testable.

Over on your real body, you spawn a tiny you in a pretty dress. This new you looks around and stares for a bit before looking at your real body. "What was I made for?" you ask.

"You're going to get pats from Abigail."

"Aww, yeah! Pats!" The new you says.

"But first, I'm going to throw you as far away as I can, so you'll only get the pats in a few thousand years." Your big body says.

The new you slumps. "But I want the pats now."

"Yes. But this way we'll see if pats gotten after being distant are better."

"Oh," the new you says a moment before being flung out into the wider galaxy at a speed that makes light look lazy and slow.

"Dreamer?"

You blink your small body's eyes (the one with Abigail and the girls, not the one screaming in happiness as it crashes through a sun two solar systems away) and refocus on the world around you. Abigail and the others have moved over to the cafeteria and are all gathering around a table near the back. "Yes?" I ask.

"We didn't bring lunch," Abigail says. "I'm going to get something. Is there anything in particular you want?"

You look over the throngs of students and towards the line where some older lady is handing out trays with plates full of food. "Lots," you say.

Abigail sighs. "Of course. Stay with Daphne and Charlotte, okay? Daphne's in charge while I'm gone."

"Quite the vote of confidence there," Charlotte says before snorting. "Go on, we'll keep an eye on your little monster."

Abigail nods and walks off to get food.

Usually you'd be saddened by the development, but this is an opportunity! Carefully shifting your floofy skirts so that they're placed just right, you sit down on the wooden bench to one side of the cafeteria table and look at your friends.

"So," you begin. Both of them look at you, Charlotte with a grin and Daphne as if you're about to steal her lunch. "I started a cult this morning. It's really cool. Do you wanna join?"

Charlotte laughs and Daphne places her hands over her face. "You're kidding, right?" Daphne asks.

"No. I started a cult about Abigail being cool."

"Did you get any members in your little cult?" Charlotte asks as she opens up her purse and pulls out some paper-wrapped food. Mostly sandwiches, but also a screw-top bottle filled with what you suspect is the juice you made the night before.

"Yes. All the familiars I could find. They'll bring food sacrifices to the altars I'm putting up around the academy and the city."

Daphne makes a weird strangled noise. "You…"

"Yes?"

"Do you have any idea how illegal cults are?"

"No. Do you want to join?"

"No!" Daphne says.

Charlotte shakes her head. "C'mon Daphne, think about it for a moment. If you're not going to join, then who's going to lead Dreamer's little cult?"

"I will," you say. That part was obvious, wasn't it?

Charlotte points at you with a triangular-cut sandwich. "See. If you leave Dreamer to her own devices, who knows what she'll do with her little cult."

"It's Abigail's cult, actually," you say.

"Does… does Abi know about this?" Daphne asks.

"No, not yet. I want it to be big and cool before she learns about it."

"A fait accompli," Charlotte says. She chomps on her sandwich, chews a bit, then swallows. "What do I get if I join?"

"Um," you say. "Well, I was gonna make it so that we all get a meeting at night while sleeping, which is always fun. But you're Abigail's friends, so you should get more than just that… what sorts of things do cults give members?" you ask Daphne. She seems to know a lot about this sort of thing.

"I think cults are more about taking from their members than giving," Daphne says. "This is a terrible idea. The Inquisition will be all over your little cult."

You frown. "If they bother Abigail I'll tentacle them."

"I don't know, it sounds kind of fun. Could the cult organize picnics and little outings?" Charlotte asks.

You're so glad that you're telling your friends. They already have such good ideas. "We can do that, yes."

"You should have better rewards for people that give more, or who are closer to Abigail. Like cool toys like the whip you gave me for some people, and maybe more power. Can you manage immortality or something like it?"

"Charlotte!" Daphne gasps.

"Yeah, sure," you say. "That's easy enough."

Charlotte grins over to Daphne. "See. Now you get to spend forever with your Abigail."

You blink. That was wrong, Abigail isn't Daphne's, she's Abigail's.

Daphne sputters a bit, her cheeks going very red. "F-fine. There should be at least one mature person at the top of this organization and I seem to be the only one to fit the bill here."

"What bill?" Abigail asks. She's carrying two trays balanced against her hips. This is why she needs tentacles, so that she can carry more food.

"Nevermind that," Daphne says. "There's a meeting of the gardening club this afternoon, I was… did you want to come?"

Abigail spends the time you eat sputtering and blushing and being very strange, but it's okay because that means you get more leftovers.

"I don't get why you're coming," you say to Charlotte.

Daphne and Abigail are walking up ahead. It's very strange, because they're walking next to each other, and sometimes their shoulders bump and that makes their faces go red. And one time Daphne took Abigail's hand and pulled her out of the way of some rude boys who were running down the middle of the corridor and they both walked with a bit of a wobble after that.

Very strange.

"Oh, Dreamer, I don't think you can begin to imagine how entertaining it is to watch those two," Charlotte says. "I actually know some of the girls at the gardening club, you know? I have money riding on this."

How does money ride on something?

Whatever, it's probably another one of those mortal things. They put a lot of importance on their whole money stuff that you just don't get.

"By the way, how's Pou-tine?" you ask.

Charlotte makes a wishy-washy gesture. "He's doing okay. There's almost always at least one girl staying by the dorm, so there's always someone to watch over him. He's become something of a little mascot. Not sure if he really likes it or not, but no one has done worse than pinch his cheeks."

They pinch his cheeks? The poor thing. You might just have to run another rescue to save him from that kind of horror. Still… if Charlotte says that he's okay then it can't be that bad.

"A lot of the older boys are jealous," Charlotte says with a growing smile. "They come over to try and woo one of the girls and find this little twerp being cuddled and hugged by every woman in the dorm."

"Why don't they get the same thing?" you wonder.

"They're not nearly as cute," Charlotte explains. Cute? You expression must tell Charlotte something because she explained a little. "That's when… humans find something worth protecting. You know, small and innocent."

Ah, then you must be the opposite of cute. You are large and you're pretty sure you ate an innocent once. "Is Abigail cute?" you ask.

"Hrm," Charlotte says. "I think so? She has that bookish girl-next-door look going on. Bit gangly, and her big glasses certainly give her a look. We should ask an expert on all things Abigail."

"An expert?" There are Abigail experts? Wait, of course there are!

"Someone that spends a lot of time gazing at Little Abi. Like, say, Daphne, for example." Charlotte says.

Ah, of course. You walk a little faster so that you've caught up with Abigail and Daphne. It's okay to ask them questions because both of them are being very quiet. "Hey, Daphne, is Abigail cute?"

Daphne's face does the reddening thing again and her mouth makes squeaky noises.

You turn to Abigail. "What does that mean?"

Now Abigail is being all fussy. "I, I don't know?" Abigail says. "But I don't think I'm cute, or anything. There are other women out there who are far more attractive. Like, um, Charlotte is very pretty."

"I am rather pretty, thank you for noticing," Charlotte agrees. "But we were talking about your cuteness. That's an entirely different metric."

"Is it? I don't think I fit in either one," Abigail says.

"That's not true," Daphne says. "You're very attractive. Perhaps not traditionally so, but to some people, myself included, your type of… attractiveness is, ah… I don't know where I'm going with this."

"Hrm," you hrm. "Maybe if you tell us what makes Abigail cute."

"Ah," Daphne says. She looks up, stares at you, then at Charlotte, then it looks like she's trying to look towards Abigail, but she fails. "W-well. Um. It's not just the whole picture? It's little things. The way she fiddles with her glasses, the way she always makes sure all of her notes and things are neat and orderly. The way she gets flustered and excited when she starts talking about all of her dreams."

"Oh," you say. And here you thought cuteness was some sort of physical thing. Truly, it's a subject with a lot more depth than you had originally suspected. "So, Abigail's cuteness has nothing to do with how good she is at patting and snuggling and cuddles?"

"I'm certain that some of those things factor in," Charlotte says. "Right Daphne?"

Daphne's mouth shuts with a click. She huffs. "I refuse to be baited this way."

Charlotte laughs, and soon Abigail joins in with a bit of giggling of her own. It sounds as if she's letting off some tension, though you don't know where the tension is supposed to come from.

Abigail opens up a door that leads outside and soon you're walking across a path, the sun beaming bright and warm down on your head. It's much nicer outside, with plenty of flowers making the air taste yum, and there are bees buzzing by that you can snap up as a passing snack.

Then you arrive near the Gardening Club's greenhouse and your group is greeted at the door by that president of the club lady whose name is so unimportant that you forgot all about it.

"Hello, Amara," Daphne says.

"Daphne," the president says. She smiles and then looks between Daphne and Abigail and back. "It's a pleasure to see you again. Especially with such distinguished guests." Then her eyes land on Charlotte and she makes a weird purring noise that you're pretty sure humans don't normally make. "You'll find that this is the season where a lot of pretty flowers are in full bloom."

"Do they taste better that way?" you asked.

The Amara lady blinks, then laughs. "I think some of our members certainly think so. Come on in, we have tea and biscuits."

CHAPTER TWENTY-ONE

YOU ARE confused.
Very confused.

The moment Daphne and Abigail move into the gardening club's greenhouse, they're both yoinked away by a group of girls who all titter and giggle and give each other weird looks while holding their hands over their mouths.

You want to follow them, but the president lady holds you and Charlotte back. "Let those two have their fun," she says. "The shipping girls aren't going to do anything more offensive than wave a fan at themselves and maybe spy on your friends a little."

This explanation does not help. "Yes, but why can't I go with her?" you ask.

"Ah, you mean Miss Abigail?" the president lady asks. "Well, you see... how old are you?"

You have no idea. "Very."

"Right, yes. Well." She shifts. "The shippers are a sort of... sub-club in the gardening club. They're very much inoffensive... most of the time. They just love seeing friends become more than just friends."

"Like me and Abigail are?" You're more than just friends, you're summoner and familiar.

"Oh. Oh my. Ah, maybe?" She snaps open a fan and waves it towards her rapidly reddening face.

"I can't be more than friends with Abigail and Daphne at the same time. That would be wrong," you say while the president tries to cool off even more.

If these mortals can't handle the hotness in their own greenhouse they really shouldn't stay in it.

"How about Dreamer and I go find a place to relax, and I can explain what's going on to her?" Charlotte says.

"Yes, yes that sounds like an excellent idea." The president's fan snaps shut. "Come along, I'll show you to one of our little gathering areas."

You and Charlotte follow after the president lady. Flowers aren't really your kind of thing, but the ones here are still very nice. They make the air smell delicious and they're really colourful. You snatch a couple with a passing tentacle and, after removing your plate and holding it in your hands, start filling it up with your second lunch.

"You can sit over here," the president-lady says before gesturing to a long bench set next to a low table. There are some girls nearby, sitting in two and threes while sipping at tea. A lot of them are doing weird things with their feet under the tables, or are holding each other's hands and have red faces.

So many red faces. There must be some sort of thing with the plants.

"Um, are those our lilies," the president lady asks. She's pointing at your plate.

"Yes," you say. "I like eating things like these."

Charlotte makes a snorting noise. "You like eating lilies, huh?" she asks. "Maybe you'll fit in here better than I would have suspected."

Out comes the president's fan again. "Well. I'll... leave you to it."

You wave her goodbye, take a lily and start munching on it. "So, what's up with Abigail and Daphne. Is this because Daphne thinks that Abigail is cute?"

"It's... something like that. When two people like each other a lot, they start to court. That means spending time with each other, hanging out, learning more about one another and generally growing closer."

"That sounds… acceptable." You think about this. "Yes. I want to court Abigail."

Some of the girls at the nearest tables gasp and start whispering to each other. Did they overhear you? Does it matter?

Charlotte's smile grows. "Then you should tell her as much. Though I think Daphne might be a little… miffed about it."

"I could tentacle Daphne until she doesn't want to court Abigail anymore." You pulled a long tentacle out from under your pretty dress, one of the skinnier ones, and wiggle it around for emphasis.

A lot of the girls go even redder. This place is not healthy, you think.

"That's… one possible solution. But I don't think it would be very nice. If Abigail and Daphne are destined to be together, then that's that. I'm sure there's enough room in Abigail's heart for you and Daphne. And I'm sure you could find some place for Daphne in yours."

"Daphne's okay, I guess. Would you want to join in too? Then there would be four of us."

Now the girls are staring at Charlotte. Charlotte doesn't seem to mind, her smile is still in place. Though she does stand up to take off her school robes, then she ties up her blouse to expose a bit of her tummy before sitting back down.

It really is too hot in here.

"I think I can take care of myself," Charlotte says. "But… apropos Daphne, she might be a hard sell."

Your eyes narrow. "Is it because she only likes cute girls like Abigail?"

"That's part of it."

"I'll just need to become more cute then. And then even Abigail will want more."

"Oh?" Charlotte asks. "And how do you intend to become more cute so that Daphne will join you and Abigail like that?"

You frown, thoughtfully shove some more lilies in your mouth, and think really hard. How does one become more cute? "Charlotte, can you help me be more cute?"

"That depends," she says. "What are your intentions? Cuteness is a weapon that shouldn't be used lightly."

"Hmm. I want to make it so that Abigail likes me even more. And then I can court her because I'm cute too. And then I can do the same with Daphne, I guess... how does courting work?"

"Usually you go on dates, eat at nice restaurants, things like that."

"I'm very good at eating. Yes. Daphne can bring me to nice places, even if that means I need to be cuter."

Charlotte's grin looks very strange, almost like Wuffles when growling. "Oh, I cannot wait to see how that will play out. Do keep me informed though, I can probably help you along, here and there."

You nod. Yes. Help would be nice. These mortal things are all so muddy and complicated.

But they're worth it if it means getting more food and pats.

"Now what do we do?" you ask Charlotte. You've been sitting in the shade of a few little trees, enjoying the way the light wibbles and wobbles across the floor for some time now. You expected Abigail and Daphne to come back, but it seems as if their whole courting thing is taking a lot longer than you had expected.

It's alright. You're very patient.

Super patient.

The mos—

"I wanna do stuff," you say.

Charlotte peeks one eye open and looks at you. She's leaning way back on her bench, arms folded behind her head in a pose that doesn't really look all that comfy. "Oh? What sort of stuff?"

You shrug. "Abigail stuff?"

"Hrm," Charlotte says. "Well... how about you wander over to the other girls in the club and chat with them? They seem nice enough."

You could do that, you decide. You could even catch two birds with one tentacle if you convince them to join Abigail's cult! It's great. "Okay. Bye," you say to Charlotte before bouncing off your bench.

Now, you just need to decide which girls to talk to.

There's one couple under a tree off to the side. One looks very studious and is holding onto a big book and the other looks tough and rough, like she wants to pick a fight with someone. But the rough girl is blushing while the girl with the book reads her some things.

They don't look like they want to meet you, so you look elsewhere.

At a table off to one end are three girls, all sitting on the same side. The girls on either end are hugging the girl in the middle whose face is very, very red. But they're also glaring really hard at each other over the middle girl's head.

You huff and look for someone else to talk with.

That's when you spot the shipping sub-club girls. They're all sitting off to one side, tittering at each other and making weird little noises like those squirrels you sometimes see running next to the roads.

They'll do.

You walk over to the circle of five girls who all quiet down when they see you approaching. "Hi," you say. "I'm Dreamer. I'm bored."

"So, are you Dreamer, or are you Bored?" One of the girls, the tallest in the group asks.

You consider this. "Yes."

They laugh, and one of them pats a free spot on the bench next to her. "Come, sit, sit," she says. There are three little benches arranged in a sort of triangle facing each other. You sit next to the girl with a plop.

"I like your dress," One of the girls says. "It's nice."

"Yes," you agree. It is a very nice dress. "I copied it myself."

The girls make agreeable little noises, then they all share looks. "So, Dreamer," one of them says as she pulls a notebook out from a bag. "Tell us… is there anyone you dream about?"

"I dream every dream," you say.

The girl's nose pinches up. "Ah, I meant more…" She leans forwards and all the other girls do the same. "Is there anyone you're really into?"

"I've been inside many people," you say.

A few of the girls giggle, but notebook-girl just shakes her head. "No no, I mean, is there someone out there that's really special to you? That you think about all the time? Who you'd want to spend the rest of your life with, and if you can't do that, then you're not sure what the point of living even is?"

Now the girls are sighing, but it's a weird sigh.

"Um. Yes. That's how I feel about Abigail," you say.

Notebook girl's eyes widen and she flips her book open to start scribbling something. "Tell us more."

Well, if they insist.

"Abigail is the best. She's fun, and nice, and gives me good pats."

"Pats?" One of the girls asks.

"Physical Attention, Time, and Sensuality," another whispers back.

"Oh. Well I for one wouldn't mind getting patted, if you know what I mean."

You ignore the exchange because it's just mortals being weird.

Notebook girl finishes taking notes and looks up to you again. "So, does this Abigail know how you feel about her?" she asks. That shushes up all the other girls who look at you with bated breath.

"Yeah, of course. I told her a lot... I think. Next time we go to sleep together I'll tell her some more if it makes her feel better."

"Oh. Oh my," Notebook girl says.

Then the tall one takes the notebook out of her hand and goes around smacking all the girls on the head with it one at a time. "Look at her, you morons, she's like... thirteen or so," Tall girl says. She turns to you. "When you say sleep together, you just mean in the same bed, right?"

"Yeah," you say. What else could you mean?

"And Abigail, she's your bigger sister?"

"She's my summoner," you say.

Tall girl looks at the others with a weird look, it's somewhere between smug and annoyed. "See. Get a hold of yourselves."

This whole exchange is a little weird. You're not sure if you want these girls in your Abigail cult. "I'm bored because Abigail is being courted by Daphne and the president lady didn't want me to be there."

"Ah, you poor thing," Tall girl says. "I guess it's normal that your summoner would pay you less attention now that she has a girl-friend."

"Less attention?" you repeat.

The girls nod. "It's normal. New couples are very lovey-dovey with each other."

That doesn't sound good. Not at all.

You think you might just do something about it.

When Abigail finally returns, she finds you sitting by a table, showing the girls of the shipping club just how good you are by eating all of their little tea cookies as quickly as you can while also playing with some cherries.

For some reason, these mortals have a game where they eat a cherry, then tie the stem into a knot.

You are very good at this game because you have lots of little tentacles that you can slip out from around the table to tie all the knots at once, and then you get to eat all of their fruit, which makes this one of the most fun games you've ever played.

"Hey Dreamer," Abigail says. "Ah, hello everyone."

The nice shipping club girls say hello, then they hush up when Daphne comes around the corner and stands right next to Abigail. Daphne is smiling really big, and so, you notice, is Abigail.

"Ah, I guess you girls will nag me if I don't say it," Daphne says. "So, um, yeah, I confessed to Abigail." Daphne looks away from all the sudden gasps.

"And then what?" Notebook girl asks. She's got her book out and is scribbling like mad into it. "Please tell us. We live vicariously through your romantic life."

Abigail reaches out and grabs Daphne's hand. They both go redder. "Ah, I said that I kinda felt the same way," Abigail says.

The shipping club girls gasp, slap hands over their mouths, and one of them falls onto the girl next to her with a sigh. Then there's clapping and giggling and the scritching of notebook girl's pen as she fills out an entire page with notes.

"Congratulations!" Tall girl says.

"Ah, thanks," Daphne says. "We'll have to go on a proper date or two, of course."

"Right," Abigail says. "We'll take things slow. Very slow. As, as slowly as we can."

You stand up, food forgotten for now, and walk up to Abigail. Carefully, because Abigail is made of weak stuff, you take her other hand and pull her after you.

She stutters a question at you, but all you can hear is the thump-a-thump of the little heart in your body and the roil of blood in your ears.

Abigail asks you a few questions, but you pretend not to hear until you're both outside of the green house and around the corner of the nearest school building. There's not much here, just a few large trash bins and a dead-end alley set between two of the buildings.

"Dreamer?" Abigail asks again.

You let go of her head.

"Abigail. I..." you pause and think really hard. "I want you to be my Abigail."

Abigail stares at you for a moment, then she gets down onto her knees so that she's just a little shorter than you.

She pulls you into a hug. "I am yours, Dreamer. Don't be silly," she says.

"But you're with Daphne now," you mumble into her shoulder.

"Yes, I guess I am," Abigail says with a laugh. "But that doesn't mean that I'm not still yours." She pulls back a little to show you her big smile. "You know, Daphne could be yours too?"

You huff. "No. I want you all to myself."

She, being very rude all of a sudden, boops your nose. "Silly. You're so big and strong, and yet so silly."

"I'm not silly," you say.

Abigail nods. "You are. But I love you anyway, okay?"

You pout. It's not nice or fair.

"Tell you what. We can talk to Daphne about it. I'm sure she'll tell you that she wants you to be part of... whatever we become. You're my familiar, there's no setting you aside."

You nod. That's fair. Probably. "I want a quota though."

Abigail blinks behind her big glasses. "A what?"

"A quota. Like, you need to do a certain number of things each day," you explain.

"I... yes, I know what a quota is. But a quota of what?"

"Hugs and headpats and cuddles," you say. "I need a certain amount every day."

Abigail laughs and gives you a pat right then and there. "I'm sure we can negotiate something workable," she says. "What about me? Do I get pats in return?"

You blink.

Have you ever given her a pat?

That… has some interesting possibilities. "Wait, don't move," you say.

Abigail twitches one eyebrow up, but doesn't otherwise move. You reach up with one of your small body's grubby little hands, then, carefully, you bring it down atop Abigail's head.

"Oh," you say.

"Oh?" Abigail repeats.

"Oh," you agree.

The hand rises and falls again. It feels good.

A smile starts to crawl across your face. "This is good," you say.

You look up so that you can meet Daphne in the eyes. The girls—Daphne and Charlotte—stepped out of the Gardening Club's greenhouse some time ago and were looking for you and Abigail when you stepped out of the alley.

"Bend over," you say.

Daphne blinks. "Pardon."

"Bend over or I'll have to use my tentacles," you explain.

Daphne looks over to Abigail who shrugs. "Okay?" Daphne says. She leans forwards a bit. It's not much, but it's enough.

You reach way, way up, splay your little human hand as wide as it'll go, then pat-pat Daphne on the head. You shiver a little. It feels real nice.

Then Abigail pats you on the head. You feel a silly smile tugging at your lips and you let it grow. Being patted while patting is the best. You summon a tentacle from between the places people forget and use it to pat Charlotte on the head. She laughs at the contact.

Patting with a tentacle doesn't have nearly as much of an effect.

This will require further study.

In fact, you're starting to think that this whole headpat business is a lot more complicated than it first seemed. You're pretty sure that cutting off Abigail's hand and patting yourself with it wouldn't do much. It's the fact that it's Abigail that's giving you the pats that make them so good, not the fact that it's Abigail's body.

Giving pats feels good too, but it feels better when you give them to Abigail than to Daphne. And giving pats with tentacles… you bring your tentacle around and pat Daphne's head with it.

Not as nice.

Strange.

You'll need a whole bunch more time spent experimenting with the art of patting. Or maybe it's a strange sort of science.

You are determined to become a patologist.

"Dreamer has discovered the whole 'it's better to give than to receive' concept, I think," Abigail explains to Daphne.

You snort. That's silly. Getting things is way better than giving them. *Morals.* You shake your head.

"So, um, what now?" Abigail asks. She's looking towards Daphne as she says this and is blushing a bit. Is this more courting stuff? Couldn't they do it some other time.

"I think we're going to have to put a pin on any plans," Charlotte says. Her voice isn't happy as she speaks.

You look around, spotting for the first time a large group of men moving towards you, all of them carrying large shields in one arm and little sticks in the other. They're wearing black, with a white 'I' shaped symbol on their shields and big swords strapped to their hips.

"Oh no," Abigail says.

You frown. These people look like those Inquisition sorts you had to deal with to save Pou-tine. You wonder what they want.

More of them show up from the other side of the school building, then even more of them appear on the roofs above and around the corner of the greenhouse. A few of the club girls are shooed back into the building by the inquisitors.

A few of the Inquisitors, those wearing long robes instead of armour, rush behind the lines of shield people and start casting complicated spells into the ground and air. You feel a bit of a tingle crawling around you, and all of a sudden your connection through the immaterial plain is cut.

Weird.

You poke at the barriers they're building with your big body and almost wince as one of them snaps. One of the mage-sorts screams out something and they redouble their efforts.

You hope Abigail won't be mad that you broke someone's thing.

One of the Inquisitors steps up. He's important. You know this because his hat is very tall and ends in a point, with little feathers and some fluff stuck to it and there are tassels around the brim handing down to his shoulder.

It's a very nice hat.

You kind of want it.

"Are you Misses Abigail, Daphne, and Charlotte? Accomplices of the Class C threat currently claiming the name 'Dreamer?'" the man asks.

Abigail's hand tightens around your shoulder. You hear her whisper "Oh no," under her breath.

Charlotte steps to your side. "They have marksmen on the roof. More in the distance. If they fire, we die."

You're frowning extra hard. You don't recall giving anyone permission to hurt your friends.

"What is the meaning of this?" Daphne asks.

"You are all under arrest for the high crimes of heresy against the non-existence of gods, the act of creating a group of worship, and multiple accounts of public disturbance and malfeasance."

"No, no, no," Abigail says.

You shake your head. "The girls didn't start the cult, I did," you say.

The man stiffens. "Don't let the creature talk. It must be disposed of. Are the shields in place?"

"They are!" One of the mages says. "It can't reach through the immaterial anymore. It's harmless."

Harmless? Sure, you can't reach through the one plane, but what about reaching through time?

Tentacles that were definitely there all along don't appear, because they were there already, and they snatch the men on the roof and wrap them up nice and tight.

And what about the imaginary?

Pretendtacles snatch shields away and make them stop existing.

And they didn't even cover the astral, mental, ancient, magical or dream planes. Terribly lazy.

There's a lot of screaming as shadow tentacles suck up some men, as grasping tentacles made of pure divine power slip through the hastily erected shields the mages put up, and some of the inquisitors fall asleep and slip into a realm that's all yours to play around in.

Meta tentacles squiggle away to go read some other story, and tentacles from the impractical plane flop around uselessly.

Then you boop the shields between the immaterial and this plane and they burst apart. Soon, everything is tentacles, as it should be.

Now you have lots of specimens to use in your patological studies.

Also, you have a new hat.

CHAPTER TWENTY-TWO

YOU ADJUST your new hat, then frown as it slowly tilts forwards until the brim covers your eyes. You need to reach up and fix it back into place atop your head, but the moment you do that, the hat will start tipping in another direction again.

If the darned thing wasn't so cool looking you would have thrown it away already. But it is cool looking, so it's worth the occasional need to adjust it.

"Oh, oh no," Abigail says.

For a moment you're worried that she doesn't like your cool new hat. If Abigail doesn't think it's nice, then it must be wrong somehow. As it turns out, she's just looking at all the dead, mostly dead, soon to be dead, and mostly non-existent inquisitors strewn about across the lawn around you.

"Don't worry about those," you say. "They're the ones that I had little accidents with. The others are much better."

The others, of course, being all the inquisitors you took for your tentacle patting experiments next to your real body. It's a chore remembering that they need to breath and such, but you're managing for now. Your experiments in tentacle-based patting are only just beginning, you can't expect them to bear fruit so suddenly.

Meanwhile, you finally get your hat to sit on straight. "How do I look?" you ask.

"Dreamer," Abigail says.

She's speechless. The hat must be working.

Then it slides down a little and you wiggle your arms in distress as the brim covers your eyes again.

Charlotte comes over and tugs the hat off, then she turns it over and fiddles with the straps on the inside. "Here," she says as she pushes it back onto your head.

The fit is perfect! Brilliant!

You skip over to the one of the glass walls of the greenhouse, wave to the wide-eyed girls within, then focus on your reflection. The hat is half as tall as your small body, with a peaked top and a brim covered in feathers and fur and intricate little folds.

You look very regal.

"What are we going to do?" Abigail asks.

You look over, to see that she's hugging Daphne close.

"They, they knew where we were, and now this. They won't stop."

You narrow your eyes. "I'll fix it," you say.

Sure, you're not the one who started it, but you can be, and literally are, the bigger person. You just need to have a chat with the nice inquisition people, tell them to leave Abigail and your friends alone, then Abigail will feel better.

A little better.

Abigail, you're beginning to truly realize, is a very complicated girl. She can love more than just one person, and she worries about all sorts of things. You suppose that it's only fair that the best human would be a little hard to understand.

You amble over to Abigail and pat her hand. "Here, I'm gonna leave you with some small Dreamers while I go take care of things, alright?"

She eyes you. "Take care how?" she asks.

Daphne squeezes her closer, which is just not fair, so you join in the hugging too, your hat leaning against the side of Abigail's face while you bury your face in her chest.

"Maybe we should let Dreamer try?" Daphne says. "Honestly, I can't see them being able to hurt her, and it would be unexpected. We... need to start seeing the Inquisition as an opposing force, I think."

"I don't like it," Abigail says.

"I know," Daphne says right back. "But we'll figure it out, right?"

"Right!" you say. Pulling back, you turn to Charlotte and give her a very stern look. "You look after Abigail, okay?"

"I'll do what I can," Charlotte says. She looks like she's having fun, at least.

"Okay. I'm leaving some of me here just in case."

You open holes into the world and drop some of yourselves out of it, just a half dozen Dreamers in pretty dresses. They look just like you, and are you, but you're wearing your awesome hat and are therefore easy to tell apart.

You see your other yous eyeing the hat with envy and smile smugly at yourself.

"I'll be right back!" you say before the ground rumbles and a big tentacle pokes out of it to grab you by the waist. With a swing and a flick, you're sent flying high into the sky, winds whipping at your pretty dress and cool hat so hard that you need to grab onto them to keep them on. Then, at the apex of your flight, you realize a small problem.

You're not sure which Inquisition people you're meant to talk to.

Shrugging, you grab one of the people next to your main body, the one that had been wearing the biggest hat, and bring him back into the mortal word.

"Hi!" you say to the wide-eyed man falling next to you.

Then you pull out the oxygen tentacle from his mouth. He starts screaming a lot.

Mortals. You roll your eyes. "Do you know where I can find the big boss of the Inquisition?" you ask.

More screaming. You wiggle the airtacle—not to be confused for the tentacles meant for flying—before his face and he stops.

"The boss, where can I find him?" you ask.

More gibbering.

You glare. You won't keep falling forever. A glance at the city way below says that you only have half a minute at most. And while you will no doubt land with grace, this mortal will go splat in a big way. "C'mon, I just need to know who sent you."

"Lord Inquisitor Shooksword! He sent us!"

"Good, good. Where is he?" you ask next.

"The, the conclave?" he tries.

You know where that is. It's the big building with all of the inquisition people in it. Easy.

"Thank you," you say as you recall your manners. You even pat the man on the head, which brings a smile to your face. Being nice to people is nice.

Then you shove the article back into his mouth and flick him back to your main body for further experimentation.

It's time to go meet the big boss and have a chat.

You land gently against the side of a big statue in front of the Inquisition's conclave building. The statue, a big stone man with an impressive hat and ugly robes, cracks and topples to the side a moment before you splat to the ground.

It's okay, your legs are only broken for a little bit before you fix them, so no harm done.

Standing up, you straighten your pretty dress, make sure your cool hat is on straight, and then you walk over to the front doors.

There are a bunch of guard inquisitors gathering at the front of the building, pointing sticks at you and opening scrolls with magical circles on them. "Halt!" One of them says. He must be the leader; he's the one with the most tassels on his shoulders and he's standing before all the rest.

You've already decided that you want to be polite, just like Abigail would want you to be, so you do as he says and stop at the base of the stairs leading into the building. "Hello."

"Identify yourself," the man demands. The other guards start circling around you, still pointing sticks and such.

"I am That Which Dreams Eternal Between Space and Time. The nightmare consumer, the tentacler and Abigail's familiar. Oh, and the leader of the Cult of Abigail." That should be enough to differentiate you from any other people like you they've met.

The guards seem a bit tense. "Right, well you're under arrest."

"But it's not nap time yet," you say. Why do these mortals have to be so confusing?

"What?" the boss guard asks.

"You said it's rest time?"

He shakes his head. "No, you're under arrest. For destruction of public property and, ah, for some other things."

"Will I get to meet Lord Inquisitor Shooksword if you do that? 'Cause that's why I'm here."

"I'm sure he'll deign to visit you in a few days," the guard says.

You're almost ready to agree when the amount of time sinks in. "No. Days is too long. Abigail will get worried and that's bad. Can I meet him now?"

The guards start moving in closer. "I'm afraid not. Please lay down on the ground and place your hands over the small of your back."

You're not doing that. Maybe if you try being polite? "Can I go meet him now… please?"

Instead of being nice and helpful, the guards start getting real handsy with you. You're pretty sure Abigail told you that if a boy you don't know tries to touch you, you can do whatever you want with your tentacles to them.

A bit of flicking and some whipping and a pinch of tossing later, and all the guards are scattered across the front of the Inquisition building. You, of course, took the guard captain's hat before flinging him through the entrance doors.

You add the new hat, which is more of a cap, really, to the top of your cool hat.

Your authority has doubled.

After making sure that your pretty dress isn't stained by any of the bits that flew off the squishier guards, you walk up to the front doors which are conveniently held open by the guard captain's slumped over form.

There's a nice little reception area, with a long wooden desk and a lot of magical lights built into sconces along marble pillars. A row of chairs off to one side has a bunch of people who are waiting around, most of them staring at the guard that you're stepping over.

You probably should wait in line. That would be the polite thing to do.

Humming to yourself (and not even a song of madness. Polite!) you step up to the very back of the line leading up to the wide-eyed secretary and begin to wait.

You're barely waiting more than a minute, watching as some of the people in the chairs move over to poke at the guard captain, that a bunch more Inquisitor types rush into the room.

"It's her!" One of them screams.

He's pointing at you.

That's supposed to be a little rude.

"Everyone back off!" One of them says. He points a stick at you and a ball of fire leaps out of it with a rumbling whoosh. It rushes across the room, screaming on a path straight for you.

You poke a hole in the world and let the fireball slip though.

There's a bit of staring after that. "So, uh," you gesture to where the line was. All the people in front of you have run away. "Does that mean I'm next?"

Your answer is another fireball.

You bat that one aside with a tentacle, then use a few more to grab and hold the guards against the walls. Then they start screaming, which is very rude so you stuff some tentacles in their mouths.

Seeing as how you're the next in line, you move up to the front desk, like a polite mortal wound, and tap the little ring-y bell next to it.

Then you tap it again for good measure.

"I-I'm right h-here," the lady behind the counter says.

"Oh. Yes. You are. I would like to speak with Mister Lord Inquisitor Shooksword… please."

"Do… do you have an appointment?" she asks.

Do you? No, no you don't. "Can I make one?"

She grabs a notepad with shaking hands. "Sure?"

"Okay, good. Tell him that I want to see him. Um. I'm Dreamer, Abigail's familiar. And I want to see him because I ate like… thirty of his people. Maybe more. They're in my body still if he wants them back, I'm practicing tentacle things with them."

The lady looks to the guards pinned against the walls. "Wh-when would be a good time for you?"

"Right now. Please."

"Of course. Do you want to go to the, ah, waiting room on the second floor?"

"No. I want to meet Mister Lord Inquisitor Shooksword." Waiting rooms are for waiting, that's the opposite of what you want to do. Now, if they had a napping room…

"There's… tea and crumpets?"

"There's food? Well, okay then." Being polite really pays!

Your wait for the big Lord guy of the Inquisition is long and boring and you're beginning to think that maybe being polite isn't the best thing ever. After all, the crumpets they had were only okay, and the tea was in a tin instead of those little bite-sized baggies you had at Daphne's place.

The room is nice enough though, all dark red woods, with a bunch of paintings hanging on the walls of landscapes and gardens and such. There's a big table that takes up a chunk of the room. It's got more square tentacles than Abigail's room before you improved it.

You're trying to think up a polite way to go tell the Inquisition to hurry it up, when the door at the far end of the room opens up and a bunch of people slip in. They form a long line at their end of the room.

Most of them are dressed entirely in white, with strange blindfolds on and little sticks in their hands, but their hats are little more than headwraps, so they can't be that important.

The people following them in, though, do look important. One is a big old guy, tall and broad shouldered. You know right away that he's the big boss. He's so important that there's a skinny guy next to him *carrying his hat.*

Crazy.

Also, you want that hat. It's got feathers, little chains, a poof, *and* a big golden medallion at the front. You could change the medallion to have a picture of Abigail on it!

The other guy is dressed in a long coat and has a sword by his hip. You can't quite remember where, but you're pretty sure you saw him before.

And finally there's a skinny woman that looks a few years older than Abigail. She has glasses too, and is wearing white robes and a very pointy bucket-hat.

The important one stands tall at the opposite end of the table as you, across from all the tea tins that you emptied out of the cabinet in the corner. "I am Lord Shooksword of the Inquisition for the protection of humanity. I have been told that you wanted to speak with me."

You nod, then remember that you're supposed to be polite. "Yes. I am Dreamer. And I did want to talk to you," you say.

"You barged in here, disabled the exterior guard and did... unspeakable things to those who tried to apprehend you," he says.

You wait for him to continue, then you wait some more. "Yes," you say at last.

"Is there any reason I shouldn't just try to get rid of you?" he asks.

You nod at this. "Yes. Because you won't even if you tried. It would be a big waste of time. Time I could be spending with Abigail."

"Abigail Normal?" he asks.

Oh, right! You realize that you forgot to tack on your new name after your shorter name. That was quite silly. "Yes. That's my Abigail. She's why I'm here."

"She sent you here?" the guy with the sword asks.

"No," you say. "I came here for her, not because she sent me. See, some guys that wear hats like this." You point to the bottom of your hat stack. "Were very rude to us. And those people are your people. So after getting rid of them I came here because you guys are bothering us and I want you to stop."

You wait for a response, then remember your manners.

"Please," you add.

"I don't think you understand what is happening here," Shooksword says.

"Well you're not explaining, and I'm not caring all that much, so that's pretty normal," you say.

Mister Lord Shooksword tightens a fist by his side and stands even taller. "What did you do to subjugation squad beta?"

"Who?"

"The group we sent to capture and restrain you," he says.

"Oh, then. Some of them I ate," you say. "I took the hat of the biggest, most important one." You point to your hat as evidence. "And the rest I'm using to experiment. They're next to my body."

The woman gasps, a hand pressing up against her face. "What are you doing to them?"

"Mostly patting their heads in different ways to see what happens," you say. Abigail explained the 'scientific method' to you, but it's too much note taking and doing the same thing but different, so you're just trying all sorts of things all the time and you'll see what works best. It's sorta like that.

"We want our men returned," Shooksword said. "And we want you gone."

You blink. "I guess I could give them back," you say. That would be kind of polite, wouldn't it. "And then I'll leave here, and you'll agree to never ever bother me and my friends?"

"We will do no such thing," sword-guy says.

You look at him a bit longer, then it clicks as one of the tentacles moving memories around in your brain accidentally bumps into a metatentacle on the way to grab something else. "Oh, you're that guy from chapter fourteen," you say.

"What?" He asked.

"Submit yourself for cognitive hazard testing afterwards," Shooksword says.

"Yes, my lord."

"Look," you say. "I'm not telling you to do something, I'm telling you to not do something." How can they not understand that not doing things is so much easier than actually doing them?

"Our entire mandate is to protect people," Shooksword says.

"The only people I've been hurting are yours because you won't just let me have fun with Abigail," you say right back.

This man, you decide, is very thick.

The thickness continues when the Mister Lord Shooksword shakes his head and basically says no to you. "You and those like you are a threat to all of humanity. We will curtail you, or die trying."

You thought that you were getting used to mortals and their stupidity. But maybe being around Abigail had ruined it for you.

Sure, Abigail was a bit silly sometimes, she is your silly summoner, after all, but she is so much brighter than all the dumb mortals in this room with you.

Now you need to figure out a way to get this guy and his friends to listen to you instead of talking past the top of your head. You frown as you try to listen to all of them. The lady that looks like a less cool Abigail is talking about dissecting your tentacles for reagents, the sword guy is glaring a lot, and Mister Lord Shooksword is going on and on about some laws and stuff that don't matter.

You look around. The guard sorts near the door are looking just as bored as you feel.

You have the distinct impression that Mister Shooksword isn't taking you very seriously.

It doesn't make sense, you're big and scary and have tentacles. You even have a hat for great authority.

It's not as big as his hat, of course but...

And like a supernova going off in your tummy, a realization burps into your head.

Of course they don't respect you! Mister Lord Shooksword has demonstrated that he thinks he's the best just by showing up with that kind of headwear.

You'll show him!

Tentacles rip out of reality and start moving across the table.

A lot of things happen at once. Sword guy takes out his sword and hacks at one of your tentacles. The scientist lady 'eeps' and falls on her bum, Mister Lord Shooksword starts screaming at you about how what you're doing is against regulations.

Some of the guards start firing spells in your general direction.

You sigh, like Abigail does before she wipes your mouth, and then—with a roll of your eyes to tell them how silly they're being—you have some tentacles eat the spells flung your way, you wrap sword guy in a bunch more tentacles until he stops, and, most important of all, a few of your tentacles grab the hat.

Carefully, so as not to unbalance things, you place your new hat atop the others.

This is a mistake, you realize.

The new hat has a pointy top, but a smaller brim, so it wobbles a lot.

You spend nearly a minute trying to get everything to fit just right while the mortals do whatever, then give up.

The solution comes to you a moment later. What if you put on the newer, bigger hat on the bottom, then the others atop that one?

It works!

You are a genius.

You stand up tall and proud, your hats of great authority fluffing and feathering atop your head with only a few tentacles holding them all in place so that your small body doesn't hurt its neck. You extend a hand across the table and point right at Mister Lord Shooksword. "You listen to me," you say.

He does not listen to you.

In fact, while you were busy with more important things, the Inquisition sorts have been trying all sorts of rude things. They put up barriers between realities, have been poking at your tentacles with all sorts of things and have generally been very poor hosts.

You huff. Now's not the time for that.

Tentacles bat away their attempts to keep you locked up, and when some of those attempts prove a little hard, you remove their very existence, then you eat that existence because wasting food is wrong.

You clap two tentacles together with a noise like the Cannonry Club makes sometimes. "Now, you listen to me," you say before climbing onto the table so that you're extra tall. Your hat is brushing the ceiling, that's how authoritative you are in that moment. "I'm going to talk, and you won't talk because you'll be too busy listening, okay?"

Mister Lord Shooksword jumps to his feet. "Do you have any idea what kind of enemy you are making here, you inhuman monster? And give me my hat back!"

"No. Also, I don't care. The time I'm here with you I'm not with Abigail. I wanted to be nice and polite like Abigail wants, and I tried really hard, but you're all very rude and I think I'll just eat you like I usually do to things that are rude or that annoy me or that look tasty."

Mister Lord Shooksword looks like he's about to say more things, so you sigh and pull out your ultimate weapon.

It's something that Abigail gave you by accident.

Over the last few days, because you're the best familiar, you've been holding all of Abigail's stuff for her. Her bags, her lunch, her spare clothes. And for the most part you only ate a bit of her lunch and then gave her her things when she asked for them.

But one thing she gave you, a thing she stuffed in her purse, you kept a bunch of eyetacles on.

It is a weapon of great destructive power and danger.

The Rolled Newspaper of Bapping.

A tentacle, one that you will cut off and burn later, grabs the newspaper of bapping and brings it into this world.

Mister Lord Shooksword is trembling with anger. "I'll see you executed, you and that summ—"

The Rolled Newspaper of Bapping lands on his head with a great loud whapp.

"Did, did you jus—"

Another whap on his head.

"Stop that!"

"No." You bap him again. "Not until you stop with the talking and start with the apologizing."

Once, Abigail explained to you how mass production worked.

It was very simple.

Mortals, because they were so lame (other than Abigail, of course) couldn't just make stuff become more stuff. They had to deal with things being a finite resource. When they burned wood, they only got ashes and smoke to show for it, and they weren't clever enough to make time go backwards so that it turned back into wood.

Still, they had some smart ideas about making lots of similar things. All they had to do was figure out each step needed to make a thing, then they would repeat the step over and over on something that wasn't complete yet.

Then, when they had all their incomplete stuff, they would go to the next step and repeat that one over and over on each incomplete thing.

In the end, it took way less time to make a bunch of stuff all at once than it did to make each thing individually.

That's why you, being very clever and attentive when you felt like it, line up all of the annoying Inquisition people in a straight line, each one held in place by a few friendly tentacles.

"You can't do this!" some say.

"We'll have you executed!" others say.

The big important one, who isn't so big or important now that he's on his knees and his hat is on your head, is screaming the loudest of all.

You ignore all of their noises and get ready to begin your mass production of less rude people.

First, you extended the Rolled Newspaper of Bapping off to one side, held at the end of an extended arm. Then you line it up with the head of the first inquisitor in the long row that loops around the room in a big circle.

You're ready.

Your little legs take off with a mighty thump-thump of your bare feet on the wooden floor.

The newspaper baps the first inquisitor on the side of the head, then as you move forwards it smacks into the second, then the third. The faster you run, the faster the baps.

There are screams of pain and torment and embarrassment as you sprint across the room, their noises only drowned out by the *smack smack smack* of the Rolled Newspaper of Bapping doing its work.

You come back to where you started and pause to pant a bit. That was a lot of running! "Did you learn your lesson?" you ask.

"You think you can intimidate us with that? We will return unto you all harm you cause tenfold!" Mister Lord Shooksword screams. There's spittle and everything.

You sigh and start running again. It's kind of fun because you need to wave your arm up and down so that the Rolled Newspaper of Bapping hits each Inquisitor right in the face. Maybe you should have lined them up by height?

No, no this is more fun. No one said that revenge shouldn't be enjoyable.

"Whoosh!" you say as you beat your arms in the air like a bird, the Rolled Newspaper of Bapping still going *smack smack* with every bouncing step you take.

Some of the mean inquisitor people start crying, others try even harder to break out of the grasp of your tentacles, but it's to no avail.

This time you go around twice before stopping to breath hard and grin at your hard word. "Did you learn your lesson?" you ask.

They reply with a bunch of sniffling and some moans. Maybe next time you'll run the other way around to make the red smack-marks on their faces match.

"You... you can't do this," Mister Lord Shooksword says. He looks most pitiful of them all.

You walk over to him, tower of hats wobbling proudly above you as you stop in front of him. "Will you hurt Abigail?" you ask.

"She, she violated—"

Smack goes the Rolled Newspaper of Bapping.

"Will you hurt Abigail?" You asked again, this time while waving the paper under his nose.

"We can't allo—" he stops to flinch when you raise the paper for another bap. "We-we." He swallows. "We could come to a compromise?"

"What sort?" I asked.

"If she unsummons you, we'll promise not to hurt her?"

You bap him again. "No. That's a stupid idea. Stop being stupid, it annoys me."

"But, but it's our duty, our job!" he says.

You smack him on the forehead. "Get another job! This is not hard. Abigail does shopkeeping stuff, you could do that instead of annoying everyone that comes from places where you can't go because you're all squishy and weak."

He starts crying, and you wonder if maybe you failed to be polite at some point.

"Please get another job?" you try.

Much better! If Abigail were here she would certainly be patting your head and cuddling you into her chest.

How long has it been since you were last with your Abigail? She's probably all worried and sad because you're not there to give her a place to rest her hands, such as atop your head.

At least she has Daphne for cuddles and Charlotte for distractions.

Your eyes narrow. You're really tired of all of these inquisition people.

"Look. I'll make it easy." A rip opens up above the table in the middle of the room and disgorges a pile of naked inquisitors. "You can have all of these, and in exchange, you stop bugging me and Abigail. If you don't stop, then I eat you. Okay?"

Mister Lord Shooksword doesn't look like he wants to agree.

You raise the Rolled Newspaper of Bapping.

"You win! You win! We'll surrender!"

Victory!

Thanks to your incredible diplomatic skills and your polite nature, you win the day.

It takes you a bit to get back to the girls. They're all sitting in Daphne's living room by the time you return, and they're not entirely alone. Pou-tine is sitting in front of Charlotte, head down while the girl runs a comb through his greasy hair.

Your eyes search out Abigail, and you find her sitting really close to Daphne, one arm around her shoulder in a sidelong hug that Daphne is returning. "Dreamer!" she says when she sees you.

"Yes," you confirm. "I'm back. And I won."

"Nice hat," Charlotte says.

You nod, setting the stack to wobbling above you. "Thank you. It's victory loot."

She gives you a thumbs up, then returns to tending to Pou-tine.

"Dreamer, I was worried," Abigail says as she hugs Daphne closer.

"We were both worried," Daphne says. "Are you well? I can get Edmund to fetch you something to eat, maybe?"

You nod. Eating sounds like a great idea, but an even better idea strikes you, and you climb onto the love seat that Abigail and Daphne had taken up, and squeeze yourself between the two in the optimal position for double-sided hugs.

Carefully, you reach out and take Abigail's hand, then look up to meet her eyes. They're big and a little scared, and a little happy, and a lot pretty. "It's safe now," you say. "Nothing's going to hurt you as long as I'm here. And I'll always be here."

She smiles, the worry fading a whole lot. "Thanks, Dreamer."

And then the evening proceeds with much hugging and some food and some better company.

You really have gotten used to all of these mortals, and you don't think you'd have it any other way.

Several Decades Later

Abigail, Empress of the South, West, East, North, and also the Other Directions, sat upon her throne of Tentacles and Bones. The God-Empress was dressed in her finest regalia. Silken robes with embroidery so fine and meticulously crafted that merely gazing upon it would drive weaker mortals into fits of envy and despair.

Across her legs lay Queen Daphne, her consort covered in gossamer cloth that hinted at the pale flesh beneath, her head and long hair laying across the Empress's lap.

Behind the throne, hidden amongst the shadows, was Charlotte, her lips curled up in a knowing smile as she looked ahead. Next to her, the form of a young man, eyes wide and filled with a heady mixture of awe and fear.

And, below the Empress' right hand, with her legs splayed out and a stack of impressive hats and crowns next to her, was a young woman in a Pretty Dress, the black pits of her eyes swirling while a contented smile adorned her lip.

"What do you think?" You ask as you turn the painting towards Abigail.

Abigail tilts her head to one side, then the other as she takes in the canvas. "I guess it's nice," she says. "You're getting better at painting."

You nod, your many hats wobbling above you. "You said I needed to capture people's essence in my art, so I took some and put it in."

Abigail sighs and picks a cup of steaming tea from her coffee table. It's the same coffee table she's always had, with one leg plunging into the abyss off in one corner and a bunch of stains scoring the top.

"What's that?" Daphne asks. She's coming out of the bedroom, hair all mussy and nightdress a bit crooked. "Oh, Dreamer made another painting?" She hugs Abigail from behind, her cheeks pressing up against your Summoners as she takes in the painting. "I like the dress I'm wearing. It's very… sheer. Not something I'd wear in public, but, maybe in private… if Abigail wants me to play the nubile servant for her?"

Abigail takes another sip of her tea to hide the way her face is going all red.

You sigh and wonder if you're going to have to sleep over at Charlotte's… again.

"I think I have a robe like that at home," Daphne continues.

"I-it's time for work," Abigail says as she gets up all of a sudden.

You sigh as she moves past you, leaving a perfectly good cup of tea behind, so of course you do your familiar duties and finish the tea for her, then the teacup because it's breakfast time.

"What will you be doing today?" Daphne asks you.

You shrug. "I'll do what I always do," you say with a big smile. "I'm going to follow Abigail and make sure she's having fun, then I'm going to make my own fun."

The older girl hums, a happy little noise that turns contemplative as she takes in the painting hanging from a tentacle behind you. "What gave you the idea of having Abigail look so… royal-like?"

"I said I don't want to be anyone's empress!" Abigail calls from her room where she's changing.

You shrug. "I guess one day Abigail might get bored of running a shop and doing naughty things with you, so she might want to take over the world or whatever."

With that, you get up, stow your painting, and walk off to follow your summoner.

She might be a bit silly, and your friends can be a bit strange, but you think that here, in this little corner of a little mortal world, you can at least be happy.

The End

AFTERWORD

Hello!

My name, as you may have guessed, is RavensDagger, I'm the idiot mortal that made this story, but I'm not the only one to blame.

I want to share some of that blame with my awesome friends on the Raven's Nest Discord! Shout out to Sam, who helped a lot with the formatting for the ebook and paperback versions. Also, Zoufii, who is the incredible artist who made the cover for this story.

This story was originally written on three websites as a quest, that is, as an interactive story. Each chapter (of which there were over eighty) were written and posted with an open poll at the end where readers could vote on the actions and events that would happen in the next chapter.

Once the votes were tallied, I'd write down the next silly bit of story and post it, usually averaging about three to four chapters a week.

It was a bit of a writing experiment that I found immensely enjoyable. And this story, after many edits, cuts, alterations and some lazy patchwork, is the end result.

I do hope you enjoyed it! I certainly had a blast writing it!

If you enjoyed this hot mess, then maybe check out my other stories. I'm afraid they're a bit more normal (though only a bit!).

And now that the self-shilling advertising is out of the way, I hope you have a great day!

Keep warm; stay cool,
Raven

Printed in Great Britain
by Amazon

23255988R00148